# BLOOD
# AND
# RAIN

## GLENN ROLFE

### POLTERGEIST PRESS

POLTERGEIST PRESS

ISBN: 978-1-913138-13-4

Originally published by Samhain

www.poltergeistpress.com

*This book is dedicated in loving memory to my brother,*
*Greg Rolfe Jr.*
*I hope you're howling up in Heaven.*

# Acknowledgements

First and foremost: Thanks to God, my family, and my friends.

Special thanks to Don D'Auria for picking this story and deeming it worthy of publication back in the Samhain Publishing days.

Special thanks to Richard Chizmar and Norman Prentiss for giving the eBook a new life with Cemetery Dance Publications.

And very special thanks to Poltergeist Press for this gorgeous new paperback edition. I always dreamed of having a book on the Leisure Books horror line. Having had Don sign the original and you guys put together this version, well, that's as close as it gets. Thank you.

To my readers: Thank you for coming back.

# PROLOGUE

*Spring 1997*

**S**TAN **S**PRINGS **STARED** at the curse in the night sky. His curse. He clenched his jaw, and bit back the grunts that demanded release from within his sweat-covered body. His muscles tightened and took turns throwing fits. He could feel his heartbeat's thunderous barrage at work inside his heaving chest. It was only a matter of minutes before the changes would come.

He ripped his gaze from the clouds, moved away from the window and knelt next to the bed against the concrete wall. He slipped one shaky hand beneath the mattress and found the small incision he'd made when he first arrived at the institution. He had traded a guard, a heavyset fella by the name of Harold Barnes, his prized Ted Williams rookie card in exchange for a copy of the key. Parting with this gold mine had been necessary. Stan Springs had nothing else of value with which to barter. Harold trusted him enough to make the swap; he told Stan there were crazies here by the dozen, but he could tell that Stan was not one of them.

*No, Harold, I'm something far worse.*

Key in hand, Stan stepped to the unlocked door and cracked it open. The hallway was clear. He moved down the corridor, as stealthily as during his heydays working on the force in New York. Hearing footfalls ahead and to his

5

left, he fell back and pressed his large frame against the custodial door. Hidden by the entryway's shadow, he watched Nurse Rozetta—a tall, thin woman with a dark complexion—pass fifty feet from where he stood, before she disappeared into the nurses' breakroom.

Barefoot and dressed in only a Red Sox T-shirt and his sleeping shorts, Stan made a break for the staircase across the hall. His breaths were coming faster now. If he didn't hurry, he wouldn't make it outside. He crept down the steps leading to the main hallway.

Through the small window on the stairwell door, he could see Harold Barnes's haunted jowls illuminated by the laptop screen in front of him. The old man's eyes were closed, his mouth open. Harold hadn't even made it an hour into his shift before he was out. Stan knew Harold also ran his own antique shop in the neighboring town of Hallowell. He'd told Stan that working both jobs on the same day, which was sometimes unavoidable, made it difficult for him on the night shift. It was another shared nugget Stan had stored away for nights like this one—the nights the beast in him needed to get out.

Easing the door open, Stan skulked his way along the shadows on the wall and tiptoed to the main entrance door. Despite the cramps now rampaging through his calves and thighs, he slipped the procured key into the lock, slow and steady. The door clicked open, and he stepped out into the night.

As the cool breeze brushed against the sweat of his brow, the tendons and bones in his face began to shift. The rest of his body followed suit. He dropped to one knee and cried out. His skin, his scalp, his eyes, his muscles were all too tight. He reached behind him and managed to push the door shut.

*If you could see me now, Harold.*

# BLOOD AND RAIN

The private roads out front were deserted. He launched from the building's stairs and landed on the lawn below, making a beeline for the woods to the left of the large property.

He was twenty feet from the forest when the change hit him like a massive wave, crashing him to the ground. His muscles clenched and squeezed and tore, while the bones of his face continued to crack and grow. His teeth began to fall out in place of the monster's.

Down on all fours, he crawled to the tree cover and vomited. A mix of last night's cafeteria meat loaf, black coffee, loose teeth, and blood splashed the ferns before him. Stan's fingers extended as his claws dug into the soft soil of spring's floor. He moaned and grunted his way through the rest of the fluid process.

In full beast mode, Stan Springs stood and howled at the cloud-covered sky. The creatures of the night became ghosts among the trees. He felt the strength flowing through him and the hunger begging to be sated.

He burst forward, headed north. Despite Stan's best effort to control the beast's killing zone, he found himself heading home.

# CHAPTER ONE

**B** RIAN ROWEL'S EVENING had been full of mind-numbing conversations inspired by an endless stream of stupid questions. Add in a devilish dark-haired temptress and this torrential downpour, and the whole damn night was a clusterfuck of tribulations that his tired mind could have done without.

The night sky had been clear and pristine as he made his departure from the Harrison Economy Inn just north of Bangor. His work for Sales Smart Worldwide—a company that worked with hotels all over the country to help desk associates make more sales—brought him up and down the East Coast. His penchant for traveling the back roads had inspired his fiancée, Shannon, to purchase the TomTom navigation system that had been a perfect guide for his trips over the last month and a half. Driving anywhere and everywhere had been reduced to a near-brainless exercise thanks to the little device, allowing him to take in more of the beautiful scenery that often came with these lengthy journeys. This trip should have been no exception. No more maps, no more fumbling around in the dark, trying to figure out what he should be doing or where the hell he was going.

Thick clouds had rolled in, snuffing out the warm glow of the stars. The light rain that followed shifted into attack mode, taking his relaxing back-road trip and turning it into an eye-straining exercise. He was forced to snail along at a dreadful fifteen miles per hour, praying that no local yokel would come bumming down the road and knock his sorry ass into the ditch.

Twenty minutes later, the TomTom lost its signal. For the rest of the night, the device's green-lit display screen would only read "Searching". He had no choice but to pull over and scrounge for the maps he had exiled to the backseat.

Under the dull-yellow illumination provided by the car's dome light, he stopped at the sight of the phone number written across the front of one of his training folders. In big, bubbly script, it read "555-2121—Amber".

Amber Cunningham had been one of the front-desk associates at the Harrison Economy Inn. Tall and thin, with an athletic build, she had flirted with him the moment he stepped into the hotel lobby. Amber made him feel young. He had arrived at the scheduled two-o'clock training course a couple of hours early. Most that time was spent standing at the reception desk, eating up every bit of Amber's infectious attention. While Shannon may have gotten a kick out of the flirting, she would have kicked the younger girl's ass for what happened later.

From the moment she entered the tight meeting space, quiet Amber's deep-blue eyes tracked his every move. Her gaze and intent was undeniable. His *uh-oh* radar screamed *Lolita*. The sudden change from fun and flirty, to sexy and seductive, was not lost on him.

He introduced their lesson and got lost midsentence as he watched Amber pout her lips and apply a glossy lip balm. She caught his stare and bit her bottom lip.

By the end of the class, he was ready to either make a huge mistake or run for his life. As the dark-haired vixen made a beeline for him, he chose the latter. Perspiring like a preteen on his first date, he gathered his papers, threw them in with his laptop and started for the door. She caught him at the staircase leading down to the lobby.

A whispered offer about an oral opportunity and a subtle nudge with her delicate hand to the front of his khaki pants had his heart pounding like a jackhammer and caused a slight stirring in his underwear. He politely thanked her for the offer, then shimmied past her, down the short stairway. A narrow escape. Nights like these reminded him that fidelity was one of the toughest jobs he had ever had.

Now, staring down at the folder with the bubbly phone number, he wondered when she'd had time to write it. He realized that in his hurried efforts to flee from the ambitious girl, he had forgotten his whiteboard.

*Damn.*

Brian found the discarded collection of warn and tattered road maps among a pile of coffee cups, empty Pepsi bottles and grease-stained Burger King bags laying on the floor behind the passenger seat. He found the Maine map and located his approximate position—twenty minutes southwest of Bangor in a town called Kingly. He spotted Route 5 and used his finger to trace his way down to Route 1.

The rain had eased up enough for him to push the speedometer back up to a decent forty miles per hour. It would be a long night of driving, but he was determined to make it home before dawn.

An hour later, his eyes began their inevitable protest. Struggling to see through the storm, while trying to read the map and keep tabs on the yellow line that centered the road, weighed heavily on his tired eyelids. He looked up from the road map in time to see a massive tree slam down across the jet-black road ahead of him.

"Holy shit." He stamped the brakes.

The car idled as he gazed upon the massive pine that would have crushed him if Lady Luck hadn't winked his way. "Fucking perfect," he said, scanning the ditch to determine whether there was enough room to get by. The pummeling rain whipping in the wind made it next to impossible to tell.

He slammed the palms of his hands down on the steering wheel before grunting on his way out the door. The tree was massive.

*Jack's fucking beanstalk.*

He'd felt the wind pushing his car around earlier, but hadn't thought it was strong enough to do this.

The large tree stretched from one side of the road to the next. A cold wind kicked up from the south, blowing the intensifying rain into his face and sending a shiver down his spine. He turned up his jacket collar and moved forward.

The thing looked like a pine on steroids, conjuring his childhood fear of the tree outside the boy's bedroom window in *Poltergeist*. Some fucked-up part of his mind was certain that were he to reach out and touch its wet bark with his hand, the walls of reality were sure to burst open and release an evil from some other hellish dimension.

He realized his fingers were inches from the tree and abruptly snapped the extended digits back. An irrational fear boiled up within him, making him feel both stupid and childish.

Somewhere within the soundtrack of the raging storm, he heard a grunt.

"Hello?" His voice died a quick death against the howling wind.

*Mrrrrrr...*

Gooseflesh broke out across the backs of his arms. The response turned his blood cold.

# BLOOD AND RAIN

The sound was animalistic, and out here in the middle of nowhere, it could have been any manner of beast.

*Mrrarrrooo*

The unmistakable howl came from the trees to his right. There was something moving in the darkness. He didn't want to look, but could not tear his eyes from the breathing shadow in the night. The rain, whipping roughly into his eyes, hindered his line of vision.

He heard branches snapping, the sound of shuffling and something else.

He began to back away, unable to redirect his gaze.

*Arrroooo*

The trees around him swayed with the rhythm of the surrounding chaos, in a mad waltz that evoked a sense of doom. His foot caught a jagged rock protruding up from the earth, sending him flailing backwards. He banged his elbow on the side-view mirror as he fell into the quickly forming mire beneath him.

Brian climbed to his feet. A deep cracking sound stole his attention. He looked up and saw another tree coming down in his direction. He scrambled backwards as the smaller pine fell through the storm and landed on the front of his car. The headlights went out beneath its weight, taking with them the only source of illumination in this Godforsaken night.

*Arrroooo*

Done trying to rationalize the situation, he grabbed for the door handle, but his fingers, slick from the rain, slipped once, twice, before finding their hold and pulling the door ajar.

Lightning flashed across the blackened sky, revealing to him his first glimpse of the thing standing at the forest's edge. He saw the silhouette of something big, something massive covered in fur, and no more than fifteen feet from where he stood.

Brian's heart tried its best to beat its way right through his chest. His knees buckled. He began hoping, more than he could ever remember hoping for anything else in his life, that this was a nightmare. More than the time he had prayed that Marie Coughlin would let him feel her up at *Scream 2*, or when he proposed to Shannon at Niagara Falls. He was praying that he had fallen asleep while traversing these damned back roads. Besides, being in a ditch would be a hell of a lot better than being right here, right now. None of this made any sense.

It had to be a dream. It had to.

*Arrroooo*

The beast was his only company on this desolate road. The sudden loss of hope stole the breath from his lungs. He had suffered from panic attacks as a preteen, but for the better part of his adult life, he had been rid of their frightening spells. He could feel the sickening wave of unsettled nerves stirring up within him and the hot flash beginning its course through his body as his mind hit overload on its capacity for the absurd.

He climbed into his car as fast as he could, nearly falling on his face as the lightheadedness that was customary with his attacks announced its presence. He grabbed ahold of the steering wheel for balance, clenching his fingers tight around the rubber cover in a meager attempt to coddle his mental atrophy. Another thunderous boom blasted the world around him.

What is that? What the fuck is out there? What in the hell is going on?

*Crrrasshhh*

*Arrroooo*

The roof of his car sunk in under the weight of the howling creature. He shut his eyes as tight as he could and began praying aloud, "Dear God, please make it go away. Please, God, I'm so, so sorry. Make it go away..."

# BLOOD AND RAIN

Lightning flashed again.

*Mrrrr...*

The beast in the storm let out a low and deep growl from directly over his head. He continued to pray, but tonight prayers were not going to be enough, and he knew it.

The car shifted beneath the weight, moaning as the beast maneuvered into position.

The entire vehicle shook. He heard the unmistakable sound of something large hitting the ground beside him.

He could sense it staring at him. The thing in the night was now on the other side of his window. Brian sat shaking behind the wheel like a child upon a bed, convinced that the bogeyman was about to finally reveal itself from behind the half-closed closet door.

He thought of Shannon, his beautiful fiancée, the woman he would never see again. The woman he loved more than anything on this earth. The one whom he had promised, less than four hours ago, that he would drive home safely, and be there to cuddle with her before dawn. Tears flowed from his closed eyes as his bladder let go.

The driver-side window shattered inward. Brian Rowel let out one final gut-wrenching scream as broken glass and cold rain slapped across the side of his face. The fur of the beast's arm tickled his nose and top lip as it reached in for him.

Its claws tore through the right side of his head, taking his jaw and that half of his face off. Blood splattered the windshield, steering wheel and dashboard.

His face and annihilated jaw landed in the mud on the side of the flash-flooded road.

The rest of his body convulsed behind the wheel.

The creature howled into the fully raging storm before vaulting itself toward the woods off the side of Christie

Road. Thunder rolled across the sky above. The deadly beast headed west, toward the city.

The body of Brian Rowel sat lifeless, drenched in blood and rain.

# CHAPTER TWO

**N**ICK BRUCE SPENT his Saturday night tuned in to Art Bell reruns on 1420 AM. The features on paranormal and unexplained events that *Coast to Coast AM* offered exclusively were right up his alley. Since graduating from the University of Maine in Orono back in '97, he'd been a freelance writer for a variety of magazines and papers. His big break came just prior to graduation, with his piece on the Full Moon Monster of Gilson Creek.

Back then, he had moved home, intent on saving up enough money to get an apartment in Portland, but after the first attacks on Old Gilson Creek Road that spring, he discovered a homegrown obsession. His vivid imagination, soaked with hours upon hours of *Coast to Coast AM* and years of reading the likes of King and Straub, went to work on the possible creatures that could cause such damage.

The picture that graced the front page of the *Coral County Sentinel* was enough to make sparks fly. The McKinneys' wagon looked like it had been rammed by a Mack Truck. Once Sheriff Fischer announced that they had been attacked and killed by either a mountain lion or bear—neither of which had bothered a soul in Gilson Creek as far back as he could recall—Nick's interest peaked. Admittedly, part of it was just a fun concept for his supernatural-based brain. The fact that the incident occurred under a full moon only fueled his fancy. He

17

decided, for kicks, he would get a police scanner and wait out the next full moon.

He was shocked when the call came in about the bodies in Paulson Park. He grabbed his camera and cruised down to the crime scene, unprepared for what he saw.

He managed to blend in with the other reporters from the county and get close enough to the scene to snap the portrait that launched his career with the *Crypto Insider*.

Unfortunately, the gruesome photo and the article he penned about the Full Moon Monster also landed him on the sheriff's shitlist. Hell, it practically branded him as a heartless sensationalist, with almost every other member of the community.

He left the Creek the following year, but after a defamation lawsuit last month from a prominent Portsmouth, New Hampshire, politician that he may have labeled a cultist, he'd been forced to move back home with his mother.

Tonight, for old times' sake, and maybe hoping for a little supernatural luck, he busted out the old police scanner. Stationed in his new basement office, researching for his latest bit on the old haunted hotel out on Route 5, he was listening to Art Bell talking about J-Rod and Area 51, while eating a chimichanga which nearly got stuck in his throat when the call came across about the body on Christie Road.

Lady Luck and the full moon above. Nick Bruce grabbed his cell phone and car keys, determined to make up for his Portsmouth fuckup.

Sonya Fischer reached for the canvas booklet of compact discs sitting at her feet. She was sick of her boyfriend's unwarranted love of the band Disturbed.

If she was spending another Saturday night cruising around the bumfuck roads of Gilson Creek, she was doing it in style.

Alex caught her reaching for the booklet. "Hey, what do you think you're doing?"

"I wanna go retro," she said. "Keep your eyes on the road."

"What are you looking for?"

"I really like that oldies mix your uncle gave you," she said, flipping through the pages of discs.

She despised most new hard rock music, and especially loathed Disturbed. Thank God for Alex's Uncle Ted. Besides looking a lot like Hugh Jackman, he worked at the local rock radio station and played guitar in the Broken Exes. They were amazing. Alex had snuck her into a show a couple weeks back at a rock club called the Rusty Nail over in Hollis Oaks.

Since then, his uncle had been bombarding him with one awesome classic rock mix after another, many of which had already migrated to her house.

Alex ejected the disc and handed it to her.

"Okay, you win," he said. "One thing though—if we're going to listen to it, we gotta crank the hell out of it."

Sonya loved to get her way. She put the disc labeled "Raise Your Fist" into the car stereo.

"Come 'ere," Alex said. "I'm being a good boyfriend, aren't I?"

She released her seat belt, slithered closer to him and touched her lips to his neck.

"I think it's only fair that if you get to pick the tunes, I get something in return," he tried to barter. "You know, *quid pro quo*?"

"Oh yeah." Sonya kissed his neck. "You mean *besides* being in the company of the prettiest girl in town?"

"Well that goes without saying." He pulled her close with his right arm, keeping his left on the steering wheel of his beloved black-and-gold 1986 Camaro.

She ran her hand up his thigh and stopped just as the first chords of Autograph's "Turn up the Radio" came blaring from the speakers. She pulled herself away and relatched her seat belt.

"Hey, where you goin'?" Alex said.

She loved it when he pined for her like this. "We've got to leave something to do when we get to Kim's," she said.

Sonya gave him her most promising smile and started to sing along with the chorus of a song that was twice her age. She would not let on just how amped up she actually was to get to Kim's too. She remained cool, but on the inside, she was doing cartwheels thinking about the night ahead.

Kim Donaldson had been Sonya's best friend since the third grade. Kim's parents had split up a couple of years back, and since her mom worked mostly second shifts at the laundromat, they had a place to hang out with plenty of unsupervised time, like tonight.

What more could a couple of kids getting ready for their senior year ask for?

Sonya looked over and saw Alex's pouty bottom lip. *Boys—they can be so sensitive.* She would definitely make it up to him.

Sonya skipped ahead on the mix and found a nice ballad. Surprised by the beautiful piano intro from such hedonistic rockers, she laid her head against the window, reached over and held Alex's hand, and watched the rain coming down as he eased the Camaro onto Old Gilson Creek Road.

A feeling of dread passed through her as she stared out at the torrent thrashing against the windshield. Lightning blazed across the night, momentarily illuminating the starless sky above, and was followed by a monstrous boom.

She'd never liked thunderstorms. The sudden blast made her shiver. It felt unnaturally strong. Behind the wall of dark clouds, a full moon patiently waited for its chance to reveal its pale-yellow face. She could handle black cats and walking under ladders, but full moons harbored bad luck in this town.

A string of horrible deaths in Gilson Creek had coincided with what her mom used to refer to as "the bright side of the dark side". She was only ten when the three kids from the high school were attacked in Paulson Park, but to this day it was still the subject of all kinds of foolish talk within the halls. Werewolves and Bigfoot.

She remembered asking her father about the rumors. He'd told her it was just a wild animal, that the kids at school watched too many monster movies. He'd laughed, but his eyes hadn't seemed to get the joke.

"You okay?"

Sonya gripped Alex's hand. "Let's just get to Kim's." She considered the black forest outside her window. "I don't like being out in this weather."

# CHAPTER THREE

"**W**HAT ARE WE looking at, Sheriff?"

*Shit.*

Joe knew there was more to his sour stomach than the horror scene he and Deputy Hines had before them. As if the dead body and a fallen tree blocking off one of his main routes through town weren't enough, now he had to deal with this annoying dipshit.

"Hello, Nick. Looks like trouble followed you home."

"I heard the call on the police scanner. Is it a car wreck?"

"You always rush out to car accidents in horrible weather like this?"

"Only when they coincide with a full moon."

Joe should've known. Not even home a month and here he was. He wasn't sure if Nick Bruce still worked for the *Weekly World News*'s ugly New England cousin, the *Crypto Insider*, but he could see the kid's hungry eyes yearning for a comeback. Joe wasn't about to hand it to him.

"As you can see, we have a tree down, and this is an active crime scene, Nick. I'm going to have to ask you to head back the way you came in."

Nick sheltered his eyes, squinted through the rain and nodded toward the car with the second tree on its hood. "Do we know what happened to that guy?"

23

Joe sighed. "Listen, Nick, I said this is an active crime scene. Your freak-out rag doesn't exactly qualify you as press. I need you to—"

"Just one more thing and I'll go. Anything—Holy shit, is that a part of the driver?"

Nick pulled his cell phone from his jacket. Joe slipped forward and bumped Bruce's arm. The cell phone bounced off the blacktop and plopped into a puddle next to the side of the road.

"Hey! What the hell?"

"Sorry about that, Nick."

"Yeah, right. You did that on purpose. You're gonna have to pay for that."

"Send me the bill."

Joe turned back to the real mess on his hands—the mutilated body in the Accord and the tree lying across his road. He shouted back over the sound of the rain, "Road's closed until further notice."

❧

"Fucking Fischer," Nick Bruce ranted to the interior of his car. He cast a glance at the ruined cell on his passenger seat. "Bullshit."

Fischer's dislike of him wasn't unfounded. Nick's graphic crime scene photo in the *Crypto Insider* had caused a frenzy in town, but that was seven fucking years ago.

He headed back toward town empty-handed. Rain hammered his windshield, the wipers tried desperately to keep visibility at more than nothing. An eighteen-wheeler passed in the opposite lane, splashing enough water to obliterate his sight of the road.

"Come on, man, what the fuck?" He slammed his hands on the steering wheel.

*Have fun turning that goddam big rig around when Fischer blocks your ass.*

# BLOOD AND RAIN

The road came back into its brief intervals of clarity with each pass of the wipers.

*Boof!*

The car pulled hard to the right. Nick's white knuckles clenched the steering wheel.

"What the fuck now?" he steamed. He knew what it was.

*Goddamn flat tire.*

He pulled the car to the shoulder. Park Street was just another minute up ahead. He opened the door, stepped out into the downpour, and grateful that he had brought his trench coat, he moved to the passenger side of the car.

Flat as shit, his right front tire lay in defeat beneath the steel rim. He stomped through the mud on his way to the trunk, popped it open and checked for a jack and a spare. He could see the handle for the secret compartment where the car companies liked to hide the little toy tires. He thought it was funny that these big companies imagined that keeping the possibility out of sight would preserve that worry-free mind-set on long drives.

Hauling the spare from the trunk, Nick put it on the ground and rolled it to the front of the car.

He trudged back to the trunk to retrieve the chrome jack he'd never used. Mud and excess water were already penetrating his sneakers and soaking his socks.

A short struggle with the lug nuts and he was able to liberate the flat tire. He got the jack in place and the car up enough to free the ruined wheel. He put the doughnut in its place and strategically tightened the lug nuts, being sure to cross from one to the other as his father had shown him.

Hunched before the freshly dressed wheel hub, he considered what he thought he'd seen on the side of the road—it looked like a chunk of flesh resting in the mud—and thought of the sensational full-moon tie-ins he could use for an article. He could have a good payday on his hands.

*Would've been even bigger if I'd been able to snap that picture.*

Nick didn't have a chance to move before he heard the growl. His spine tingled milliseconds before the animal at his back slammed him face-first against the wheel well.

Stars exploded in his vision; then his front tooth jammed into his top lip.

There was another loud, guttural growl. He reached out for the jack encased in the mud and felt an immense pain tear through his hand.

*HONK*

Bright lights tore through the darkness. The thing that attacked him grunted and disappeared into the tree line.

The encroaching truck stopped.

"Buddy, hey, buddy, you okay?" a male voice said.

Nick's head swam for the shore. Thoughts of tetanus, rabies and amputation passed by like cars down I-95. A hand was on him, helping him to his feet.

"Hospital..." he managed.

"Not this way," the man said. "Road to Hollis Oaks is closed off. It'll take a bit longer to get around through Jackson."

"Can you give me a lift...to my house...in town?" Nick steadied himself with his good hand on the hood of his car. The world and the crap weather came back into view.

"Looks like it gotcha."

Nick gazed drunkenly toward his bloodied hand.

"Not sure what in the hell that was. Big son of a bitch. You're lucky I came back around when I did or it might have finished you off like that other fella up the road."

"What...what did it look like?"

"Not sure. Big and hairy. Eyes shinin' like two fat yella moons. I scared it off."

# BLOOD AND RAIN

Mike Ouellette needed to get up. The whole world seemed to be coming down around him. He'd crawled beneath the children's slide to remain as dry as he could.

The downpour was too much. It was coming through from every which direction. He curled on his side, pulled the collar of his dirty denim jacket tight against his neck and clutched the fifth of Popov vodka for dear life.

Too far from his own house, he knew he should climb out from under the slide in the playground and try Gil Laverty's. Gil owned the tavern on Brighton Circle. He sometimes let Mike stay on his couch. Usually when nature got nasty and he was too drunk to stumble home, like tonight.

The booze was making his head spin. He wasn't sure he could climb to his feet. Instead, he closed his eyes and sent a little prayer to the Lord. "Please, Jesus. Don't lemme drown out here tonight. Not unless ya have ta." A warm grin spread across his face. Lightning lit up the world beyond his closed eyelids. A thunderous boom answered. The storm was right over town.

A shuffling sound from the trees off to his right caused him to open his eyes. "Huh?"

He propped up on his elbow and tucked the bottle of vodka against one of the legs supporting the slide. He scanned the swirling trees for signs of movement. A shadow emerged.

"Oh no, oh no, oh no..." Old Mike's heart hit Mach 1.

He'd forgotten what day it was. He knew this day every month. How could he have forgotten today? All these years, not one slipup, whether sloshed or otherwise. He always knew to find someplace safe to sleep during the full moon. Tonight, he fucked up.

He didn't have a chance to scream. The beast flew at his extended arm. He felt its incredible strength and fury as it clawed into the flesh just above his elbow and pulled.

He watched the rest of his arm detach from his body. He managed a high-pitched moan as the monster's ugly yellow eyes lowered into sight.

Old Mike tried to push himself down and out, and even got his bottom half out on the other side of the slide. He heard the growl in harmony with the next blast of thunder. The paw of the monster palmed his face, its nails puncturing the flesh under his jawline.

Dragged out from under the slide by his face, Old Mike's last fleeting thoughts were of Gil Laverty's gentle hazel eyes and toothless grin.

*Should've known better, Gil.*

The werewolf burrowed its snout into his stomach.

The storm screamed for him.

**❄❄❄**

The big rig he'd cursed earlier, and its driver—Tom, Don... or one of those names he couldn't remember—drove him into town and dropped him off at his home. Nick rushed inside without a thank-you, grateful his mom hadn't returned from her boyfriend's. He snatched her half-empty bottle of whiskey from the kitchen counter and staggered to the bathroom.

He took a swig from the bottle and held his injured hand over the pristine porcelain sink. The wound was black.

*Don't let it be rabies, don't let it be rabies...*

He hated needles, and knew about the series of gut punctures the doctors would have to deliver.

The alcohol splashed over the wound. He screamed at the intense burning in his throbbing hand, stumbled backwards, and plopped down upon the toilet.

He slid to the linoleum floor and crawled to the cabinets under the sink. His mom kept the first aid kit under there. His arm shook as he unrolled the gauze and wrapped the injured hand. He should have cleaned the bite properly, but hoped the booze would kill whatever the goddam animal left behind.

*Animal.*

He never even saw the damn thing. It could have been the same animal responsible for whatever happened out on Christie Road...or something worse. He took another swig from the bottle of Jack and tried to wash the thought away. He'd have to go to the hospital in the morning.

Nick kicked off his shoes, worked his way out of his wet jeans and hauled the bottle of Old No. 7 to bed with him. He placed the whiskey to his trembling lips and accepted its fiery blessedness over his tongue.

Three swallows later, he put the bottle on the nightstand and looked at his alarm clock: 12:22 a.m.

He needed to call AAA to collect his car, but suddenly felt sick to his stomach. The room began to spin. His eyes fluttered. His head hit the pillow. He stared at his bandaged hand and allowed the whiskey to numb him to sleep.

# CHAPTER FOUR

"**TURN THAT DOWN,**" Sonya said. Kim slapped Heath's hand from her ass and turned the stereo down.

"Hello, Dad."

"Hi, honey."

"What's up?"

"I figured you kids would still be up. I need you to do me a favor."

"Sure."

"I need you and your friends to stay put at Kim's tonight."

"Why? Has something happened? Are you okay?"

"Yeah, I'm fine. We found a body out here on Christie Road."

"Oh my God."

"Looks like an animal attack."

"In this weather? What was someone doing out there in this storm?"

"Well, there's a pretty big tree lying across the road. Unfortunately, it looks like this fella stopped, got out of his car and ran into something else."

"Was it somebody from town?"

"No. Listen, I want you, all of you, to stay put, okay? I know Alex and Kim's boyfriend are there. You just let Shauna know that I don't want any of you leaving. Not until we find out what we're dealing with here."

31

"I'll tell her. Please be careful."

"I always am, honey. I'll call you in the morning."

"Love you, Dad."

"Love you too."

"What the hell was that about?" Alex said.

"My dad said there's a tree that got knocked down on Christie Road. Some out-of-towner stopped, got out of his car and was apparently attacked by an animal."

"Holy shit," Alex said.

"I bet it was the Full Moon Monster!" Heath said. He made claws with his hands and stalked toward Kim.

"Quit it with that dumb shit," Kim said. She broke into laughter as Heath tackled her and nuzzled his face into her neck.

"What's all this about?" Kim's mom appeared in the doorway in her pink, fluffy housecoat.

"Oh hey, Shauna. My dad called. They found a body out on Christie Road. He says looks like an animal attack. He says he wants us all to stay here tonight."

"Absolutely. Boys?" Shauna said. She looked at Heath and Alex, who were both peeking out the window. "Boys, you can stay downstairs. I don't want any funny stuff."

"Okay," Alex said.

Heath nodded.

"I'm going to bed. Why don't you kids settle down for the night? I have to work in the morning."

"Okay, Mom," Kim said.

Sonya watched Shauna scoot down the hall and back into her bedroom.

"Do you guys think it was for real?" Sonya said.

Kim sat next to her on the couch. "You know what these two are gonna say."

"Yeah, well, I don't believe in the Full Moon Monster. It's just a bunch of bullshit from the *Crypto Insider*." Sonya thought the weirdos behind the weekly bizarro paper were a bunch of bored creeps who probably huffed gas or sniffed too much glue.

Heath squeezed in next to Kim. Alex plopped down Indian-style on the floor facing the couch.

"You know what Old Mike told me," Alex said.

"Oh yeah, listen to a drunk," Kim said.

"Last summer he told me and Jason Schneider that Gilson Creek was home to a werewolf."

"That's the same thing as the Full Moon Monster, idiot," Heath said. *"Full. Moon."*

"No, dude. The Full Moon Monster is something made up to sell copies. I'm talking about a real werewolf."

"I vote we watch a movie," Sonya said.

She'd heard enough of this crap years ago. She remembered being in fourth grade when practically everyone in town was talking the same nonsense. She even got yelled at by Paul Glidden's younger sister who was a grade ahead of her. She'd said that the sheriff should be fired. That he let her brother die. It wasn't fair then, and she wasn't about to start listening to that crap now.

"My uncle thinks it's real too. He says that it killed all those—"

"Shut up, Alex."

"What?"

Sonya fought back the tears. "I don't want to talk about this stupid werewolf shit tonight, okay?"

Alex put his hands up. "All right, I'll shut up. I'm sorry."

She put the attacks of 1997 in her rearview years ago. Outside of Kim and her mom, no one understood all the shit she and her father went through that year.

The beast made its way out of town and passed through a little patch of trees that gave way to a small field. Just ahead, it spotted a hideous green-and-yellow trailer. Beside it sat a two-car garage painted the same ugly colors. Lights and loud music blared from the garage.

The beast broke for the small building.

Keith Turcott was trying to figure out how to change the oil in his old Escort. His father was useless when it came to teaching him anything. Keith always had to figure out these kinds of things for himself. He'd been doing things this way for sixteen and half years; all things considered, he thought he was doing pretty well. His drunken father could just sit in that piece-of-shit trailer and waste away, for all he cared. His mother was no better. She parked herself in the back room and watched episode after episode of *Law & Order: SVU*, smoked her menthol cigarettes, drank coffee and Kahlua, and stuffed bags of Doritos into her face.

They were a couple of fucking losers. No way was he getting stuck here with them. He wasn't about to grow up and grow old, just to give up. He was moving to Boston after graduation, if not sooner. He'd paid for this piece-of-shit Escort with his own money, fixed it himself, and once he got that diploma, he was good as gone. He was ready to get the fuck out of this house and this goddam town. Hell, he could—

Just outside the side door he'd left open a crack, something growled loud enough for him to hear it over the storm.

His first thought was of Bailey, his old husky who'd died two weeks ago. Obviously, not possible.

*A coyote maybe? Did coyotes growl like that?*

He put down the red, oil-stained rag, picked up his flashlight and shone it toward the door. He didn't see anything.

*What the fuck? Maybe I'm just hearing things.*

He reached for the rag he'd dropped. Just as he did, the door flung inward and smashed the stack of paint cans behind it to the concrete floor. Before he could retrain the flashlight, the car sunk down on top of him, the light fell from his hand, and the car pinned him to the ground. His feet kicked at nothing as he let out a muffled whimper. He could barely breathe, as the car was sitting right on top of him. Being as small as he was, he hadn't bothered using a jack. Something was on top of the car.

"Hey..." he said in a strained whisper.

Another growl came in response. This time, it was deeper and somehow more menacing sounding.

He tried to reach for the flashlight again. Just as he got hold of it, he felt someone, or something, grab his right ankle.

*What the f–*

"Aarrrgh!" The grip tightened, then ripped his foot and lower half of his leg from his body. All of Keith's thoughts smashed into a wall of pain as his body was sent into a series of convulsions, and he was unable to prevent his face from hitting the rusty bottom of the Escort.

Theresa Turcott came running out of the back bedroom, making her way down the small, confined hallway of her beloved trailer. She'd heard the bone-chilling screams of her son coming from the garage. She rushed past her husband, Rusty, who was in his usual passed-out position in his recliner. She was scared, but hoped Keith had just dropped something heavy on his foot or banged himself with the hammer again. In the back of her intoxicated mind, she knew better. She knew his screams.

Theresa Turcott opened the front door. She nearly fell back inside as the garage doors exploded outward and she took into full view an enormous beast among the splintered wood and shattered glass. She clutched at her housecoat and struggled to catch her breath.

*Keith.*

The large animal raced away toward the woods. Barefoot and bewildered, Theresa scurried down the front steps, too frightened to call out to her boy. She stopped at the destroyed garage entry and screamed.

# CHAPTER FIVE

**"S** HERIFF," **DEPUTY RANDY** Hines said.

"What is it?"

"Earl just radioed. Looks like we've got another attack at the Turcott place."

Joe looked at the dark clouds. The rain was letting up, but his bad feeling had just gotten worse. "You stay here until Seth Kimball shows up for the body. I'll check on the Turcotts."

He saw the fear in Hines's eyes. "Sheriff, you shouldn't go over there alone."

Joe started for his Range Rover. "I'll call Clarke over to join me." He turned and nodded toward the hidden moon above. "Don't go jumping to conclusions. Could be a bear or mountain lion."

"Like last time."

Joe knew he was grasping at straws. *Too many damn coincidences.* "Yeah. Maybe."

He climbed into his vehicle and headed back toward town and thought about the body he was leaving behind. The lumps of flesh and bone he had found half-buried in the mud off the side of the road. The *rest* of his body sitting behind the wheel of the car. The driver-side window smashed inward. There was blood all over the interior that the rain couldn't reach to wash away. Tufts of fur clung to the shards of glass that still rested in the window frame.

And those goddamn coincidences. There *was* a full moon tucked up behind the clouded sky and a victim's partially mangled body on its way to the morgue in Hollis Oaks. He could only guess what waited for him at the Turcotts'.

Now it was Joe's job to figure out a way to hold off the wave of impending consternation, while wrapping his mind around exactly what happened to the body on its way to the morgue. He could feel a strong headache waking in his temples.

He met Deputy Dwayne Clarke in the driveway of the Turcott place. He could see Theresa and Rusty clinging to each other just inside the trailer's front door.

"It's over here, Sheriff," Deputy Clarke said.

Joe followed Clarke over to the trail of debris that led to the garage.

"There's a part of a leg over there in the workspace."

Joe could see the blood splatter from the car to the work area. "And the rest of the body?"

"Under there." Clarke pointed to the car. The caved-in roof matched the one he'd just left on Christie Road.

Joe gestured toward the trailer. "Did they see anything?"

"Theresa says she saw something...burst through the garage door."

"Something?"

"Yeah, she says it was huge. Says it was big and black. You thinking black bear?"

"I'm not thinking anything just yet." Joe didn't know of too many black bears that waltzed into garages, tore off limbs and knocked cars down on top of people. "You call an ambulance?"

"Yeah. They're on their way. Said it will take longer since they have to come in through Jackson."

"Better let Kimball know he's got another pickup."

# CHAPTER SIX

**T**ED MCKINNEY WAS winding down his local morning radio show with a little Twisted Sister. These early Sunday shifts were by far his favorite. He could always count on the Saturday-Night Hangover Crew tuning in. There was never a shortage of gory stories or great requests from his faithful listeners. How could you go wrong?

The little orange light above the station's two phones lit up.

"WRKU, Ted here."

"Hey, Ted."

"Good morning, Dwayne. Can you hold for a sec? This song's almost over."

"No problem—"

Ted put Dwayne on hold as he addressed his loyal flock, "Ohhhhh yeah, you better believe I'm an S.M.F., but you all know that by now. That's a little Twisted Sister for all you other S.M.Fs. and Saturday-night Aftermathers out there in hangover land. Right now, it's just about time for Wild Ted to wind this beast down, so go ahead and call in with your last-minute requests and I'll try my best to squeeze something in for ya before you get to those church doors. REPENT! REPENT! It's your last chance before Wild Ted's grand East Coast vacation! I'll be hitting the road with the Broken Exes for the next few weeks. So get your last-minute requests in now. Be back in a flash—hold on."

Ted cued the station call sign, which gave way to a Hollis Oaks used-car dealership spot from Timothy's Honda. He grabbed the phone and hit line one.

"What's the story, morning glory?"

Deputy Dwayne Clarke was in a conversation with someone else. His voice was too far away from his phone for Ted to make out what was said, but he did manage to pick out the voice of a female, instantly identifying it as Deputy Shelly Glescoe.

Dwayne and Shelly had a real thing going. Ted, on the other hand, was much more the playboy type. He had plenty of fun, with plenty of lady friends, and appreciated having his castle to himself. He loved his own life too much to ever let one of his overnight companions stay at his place for more than the night. His Aunt Janice joked that he was Gilson Creek's answer to George Clooney. He knew what she meant by it—he even agreed—but, boy, did he fucking hate George Clooney.

"Hey! Lover boy! Mr. 867-5309, Deputy Dwayne, are you on the line?" Ted said.

There was a pause before Dwayne came back to the phone. "Hey, Ted, sorry about that, man. Shelly just swung by to let me in on the boss man's mood."

Ted sensed Dwayne's tone had changed.

"What's up with Joe?" Ted said as he cued up the next song.

"I imagine you saw the news this morning, right?"

Ted's stomach fluttered. Two bodies were found on opposite sides of town during last night's storm. Apparently attacked by animals.

Dwayne continued, "I just wanted to make sure you were okay. You wanna meet for coffee?"

Ted's head flooded with ghosts from his past—his brother's and Michele's funerals and that horrifying photo on the cover of the *Crypto Insider*. The official report was a mountain lion had been responsible for the killings. The whispers among the more open-minded suggested something more sinister.

"Ted?"

"Yeah, yeah, I'm here. I can do that. I'll meet you at Mel's as soon as I finish up."

"Ted, we're trying not to jump to any conclusions here, so don't you go jumping off the deep end with your wild theories. We're still investigating the scene."

"Well, my *theories* might be shit, but something sure as hell tore apart most of the people I loved in this fucking town, whether you believe it or not. I'll see you at Mel's." Ted slammed the phone down. Line one instantly lit back up, and line two had already been sparking to life throughout the entire conversation. He couldn't bring himself to answer either.

He didn't give his normal sign-off. He cued up this week's live concert and headed straight out of the studio. He didn't say bye to Station Manager Cindy Hues or to Doug Jenks, the station custodian. He had bad things on his mind. Very bad things.

Ted got on his black Honda Rebel and headed over to Brighton Circle. The brilliant morning sunlight that felt warm and invigorating on his smoke break an hour ago had lost all of its shine. Even in the already hot morning, a cold spell cast its way down his spine. He leaned his bike and rounded the corner of Gilbride and Brighton. He could see Dwayne waiting ahead, standing beside his cruiser in the parking lot of Mel's Café.

Visions of full moons and dead loved ones crawled across his mind. He didn't think he was going to like what Dwayne had to tell him. He just hoped he didn't wind up punching out his best friend.

Ted parked his bike next to the black-and-white cruiser, pulled a cigarette from his right breast pocket and lit it. He was trying hard not to allow every emotion to parade across the features of his unshaven face.

Dwayne let Ted finish his smoke. "Coffee's on me."

Ted tossed the butt and followed him into Mel's Café.

The place was at half capacity. By the time the tired, the ashamed and the atheists came wandering in, the early birds had already left for morning service at Saving Grace Baptist.

After a night of house parties and forgotten mistakes, Mel's "Best Stack in Town" special was the perfect elixir for both guilt and hangovers. The special's name served as a bit of a double entendre. Mel's bountiful bosom, which rightfully had fans aplenty for, was in close competition with the most rich, fluffy, delicious stack of golden pancakes in all Coral County.

Ted and Dwayne took a booth in the far corner of the shop. Ted knew they were about to discuss what was a very sensitive subject here in Gilson Creek and wanted a little privacy.

In truth, Mel's was probably not the best choice for this conversation, but Ted had a mad craving for a pile of perfect pancakes and a great cup of joe. Mel's was the best place for both.

Katie Brooks, a blonde high school girl with a lazy eye, poured them each a cup of coffee and took their orders. They sat in silence, sipping their beverages, until she returned with two stacks of pancakes and a side of bacon—Ted's idea of a breakfast dessert.

"So, tell me straight. Is it like last time?"

Dwayne put down his mug and sighed. "Man, I'm sorry for what I said about your theories. It's just...it just...I don't know, it's not possible."

"What? That *something* did that to my brother, to Michele? That there are people in this town who know a hell of a lot more than your boss told us?"

42

Dwayne crossed his arms over his chest and stared out the window.

"What's Joe's story this time? Murderous mountain lion's cub returns to finish what—"

"Dammit, Ted. You know I wasn't here when all that stuff went down. All I know is what Joe told me, all right? That and this beast-in-the-woods nonsense of yours."

"Fuck you, Dwayne."

"Hell, man, you gotta look at this from my end."

Ted leaned back and shook his head. It did sound fucking insane. Beast in the woods. *Bigfoot, werewolf, ravenous fucking mountain lion*...It did sound stupid, but nobody was convincing him otherwise. Not Dwayne, and certainly not Sheriff Fischer.

On the other side of town, Sonya Fischer was awakened by the music blaring from her cell phone. She was lying comfortably on Kim's big brown couch with Alex fast asleep behind her. A smile broke out across her face at the warmth of his body. Her father had called late last night and told her that she and her friends were to stay put for the night.

He'd even known that Alex and Kim's boyfriend, Heath, were there and made sure to let her know that they were to stay as well. She could tell that her Dad was shaken by whatever it was that he had found out on Christie Road. She'd heard the tightness in his voice. For something to affect him enough to give him away so easily, it had to be downright awful.

Sonya picked up her cell.

"Hi, Dad." Sonya cringed at her own voice. She sounded like a girl who had stayed up all night drinking and smoking.

43

"Hey, honey, did I just wake you up?"

He didn't sound so well himself.

"Yeah, we were up half the night watching Harry Potter movies. Is everything okay on your end? Was anyone hurt?"

"Yeah, for the most part everyone's okay. There was an incident, like I told you last night. Looks like an animal attack," he said. "That storm was a pretty nasty one, knocked down some power lines and such. We're getting Christie Road cleared up right now. Is the power still on out there?"

She reached for the remote-control laying amongst the collection of empties on the coffee table and clicked on the television. Steve Carell and Seth Rogen were discussing masturbation.

"Yup, looks like it. You sounded a little...out of sorts last night. Are you sure you're okay?"

"Yeah, honey, I'm all right. The man we found out there was dead when we arrived on the scene. Never like to run into that," he said, before redirecting the conversation. "Those boys behave themselves last night?"

"Of course they did, Dad. Shauna was here to chaperon, remember?"

"I know, I know. I was just giving you a hard time."

"So a guy died, huh? Was it somebody from town?"

"No, it wasn't anybody from around here. It looks like he was just some unlucky guy passing through." He paused. "There was a second attack, as well."

"Oh my God."

"Keith Turcott."

She didn't know Keith personally—he was a senior—but she knew who he was.

"Look, honey, I was just calling to check up on you kids and also to let you know I'm all right. But with everything going on, I'm going to be tied up for most of the day. I want you to hang out at Kim's, if

44

that's all right with her mother. At least until I can get home, okay?"

Sonya knew there was more to all of this than he was telling her, but she knew the last thing that he needed to be doing was worrying about her while he was investigating. She had no problem hanging at Kim's. "Yeah, Dad, that's fine. Pick me up when you're done?"

"You bet, but I can't make any promises as to when. I'll check back in with you this afternoon, okay?"

"Okay, Dad. I love you."

"I love you too, honey."

Sonya hung up, shut the TV off and lay back down next to Alex. He had not so much as flinched during her phone conversation. Poor guy was out cold. She brushed his hair back from his face and kissed his temple.

Her mouth tasted like shit, and she wanted more than anything to brush her teeth and get a glass of ice-cold water, but lacked the actual initiative to get up to do either. She closed her eyes and slipped into a dream of wicked things that howled in the night.

# CHAPTER SEVEN

**D**WAYNE SIPPED HIS black coffee and watched his best friend wrestle with his skeletons.

Last night's attacks were similar to what he knew about those of 1997. He and Ted had been friends with, or had known people who were friends with, the three Gilson Creek students who were found torn apart.

Ted dated Michele just a few weeks prior to the tragedy, before she dumped him for Paul Glidden. No one knew how deep her leaving Ted had cut his best friend, and it only worsened when hers was one of the three bodies the police found decorating the park.

Dwayne wasn't even sure if Ted had been in any kind of lasting relationship since then. The sad part was that Ted had bought into all the beast stories whispered among the town's more superstitious types. Ted was so desperate to understand, to place blame for what happened to Michele and his brother Jack, that he was open to anything. It made it next to impossible to discuss the situations with him.

Katie Brooks returned to their corner booth. "More coffee, Deputy?"

"Yes, please."

Katie scooted away.

"So Joe is chalking it up to random wild animals again?"

"Jesus, Ted. Would you just drop the goddam werewolf bullshit already? You're not a fucking kid anymore."

Ted jumped up from his seat and grabbed Dwayne by the collar. "Fuck you, Dwayne."

Dwayne shoved him back. Ted countered with a haymaker that caught him in the eye. Dwayne held his face and pointed at his best friend. The customers stared at them. No one moved a muscle. Katie Brooks froze next to Kenny Larson, still holding his order of pancakes. Mel came out from behind the island that separated the front counter from the kitchen, frantic at the sound of the commotion. "Just what in the hell is going on here, Ted?" Mel said.

Dwayne slid out from his seat.

Ted started for the front doors.

"I'm sorry about this, Mel," Dwayne said. "I'll be right back."

Ted couldn't believe what he'd just done. He was sick of Dwayne treating him like a child over this. If he wasn't coddling him over Jack and Michele, he was taking shots at him about what he believed might be responsible for their deaths. Ted burst out through the café doors. The bright sun felt warm again on his face. He wiped the tears from his cheeks and headed straight for his bike.

"You okay?" Dwayne said.

Ted reached into his shirt pocket, pulled out another cigarette and lit it. "Yeah, I think so. I'm sorry I hit you. I don't know what the fuck just happened. I don't know how—"

"Fuck you, Ted. Don't apologize to me. I know what you've been through and how much this stuff means to you. Shit, you don't have to explain a thing. I'm sorry."

"Aw fuck." Ted watched as Sheriff Fischer's Range Rover pulled into the parking lot, then sidled up next to Dwayne's cruiser.

The sheriff leaned out his window and stared at Deputy Clarke. "Didn't Glescoe give you my message?"

"Yeah, Boss. I had to stop and see Ted real quick."

"What happened to your face?"

"Ah, just...a little horseplay. Ted got the better of me."

"Well, you're on the clock now, so let's go. We've got to get out to Hollis Oaks General before noon. You know how those morgue guys like to keep to their lunch schedules."

Dwayne slapped Ted on the shoulder and got into his cruiser. "Gotta go, Ted. I'll catch up with you later."

"Yeah, man. Thanks for breakfast. And I really am sorry."

"Don't worry about it." Dwayne turned to the sheriff. "Ready when you are, Boss."

Joe gave Ted a nod.

Ted nodded back, pulled and lit another smoke, and got on his bike.

Still mortified by the spectacle he'd just made of himself at Mel's, Ted decided to cruise by Paulson Park. Michele, Paul and Paul's friend Luke had spent their last summer night there. He rode up to the entrance and cut the engine.

The place was in disarray. A fallen branch took up the entire circumference of the sandbox to his left, a couple more limbs poked up through the jungle gym just beyond that, and a much larger one leaned against the swing set to his right. Ted started to go for another cigarette when he noticed something odd covering the surface of the merry-go-round just up ahead. The golden rays shone down over the debris-covered play area that was like something out of a nightmare. His stomach squirmed. He gripped the lighter in his hand. He inched toward the merry-go-round. There was blood and...displayed across the surface of the park equipment, a severed arm. The dark, soaked sleeve with a blood-covered hand at one end, and a string of tendons and ripped flesh at the other, sat still and frighteningly tangible in the thick, coagulating mess. Just a few feet farther, he caught sight of the rest of the body lying facedown on the ground.

Ted McKinney dropped to his knees and vomited.

# CHAPTER EIGHT

**W**ES **KAPLAN PACED** in one of four small offices at the *Crypto Insider*, his cell stuck to his ear. The phone on the other end of the line continued to ring.

"Fuck, Nick. Answer your phone."

There was a knock on his door.

Joel O'Brien's Mohawk peeked in. "Still no luck?"

"No. I've left him like twelve fucking voice mails already."

"Jesus, you'd think he'd be all over this."

"Yeah, well, he should be."

Wes tossed his cell amongst the pile of crap on his desk. His little weekly publication had suffered quite a shot from Nick Bruce's Portsmouth fuckup, but, dammit, this was their chance to make things right. This was Nick's opportunity to make things right.

"What do you wanna do?"

Wes gnawed at his piercing in his bottom lip and locked his hands together on his head.

"We're gonna have to go up there."

Joel stepped into the office and picked up a book from Wes's shelf by the door. "You don't think he just forgot his phone at home or something?"

"I don't know, maybe, but we can't fuck this up. I'm going and you're coming with."

"When do we leave?"

Wes snatched his keys from the desk. "Right now."

They hit I-95 and headed north from the small building Wes leased in downtown Portsmouth. Wes had never driven north of Portland, but had heard Maine was fucking beautiful.

"Where we stayin'?" Joel said. "With Nick and his mom?"

"No. I checked online. There's a Motel 6 in the next town over, which is Hollis Oaks. Use my phone and get us a room for the next couple of nights. I saved the number in my contact list."

While Joel made the call, Wes imagined a return to glory for the *Crypto Insider*. The animal attacks were all over TV. He was amazed that Nick hadn't called him first thing this morning with a full report and a gallery of photos. The fact that the guy wasn't responding to his phone calls, or the emails he'd sent, bothered him. Nick lived for this stuff, just like he and Joel did. No way Nick had just blown it off. Not even with the embarrassment of the Portsmouth gig. Imagine, Representative Jonathan Haim as a Satanist. Hey, it made for good copy. Nick's story was brilliant. Problem was it was also a lot of misconnected dots and a wonderful practice in fiction.

"Done. One smoking room with two doubles."

"Thanks. We're gonna stop in Portland and grab a map and a bite to eat."

"Cool. Can we go to the Great Lost Bear? Wings and PBRs?"

"No. Drive-thru. We don't have time to waste. I wanna get up there and see what the hell happened." Wes knew how fast these types of things got covered up, especially if it was what he thought. Nick thought he was clever coming up with the Full Moon Monster, but Wes called it what it was. A *werewolf*.

Joe Fischer thought about the body of Brian Rowel. The portrait of mutilation, the blunt, sheer gruesomeness of it. It was too close, too similar in style to the way they found the groups of bodies that unforgettable summer. It was the beast's signature.

Gilson Creek was like a wife trying to cover up the scars of spousal abuse, both physical and mental; it dwelled in denial and guilt. The darkest of such secrets involved the vicious attacks and deaths of three separate sets of members of their quiet community.

The first attack of 1997 took place at the end of spring that year.

Joe, then just a rookie sheriff, and his deputies walked into a scene out of a horror film. The forest-green Saturn wagon they found smashed and battered all to hell looked like something that had been through a war zone. The windshield was gone, both the driver and passenger-side windows were smashed in, and the driver-side door looked as though it had been rammed by another vehicle. The result was the car leaving the road and landing on its side in the ditch. Troubling thing was there were no signs of another vehicle having been involved. No mismatching paint on the points of impact or one fragment that could have belonged to anything other than the wagon. It was obvious *something* had slammed into the car as it made its way up Old Gilson Creek Road.

It was what they found inside of the demolished car that really sent their heads and stomachs spinning. Crimson covered the dashboard and the police detector gadget attached to it, the stereo console, the steering wheel and the seats. Even the cup holders were filled with pools of the dark fluid. The bodies were worse.

Only the lower halves of the two people remained inside of the vehicle. The lap bands of the seat belts were still engaged, securely holding the bottoms of both bodies in place. What on God's green earth was capable of such a savage act? At the time, he had no idea. What his deputies could find of the rest of the bodies was scattered and strewn throughout the woods beyond where they found the vehicle.

It was the same viciousness executed upon the body of Brian Rowel. Only, Rowel was a stranger to this town. Whereas, the two people they had found that spring night were some of his best friends. Jack McKinney was Joe's best friend in high school, and Jack's wife, Kelly, was one of the primary nurses who'd cared for Joe's wife, Lucy, as she battled, and ultimately passed away from, cancer. Tears began to well up in his eyes as he tried to stop this long and very painful train of thought from rolling along any further, but he couldn't. Lucky for him, Rita came over the police radio and did it for him.

"Sheriff?"

Joe snapped back to the here and now. He picked up his police radio. "Go ahead, Rita."

"Sheriff, you'd better get over to Paulson Park. Someone just reported another body."

Joe pulled up to the entrance to Paulson Park, followed by Deputy Clarke. The sheriff climbed out of his vehicle and motioned for Deputy Hines to join him.

Deputy Clarke followed close behind. "Now what the hell do we have here, Randy?"

"McKinney says he pulled up to the park, all upset about something that happened down at Mel's. Says he walked into the park and found the body on the other side of the merry-go-round. He showed up down at the station looking like death."

"Where the hell is he now?"

"We sent him home."

"Well, I need to talk to him."

Joe turned his attention to the playground. "Clarke?"

"Yeah, Sheriff?"

"Put the lines up around here and then get Ted back down to the station."

"You got it, Boss," Deputy Clarke said.

Deputy Hines led the sheriff over to the playground equipment. There were broken tree branches everywhere; it looked like a damned tornado had come through in the night. "There's the first thing Ted says he came to," Hines said as he pointed at the merry-go-round. A severed human arm lay across it. "Body's just beyond, over there by the tree line."

Joe looked at the ravaged form lying facedown in the grass just before the woods. He could see the bloody mess left at the shoulder where the arm should have been. A pool of blood held what was left of the person in a final congealed caress to the grass and dirt.

*Ashes to ashes, dust to dust.*

"Anyone we know?" He made a quick prayer for another stranger, but his gut was already telling him it wasn't.

Deputy Hines put his hands on his hips. "Can't be a hundred percent sure—the face, or what's left of it, looks a lot like that shoulder. No wallet, no ID, but the red hair makes me think it's Old Mike."

"Old" Mike Ouellette was the town drunk. He was a small, withered old man in his early fifties. He had greasy red hair that was always jutting out the sides of the dirty, old Red Sox baseball cap he wore every day. What he had left for teeth was brown and decayed. He lived in a crappy little hovel of a house that was closer to a shack than an actual home—broken windows, crooked door and yard covered in useless piles of random junk. The centerpiece of it all was an old, broken-down 1970 Pontiac Tempest that probably used to be red before it was bleached into the pale-pink lump of automobile that it was now—no wheels, no windshield. Damn shame. The old man kept to himself, for the most part. They had to pull him out of Jenner's Grocery a couple of times a year for getting loud, spouting nonsense and scaring kids with his tall tales.

He was the one person around Gilson Creek who would openly mumble about what happened in the spring and summer of 1997. It was on those rare occasions at Jenner's that he'd start howling and going on about werewolves and shapeshifters. That was always sure to get him a free night down at the station. Otherwise, he'd be out there until dawn, barking at the moon or whoever happened to pass him by. They would bring him in and let him howl the night away in a cell where he would bug the shit out of whoever drew the late shift.

"It's Old Mike all right." The sheriff pointed back over toward the playground equipment, without looking away from the body. "See that bottle under the merry-go-round?"

Deputy Hines looked back.

"You know anyone else who likes a little vodka in the park?" Joe said.

Hines looked at the sheriff.

Joe was half-lost in thought, zoned out in the direction of the body of Mike Ouellette, but not really looking at it. He could still hear the old man howling as he hauled him out of Jenner's about this time last year. Joe shivered and hoped Hines didn't notice.

"Did you call Seth Kimball yet?" Joe said.

"On his way, Sheriff. Should be pulling in any minute."

"Wait here for him." He turned back to face Hines. "I have something I need to go check on before I head back."

Hollis Oaks Coroner Seth Kimball pulled up to the police line just as Joe drove around it. Kimball waved, but Joe just drove by without so much as a look in his direction.

The sheriff knew what a werewolf attack looked like. He had seen the ravaged victims too many times already in his forty-two years. He also knew that he had shot and killed one of the fucking things seven years ago.

His stomach curdled as he passed the road to the station and headed north. He needed to make a stop at his house and place a phone call to check in with Sonya. He also needed to check on a grave.

# CHAPTER NINE

**S**ONYA TRIED TO focus on the cheesy eighties horror movie playing on the TV, but her gaze kept darting to Heath and Kim on the couch. She could see that Heath's hand was under Kim's skirt. Sonya found Alex's hand and gave it a squeeze. She considered moving it someplace warmer, but held off. She was horny, but she wasn't an exhibitionist. She glanced at Alex to see if he was witnessing their friends, but he was lost in the film. She preferred to read horror over watching it. Something was always lost in the translation, some intimate connection that only came from sitting down for hours with the characters caught in the madness.

"I think we're going to head upstairs," Kim said. Heath in tow, they headed to her bedroom. "You two can help yourselves to the guest room." She screamed as Heath picked her up and threw her over his shoulder.

"Me Tarzan, you Jane, now you do me," Heath grunted as Kim's laughter traveled down from the second floor.

Sonya and Alex were finally alone. She leaned in and kissed his neck letting her lips linger, tasting the saltiness of his skin. She placed her hand on his thigh and slowly moved it up to the front of his jeans. Letting her tongue trace his neck, she felt him stiffen under her hand. His attention officially diverted, Sonya stood, grabbed him by the front of his t-shirt and guided him to the guest bedroom.

"Wait right here," she said. She moved to the nightstand and lit a couple of candles. She grabbed the bottom of her T-shirt and pulled it up over her head. Alex stepped into the warmly lit room and followed suit. Sonya undid her leopard-print bra and tossed it to the floor.

Kim and Heath's moans floated down from above. The thumping of the headboard like a primal drumbeat stirred Sonya's own hunger. She grabbed Alex by the front of his jeans and pulled him to the bed.

"Do you want me to turn the radio on?" he said, pointing to the small gray CD player on the bureau next to the door.

The sounds of their friends fucking turned her on. She wanted Alex so bad. Maybe it was the anticipation of finishing what they'd started on the ride over last night. They hadn't had sex since summer vacation started three days ago.

Alex crawled toward her. "Do you want the radio—"

Sonya lunged forward, climbed over him and slipped her tongue into his mouth. His hands went to her breasts as he pulled her down on top of him. She felt like an animal uncaged as she reached forward and undid his pants. He grabbed her by the wrists and guided her onto her back, meeting her mouth in a deep kiss as he slid his hands down her arms, then her chest—she flinched as his fingertips fluttered over her erect nipples. Sliding his hands across her flat stomach and on to her hips, he grabbed hold of the waistband of her black stretch pants and pink-lace panties, and pulled them down over her ass in one fluid motion. Overcome, she needed to touch him, feel him inside her. She was panting and sweating as she helped him shed his pants and pulled him down on top of her.

"Fuck me," she whispered, as she put her hands on his hips and guided him inside.

Loud music erupted from Sonya's cell.

"*Oohhh*, not *nowww*," she said. She swatted the phone off the bed.

Alex thrust into her, his pace slow and deep.

"Harder," she said, grinding against him, tightening herself around him. She knew this drove him crazy and made him cum a lot faster, but right now, she didn't care. She just wanted all of him.

The phone fell silent.

"Oh my god, Sonya, yes...I'm gonna cum," he said.

"Give it to me."

The ringtone blared to life again.

"Yeah, mmm, yeah," she moaned, sensing he was close. She wasn't nearly ready herself, but that was fine. She'd get him to go down on her after they showered.

She felt him explode inside of her as his hands clenched her ass. His nails digging into her flesh. He collapsed on top of her, huffing and puffing.

"Oh, fuck," he wheezed.

The phone went silent before starting up again.

"Goddamn it," she said. "I better get that."

"Damn, Sonya, I mean...damn."

"You can thank me later," she said, tapping his shoulder. He slipped out of her and slumped at her side.

"It's probably my dad calling. He's acting a little strange since last night."

She leaned over, gave him a kiss, and then went for her phone on the floor.

"Hi, dad," she said.

"Hey, honey, I just wanted to let you know that I've got a long day ahead of me. You're going to have to fend for yourself for supper."

"No problem, I can probably just hang here. Kim's mom promised something good for dinner if we were all still here."

"I hope you kids are behaving yourselves."

She felt Alex's hand tracing her spine. He moved her hair aside and pressed his lips against the back of her neck.

"Yep," she said, trying not to moan or purr. "We're just watching scary movies."

"Well, I'll try to give you a call later to check in, but if I don't—"

"I know, I know, dad, I'll be fine. Do what you have to do."

"Okay, I love you."

"Love you, too, dad."

She closed the phone as Alex slid his hand between her legs.

"Mmm, you're asking for trouble," she said.

"I'm not scared."

She spread her legs for him.

"My dad's the sheriff, you know."

"Well, I'm a very bad boy."

She reached behind her found his cock and wrapped her hands around him.

He kissed her clavicle, his long hair spilling over her shoulder, his hand on her working its magic. She jerked him off, and felt herself spiraling toward orgasm.

Swerving her hips, pressing herself against his hand, she let out a cry as she came.

He followed suit, exploding in her hand.

❦

Cleaned up, showered, and dressed, they returned to the couch.

"Think they fell asleep?" she said, snuggling up next to Alex, her head on his chest.

Alex aimed the remote and started the next movie, *Halloween III: Season of the Witch*.

"I'm sure they did," he said. "Sounded like they were working pretty hard up there."

"Speaking of which," Sonya said, "don't expect me to make it all the way through this Michael Myers movie."

"Michael's not in this one."

"Well, whatever, just let me snuggle you until I fall asleep."

"Nap away," he said. He leaned over and kissed her forehead.

Sonya closed her eyes, a smile glued to her face, and drifted off.

# CHAPTER TEN

**J**OE SLOWED THE Range Rover, pulling off Old Gilson Creek Road, and headed between two large pines. The path, overgrown with tall grass and sporadically birthed blackberry bushes, was much as it had been the night he transported the carcass of the dead creature to what he believed would be its final resting place.

Joe reached for the pack of Marlboro Reds on his dash. He had started smoking again—another secret he was hiding from his daughter. He kept telling himself it would all be over soon...at least, that's what he was hoping. They could just go back to having the wide-open relationship he cherished so dearly. Until then, he would continue to be evasive when answering her questions, he would remain vague when telling her where he was heading and what he was doing, and he would continue to smoke his way through his anxieties.

About a hundred feet in, the path disappeared. He parked the truck before a small group of trees and cut the engine. Horace Cemetery was a little farther within the woods. He could find his way to the small group of crumbling gravestones that made up the old graveyard with his eyes closed. As the first of the old headstones came into sight, Joe was flooded with a rush of memories.

His introduction to Horace Cemetery, the first and original graveyard of Gilson Creek, and its haunted past was something he would never forget. He was out on his first hunting trip with his father and his uncle when they happened upon the old burial site. The graveyard was ancient and brittle, the result of being uncared for and forgotten, which had only made it that much more frightening as a child. It seemed so out of place, cast out like spoiled meat and left to rot in the middle of the woods. Joe's father only increased his unease by telling him that the place was haunted. His father did not elaborate on the subject; he just ushered them away with a quiet but stern sense of urgency.

It was his best friend, Jack McKinney, who told him about the soul who contaminated the place. According to the legend, a murdering monster of a man by the name of Gordon McDonough had been hanged and buried in the cemetery in the late 1800s. McDonough killed thirteen people in all—four adults and nine children. He then walked right into the town's small saloon, carrying an old potato sack that was dripping with blood and, supposedly, filled with body parts of two massacred families. The townspeople dragged him out to the cemetery to meet his judgment. They say he never said a word as to why he committed the murders, that he just smiled as they grabbed ahold of him, and kept on grinning whilst being dragged up and down the dirt roads leading to the graveyard. They also say he was wearing the same ugly smile when they slipped the noose over his head and raised him up. The smile was said to have still been on his face as the cold, dark earth was shoveled upon it. Townspeople, from then on, claimed to feel an evil presence lurking around them when visiting the graves of their dearly departed. Gilson Creek made a new graveyard the following spring, leaving

# BLOOD AND RAIN

Horace Cemetery to the surrounding forest and the ghost of Gordon McDonough.

Joe had not returned until the night he brought out the burnt body of the beast he shot down, burying it toward the back with the older, smaller and mostly unreadable headstones. He couldn't think of a better place than Horace Cemetery to put to rest such a hideous creation.

Standing now, in the presence of such wicked history, in the high-noon sun, Joe walked into the town's abandoned burial ground. The sky above was clear; the blanket of silence around him set his senses on high alert. Despite the eighty-eight-degree temperature, a cold chill full of sleeping skeletons, smiling demons and all things unnatural trickled carelessly down his spine.

It took him a few minutes to find the exact spot that he had dug for the monster, as the small wooden cross he placed to mark it had been knocked over. He found the crudely made cross laying at the foot of a tall pine standing ten feet from the otherwise unmarked grave. Joe plunged the shovel he had carried with him from the Range Rover into the soft earth and began to dig.

"Hey," Dwayne said.

Ted leaned against the stairs to his apartment. The cigarette wobbled in his palsied hand, his eyes swam for the shore. When he brought his gaze up to meet Dwayne's, they ignited.

"Did you see it?"

"I need you to calm down."

"Did you see it? The arm? The body? Did you?"

Dwayne stayed just outside the door. "I..." He hadn't had time. Not that he wanted to see it. Joe had sent him to grab Ted before he could walk the scene. "No."

"Well I did, Dwayne." Ted took a drag. "I don't know *what* did that, but I know what *could*."

"C'mon, Ted."

"I'm not asking you to believe it, but I suggest you open your eyes. Three bodies, Dwayne. This makes three."

"I don't want to get back into this with you."

"Then what the hell do you want?"

"Joe wants you back down at the station."

Ted dropped the cigarette butt, stamped it out and lit another.

"He needs to talk to you about the body."

Ted shoved past him and climbed the first couple of steps before he turned back. "Tell him he can come and see me. I'm not going anywhere."

"Ted."

He watched his best friend tromp up the stairs and disappear inside.

*Shit.*

Soaked with sweat and grimed with dirt, Joe put down his shovel, giving up the slim ray of hope as he realized what he already knew on some level to be true—the grave was empty.

The thing he had shot down and buried in this very spot was still alive. He didn't know how it had survived. All he knew was that it hadn't been breathing when he stuck its charred carcass in the ground. Nothing about the creature made any sense—not its murders, not its existence— so why should its demise?

He made a stop back home, took a shower and had a few swallows of whiskey before heading back out. The whole time he was thinking about how much this felt like some kind of never-ending nightmare. The one thing that protected his sanity was the fact that if this was the same beast, then that meant he had time to prepare. And he would.

After checking in with Sonya again and informing her that he was going to be tied up for the next few days with the investigation, he stopped by the laundromat and asked Kim's mom if Sonya could stay at her house for the time being. Sonya had tried arguing that she was almost eighteen and that she could handle being home by herself, but he'd told her the issue wasn't up for debate. He did not mention that they had found Old Mike, severed arm and all, down at the park in a pool of his own blood.

He arrived at the station, greeted by deputies Clarke and Hines.

Deputy Clarke noticed the change in the sheriff right away. He looked like someone being tormented from the inside out. The lines on his face were deeper than they had been earlier in the day. Dwayne didn't want to be the one to tell him that Ted had refused to come in, but his friend was his responsibility.

"Sheriff," he said, "Ted's at home. I went to see him and, well...I didn't fight him. Hell, he looked..." Dwayne wanted to say "like you", but did not, "...tortured."

He waited for the sheriff's verbal scolding, but the admonishment never came.

"That's fine, Dwayne. I know where to find him."

The sheriff turned to Deputy Hines. "Did Kimball get everything all right?"

"He brought the body over to Hollis Oaks General Hospital with the rest of them. Should be there by now.

Said he'd get to it right away and ring you directly when he had something," Hines said.

The sheriff turned to Deputy Clarke. "You and Glescoe are on tonight, aren't you?"

"Yes, sir."

"Keep your heads on straight tonight. No fucking around. I want you armed and loaded at all times this evening. Understood?"

"Yes, sir."

Joe looked him in the eye. "I mean it, Dwayne. Keep your sidearm and a shotgun with you at all times while you're out in the cruiser. I want you guys to be on high alert for the next couple of days, understood?"

"Yes, Sheriff," he said.

Joe looked to Deputy Hines. "You too, Randy."

Hines nodded in acknowledgment.

Dwayne watched Joe take his Stetson off and hold it to his chest, lost in thought.

"Everything okay, Sheriff?" he said.

"Huh? Yeah, as good as it can be, I guess. You guys just be careful."

Dwayne couldn't recall ever seeing Joe like this. He might just be tired, but Dwayne had a feeling there was much more going on than any of them knew. He just hoped Joe knew they were all here for him.

# CHAPTER ELEVEN

**J**OE PARDONED HIMSELF and strode to his office. Regardless of what Kimball had to say, the three bodies they had found in the last twenty-four hours meant one thing. They had another month before the next ones showed up.

Joe thought about the people who had been there to help the first time around. He thought of Stan.

He hadn't spoken to Stan since the day the man first came back from the mental health facility. That few moments of trivial conversation had taken place at Mel's Café while Joe stopped in to grab his morning coffee. He wasn't even a hundred percent sure as to why he had been avoiding the former sheriff, just that he had.

In the time since their last conversation, he had grown leery of the man. Stan's gruff, disheveled appearance, coupled with the fact that he was normally only seen while walking to or from the café, all added to Joe's ever-growing apprehension.

Stan Springs had been his mentor, practically grooming Joe for his present position. He thought of the day Stan resigned. He remembered how scared he was when Stan said *"Joe, it's your turn to soar"* and handed him the gold pin of an eagle in flight, which he still had to this day. Joe had admired many things about the former sheriff and did his best to emulate those same honorable traits, along with his top cop etiquette.

Prior to Stan Springs's sudden and rapid mental atrophy, he had been everything that was good and right about Gilson Creek. He could have easily run for mayor and won. It wouldn't have even been close. Stan had been a straight-talking, no-nonsense type of guy with a penchant for making you feel as cool and calm as he was, even under the most intense or devastating conditions. It was Stan, along with the McKinneys, who had been there with Joe as he watched Lucy deteriorate from the cancer that had ravaged her body. After her death, it was Stan who, even in the midst of his own psychotic breakdown, had lent an open ear and broad shoulder for him to weep on.

And Stan was there again for Joe after the unexpected and messy demise of the McKinneys. And then, of course, there were the weeks of research and brainstorming that ultimately led to helping Joe rid the town of the curse that would be responsible for at least nine deaths over the spring and summer of '97.

That was the place Joe had been trying so hard to divert his thoughts from going since last night when he first laid his eyes on the body of Brian Rowel.

Joe's mind broke like the levees of Galveston, flooding with the memories of the sweltering summer night he faced down and shot the murdering beast terrorizing his community.

*After* piecing together the evidence and coming to grips with the idea that they might be facing a creature that was a supernatural entity, they began studiously researching every inch of fact, fiction or gray area concerning werewolves. They looked at all of the folklore surrounding a wolfman, lycanthrope, *vilkacis* or as the Native Americans referred to them, shapeshifters.

Each legend described the werewolf or shapeshifter as being, at least at one point or another, a human being. A man or a woman who may or may not even be aware of what they were becoming or what kind of acts they were perpetrating while under this spell, or curse, or condition—whatever the case. They had abnormal strength, more powerful than any man or wolf. Some were supposedly rapid healers, while others were just as susceptible to pain and injury as their human counterparts. Silver, wolfsbane and in some cases they had come across, mistletoe—all were listed as weapons that could be used to either cure or kill the beasts. The curse caused some of the creatures to kill when under a full moon, while others could kill on a nightly basis if they so desired. Targets could be completely random acts of extreme violence or be preselected based upon people they despised in their human forms, whether a neighbor, town official, townsperson who may have scolded them at one point or another, or in the scariest case, who may be a threat—in other words, someone who may have suspicions about what they really were.

There were supposed to be ways of identifying a man or woman who might be a werewolf as well. Some of those were as silly as a person having eyebrows that connected above the bridge of the nose, or fashioned curved fingernails, or even arms that swung too low. One article told of how medieval Europeans would cut open the skin on the people suspected of being cursed, expecting to see fur within the wound.

All that considered, Joe and Stan decided that going at this thing armed with silver bullets was the most likely way to be sure of taking the monster out. Maybe it was a gut call, maybe it was from seeing too many Hollywood horror films, but, either way, it was the most attainable weapon and one which would allow them to strike from the safest distance.

Stan suggested going to Barlow Olson over in Hollis Oaks. Olson was a trusted friend to all of the neighboring police departments and a man with some unique tastes in weaponry. He had a collection of samurai swords, medieval broadswords, maces, flails and battle-axes, and an even stranger collection of silver stakes, crossbows, throwing knives and flamethrowers. Joe simply name-dropped Stan to Olson, and placed an order for two hundred silver bullets. They arrived at the station two days later.

Joe brought Deputy Randy Hines in on what he and Stan believed to be the culprit in the town's vicious deaths. Hines told them they were both crazy and suggested Joe check into the room next to Stan's.

Joe knew Randy had also held Stan Springs in high regard, and that—coupled with seeing their stone-cold gazes—had been enough for Randy to at least open his ears and hear the two of them out. They had zero suspects in either of the attacks they had encountered, but the severity and maliciousness of the slayings were congruent with those only capable of being committed by a monster. Whether that meant there was a large animal or a mythological creature on the loose, they didn't know.

Once they had Hines on board, theoretically they knew that they would have to wait for the next full moon since both the McKinney and the high school student killings had fallen in its glow. In the meantime, Joe found himself eyeballing numerous people in town with unibrows, staring at people's nails, and even watching the few dopey rednecks who swung their arms like apes.

Days and weeks went by. Joe concluded that none of his townspeople could be the beast. He hadn't seen anything that pointed to one of them, and started to wonder if maybe it could be someone from either of the neighboring towns, Hollis Oaks or Jackson.

He called Police Chief Tom Healy over in Hollis Oaks and Sheriff Paul Dumas over in Henderson County (who patrolled the town of Jackson) to confer with them about any out-of-the-ordinary accidents or incidents within the last year that either town might have had. But neither had anything for him. It seemed to be only Gilson Creek being targeted and threatened by this evil they were dealing with.

Joe decided to keep the details of the crimes vague. He simply left "animal attack" as the probable cause in the case of the three slain high school students and issued a town curfew of 9:00 p.m. He felt tense, nervous, scared and guilty about the whole situation. He never felt quite right about not opening up to the public that there was a murderer amongst them. Whether it was watching from the woods or from the barstool next to him, he had no way of knowing. He would have to wait and keep an eye open.

Two days before the night of the full moon, Stan Springs called Joe to inform him that he could no longer discuss the deaths or the werewolf or, frankly, anything else. He told Joe that one of the nurses had stumbled across his books and notebook, and forced him to turn them over to his doctor.

Joe found it hard to believe and in his gut thought Stan might have just reached the last frayed end of his sanity, and wanted out before he fell too far to come back. Either way, Joe had not felt that sense of abandonment or loss since Lucy's passing.

He wanted to pack up Sonya and leave Gilson Creek right then and there. He thought about moving to New York City, where at least the murderers had human faces and were only monsters on the inside. That made sense, this did not.

The night fell without as much as a shouting match near Gil's Tavern. He had all of his deputies on duty, for the first time in Gilson Creek history. Randy Hines, Patrick Somers, Lyle Paulson and rookie part-timer, Brett Curry, were all out on patrol. Somers and Paulson rode together. Curry was with Hines. Joe flew solo while Rita manned dispatch.

No one, not even the rookie, questioned the sheriff earlier in the day as he handed out the silver bullets. Neither Joe nor Deputy Hines had shared the idea of a werewolf with any of the other men, but small towns tended to have big superstitions. The young group of officers took and loaded the ammunition on the spot. Joe informed them that they were looking for some kind of large mammal and ordered them to shoot to kill on sight. Somers and Paulson patrolled Main Street and Brighton Circle. Hines and Curry were covering from Nelson Street to Arcade Lane, where about half of the town lived. Joe was cruising back and forth from Park Street to Old Gilson Creek Road.

At just after midnight, Somers and Paulson got the obligatory call to Gil's Tavern. Allan Buck was three sheets to the wind and swinging his big mitts at any man within his long reach.

It turned out Allan's best friend, Tom Frost, had been sleeping with Allan's live-in girlfriend, Charlene Deaton. Allan, who was normally a very timid, quiet guy despite his six foot five, 325-pound frame, had left the best friend and girlfriend, after walking in on them having sex on his bed, and headed into town on foot. Once he had drunk himself sideways, the anger and betrayal set in. That's when he reportedly started grumbling at everyone in the bar, just before bashing Keith Jones's head into the face of his girlfriend, Janet Lilly.

Chaos ensued as the other patrons tried to stop the giant of a man from hurting anyone else. Unfortunately for Janet, they weren't successful until after he had broken her left eye orbit, nose, and knocked two of her front teeth down her throat. All while using her boyfriend's head as his weapon. It was sudden, brutal and totally out of character for Allan Buck.

Somers and Paulson walked in, cleared out the area and from ten feet away Tasered the large man without a moment's hesitation. Buck shivered and convulsed before dropping to his knees and falling face-first to the dirt-covered wooden floor. They dragged his enormous girth out through the front doors, loaded him into the back of the squad car and locked him up down at the station. Paperwork would have to wait until dawn, per Sheriff's orders. They were back out on patrol within minutes.

On the outskirts of town, deep out on Old Gilson Creek Road, Joe Fischer was moving thirty miles per hour, as opposed to the posted speed limit of forty-five. His hands were white-knuckle tight on the steering wheel. He had given up cigarettes the day Lucy was diagnosed with cancer, but had purchased a pack at Gary's General Store after prepping his men for the night's watch.

He'd already gone through half a pack in the four and a half hours since. His mouth tasted like ash, his throat hurt, and his tired eyes stung. The cigarettes hadn't done shit for his anxiety, either. If anything, they'd just made him feel sick on top of everything else. He let go of the steering wheel with his right hand, reached over for the pack of Camel Lights and threw them out the driver-side window. That's when he saw it.

Against the screaming voice in his head telling him to floor it and not look back, against every sensible emotion asking him to ignore the *nothing* that he thought he'd just seen staring out at him from just beyond the tree line, he stamped his foot on the Range Rover's brakes and brought the vehicle to a screeching halt. His heart beat out of control and his hands were soaked with perspiration, but the law in him had turned the switch and had taken over for his weaker sensibilities.

He eased the truck around and pointed its bright-white headlights into the thick black forest lining the desolate back road. His eyes darted back and forth along the skeletal-looking branches and he could feel the pulse in his neck as he scanned the enveloping darkness.

Nothing.

He set down his Magnum revolver, not realizing he had already unholstered the massive weapon, and rubbed his worn-out eyes. There was a snap from off to his left. Something was out there with him. He grabbed the gun and the Maglite off the seat, then stepped out of the vehicle and into the dark night. Within seconds of the move, he decided better of it, climbed back into the cab and picked up the radio.

"Somers, Hines. I think I've got something out on Old Gilson Creek Road, almost to the Hollis Oaks town line. Hines, you should be closer—get your ass out here. Somers, patrol sectors one and two, unless I get back to you, over?"

"Hines, Curry, on our way."

"Gotcha, Sheriff," answered Paulson. "Keep us posted."

Joe Fischer dropped the radio, picked the flashlight back up and exited the vehicle for the second time. He lit up the spot directly off to his left where he had seen the movement moments before, but the sweeping light caught nothing.

Then, there was another snap, followed by a growl.

Joe stood paralyzed. He thought of Sonya, of Lucy and of Jack and Kelly McKinney. Ashamed of his flash of cowardice, he shone the light near where the growl had emanated. The night—black and silent—echoed with the sounds of crisp-snapping twigs and branches. He could hear the creature staying close to the road, just out of sight. Almost as if it were taunting him as it started toward town.

He pursued it on foot, choosing to stay on the blacktop and follow the creature from the road. He quickened his pace until his feet were pounding the pavement. The creature was distancing itself from him. Joe turned back around, ran to his vehicle, jumped into the Range Rover, and threw the vehicle into Drive.

Watching the road before him, and the trees off to his right in his peripheral vision, he caught sight of a large shape just up ahead. An enormous dark mass moved in the blackness beyond the reach of his headlamps. He shouldn't be able to see it, but there it was—up ahead, running quickly along in the shadows of the pines.

Lights and sirens came from up the road. Joe grabbed the radio. "It's coming your way, on your left, just in front of the trees. It's big, and it's fast."

He saw the deputy suddenly slam on his brakes. Both Hines and the rookie, Curry, stepped out of the car, taking aim at the woods. Between the deputies and himself, Joe saw what he couldn't believe.

There it stood—the beast's monstrous form perfectly silhouetted in the moonlight. Joe stopped short of where the beast reared. He climbed out of the Range Rover and went for his revolver, ready to aim. The monster made its move without hesitation.

Curry stared in shock and awe as the creature launched itself in the air and crashed down on Hines's cruiser. The weight of the large beast's impact smashed out the car's side windows and crumpled the roof.

Hines stepped away from the vehicle and tripped over his own feet before falling in the middle of the road.

Curry squeezed his eyes shut and pissed his pants, also blindly discharging his weapon. He completely missed the beast as it slashed its elongated, fur-covered arm across his face, neck and chest. One of its large claws caught his jugular, leaving the twenty-two-year-old rookie dead in seconds.

Joe fired once, twice, then three times, nailing the beast directly in its wide, muscular back. The beast shook with each shot and dropped forward, falling out of Joe's sight as it crawled down the cruiser's trunk and dropped behind the car.

Hines froze. He was laid out flat on his back in the middle of the road, staring wide-eyed at the abomination.

Joe wanted to yell to him, to ask him what he could see, but then thought better of it. Randy Hines had not moved since falling down and was probably in shock. Yelling to him might only draw the attention he was sure that he himself owned since he had shot the thing, back to his other deputy and unnecessarily put the man in mortal danger. It was best to move slow and cool.

Joe wasn't even halfway around the side of the car, where the body of rookie Brett Curry lay dead in a pool of blood, when the beast arose as best as it could.

The monster growled, sounding more like a wounded dog than a massive creature. Joe stared up into a dark pair of flickering eyes and caught a glimpse of something familiar. It let out a howl that instantly turned his blood cold.

He fired the last three silver bullets from his revolver, burying them into the chest of the beast. The howl died in its throat. Its bulk dropped backwards. The eyes closed, it lay there motionless.

Joe wasted no time reloading the silver bullets from his belt clip into the gun. He moved past the body of Curry and stood before the monster. His mind half expected the thing to lunge back up instantly and rip his head off. Without a second thought, he emptied the weapon into the chest and head of the creature lying before him.

# BLOOD AND RAIN

The replay of that awful night pressed on him. Atlas might shrug, but Joe needed something with fire. He pulled a silver flask of Jameson from his coat pocket, took a swig and reveled in the burn trickling down his throat. He would need to man up and pay his former mentor a visit. Stan had helped him before and would prove most resourceful if this situation blossomed into what he thought it would. Another full moon bloodbath was not on his list of things to do this summer.

# CHAPTER TWELVE

**S**TAN **S**PRINGS **DREAMT** of the old night watchman at the Augusta mental health facility, Harold Barnes. He watched Harold's eyes strain as he gazed through the bright ray reaching from his flashlight. Stan had had this dream before. Harold had passed away the year Stan left the psychiatric hospital, but lived on to die over and over again in Stan's dreams.

This time Harold walked right over to Stan's hiding place just behind the pond. The dumb bastard normally had the sense to flee. Stan would give chase, but usually Harold's old legs carried him quick enough to survive another nightmare. Since falling off the wagon, Stan's dreams had not been so kind to Mr. Barnes.

"Whoever you are, you're on state property and I've got every right to drop you on sight."

Stan shuffled left, hidden behind the large stone at the edge of the pond. The forest at his back held its breath as the beast in him prepared to introduce itself to the unsuspecting night watchman. Saliva pooled above the fingers he had firmly planted in the lawn. The change was swift, faster than it was in real life.

"Oh...my...God..." The light dropped from Harold's trembling hand and rolled down into the black pond.

*Arrroooo*

The beast rose to its feet. A hulk in the darkness. Harold's lips moved, but no words came out.

The monster jumped the man-made pond and reared back a clawed hand.

"No, Stanley, no."

It ripped out Harold's throat in one swipe, nearly decapitating the man. Harold's body dropped to its knees, falling forward.

The beast roared at the heavens before descending upon its kill.

Stan Springs awoke. His bedsheets clung to his naked form. He wiped at his mouth. Harold's blood was not there. The dreams—he no longer considered them nightmares—were so vivid he could hardly tell them apart from the nights he surrendered to the monster within.

He stretched, then swiveled his feet to the hardwood floor. At his age joints should pop, bones should creak, and his muscles should ache after the kind of night he'd had. His secret held those problems at bay. Secret. The dark, dirty, not-so-little secret secured him from the degenerating effects brought on by old age. It also left him alone and fucking hostile.

For years he'd held the rage in check, managing to drown the beast in a concoction of Klonopin and other opioids that kept him next to dead on the nights of a full moon.

The true surprise came after he left the facility sans drugs. He came home to Gilson Creek, ready for whatever fate awaited him. Should the beast return, he was confident Sheriff Fischer would put him down for good.

The full moon came and went. The change, MIA. He'd read about a cursed Lithuanian priest who claimed a similar dormant state, but Stan had just swiped the story aside with the plethora of false myths he'd studied. The priest was said to have died alone in the mountains.

Despite returning home, Stan adopted the priest's solitary lifestyle. He spoke to no one. And they returned the favor. Even Fischer, whom he thought would engage him, seemed to sense that something wasn't right. As if he gave off a certain scent. A distinct pheromone. And maybe he did. Whatever the case, Stan had managed to hide away from the monster and the town.

Until last night.

A storm had raged outside and within. This time he relished the curse. He'd grown nasty in the years since he returned home. In a way, he'd hoped for the beast's return. The dirty looks from the people in his community, the way the punk kids giggled and mocked him as if he were no better than that dead fuck, Old Mike. While he'd initially been relieved by the sheriff's distance, there came a time when you acknowledged old friends, out of respect, if nothing else.

No, this town had grown putrid. It was the *town* that was cursed. It was *his* job to deliver the dark enchantment's promise. It was his job to bring Gilson Creek to death's gate.

# CHAPTER THIRTEEN

**"YOU GONNA KNOCK?"** Wes nudged Joel in the back.

"All right, man, but if his mom doesn't answer because there's a strange dude with a Mohawk at her door, that ain't on me."

"I'm pretty sure she knows what kind of bizarre shit her twenty-nine-year-old son is in to."

"Fuck yeah, good point." Joel knocked.

A short, dark-haired woman with glasses and her hair pulled back in a tight bun answered.

"Hey, is this the Bruce residence?" Joel said.

"It's actually the Hersom residence; Bruce is my ex-husband's name. Are you boys looking for Nick?"

Wes stepped up next to Joel. "Ah, yes, ma'am. Is he in?"

"He's here." She nodded for them to follow.

Joel looked to Wes and shrugged.

"He's been in his room since I got home this morning. Says he doesn't feel good."

She led them past a bathroom and down a short hallway that stunk like cat piss and was taken up mostly by a washer and dryer. She rapped on the door. "Nick? You got visitors."

There was no answer.

"Nick?" She turned back to them. "If he don't answer, feel free to walk on in. I gotta go get ready."

Another shrug from Joel. Wes put his hand on the doorknob and turned.

"Nick?"

He was on the floor, tangled up in a faded blue sheet and sweating like a pig. Wes walked over to him. "Hey, Nick. You okay?"

"Huh...uhh..."

"It's Joel and Wes, man," Joel said.

Wes watched Nick's eyes open. They rolled back in his head almost instantly. He moaned and clutched at his stomach.

"Shit, Wes. I think he's gonna throw up."

"I saw the bathroom at the start of the hall. Help me get him up."

"Look at this. Man, it smells too." Joel held his head back from the bandaged wound on Nick's arm.

"Hurry up," Wes said.

They got him down the hall and into the bathroom just in time. Nick flung himself at the toilet and hurled.

"I can't watch this, dude. I'll blow too." Joel squeezed past Wes.

Wes heard the front door open and close.

Once Nick stopped puking, Wes spoke up, "Hey, Nick, you want us to come back tomorrow?"

Nick moaned and belched in response. The burp brought forth another round of vomiting.

"All right, Nick. We're staying at the Motel 6 in Hollis Oaks." Wes pulled a business card and a pen from his pocket and scratched down the phone number and their room number. "This is where we'll be. Call me tomorrow when you're up and feeling better." Wes stepped toward the door. "Do you need help back to your room?"

Nick didn't answer.

Wes met Joel at the car. He couldn't help but eye the moon. It looked full.

"Where to now?" Joel said.

They rolled down the road, heading toward town.

"Let's see if we can find the crime scenes," Wes said. "Maybe we'll luck out and find something."

"Fuck yeah. Let's do it."

They headed past the last set of lights and headed for Paulson's Park.

"This is it. This is where Nick took the picture." Wes remembered the shock and the gruesomeness of that photo. He also recalled the extreme, twisted glee it filled him with. That was the shot that put the *Crypto Insider* on the map.

"Keep going, man," Joel said.

He was right. Police lines blocked off the park entrance. Something bad had happened. He slowed as they took in the scene, or at least what they could see of it.

"Shit," Joel said, craning his neck. "Looks like we had another attack. That makes three total."

"We don't know that for sure. This could be anything."

Wes didn't believe it, but the scope of last night's events demanded he find out.

Nick tried to get up from the toilet. The chills that hijacked his body raked icy claws from the nape of his neck to his tailbone. All he could smell was the sour scent of death, like the time the squirrel curled up and died in the wall next to his bed. It was a sickly sweet rot.

His stomach tensed. Another hot wave of bile splashed the murky toilet water under his nose.

*I'm dying. I'm fucking dying here.*

His stomach lurched again, but this time came up empty. Had he heard Wes and Joel? Or was that a fever dream? He couldn't think straight. The walls inside his skull kept going from black to red, to dots and tracers. Awful, awful dreams. He couldn't recall of what, but knew his few waking moments had been filled with terror. Yet each time he reached for help, he was dragged back under.

Nick's arms shook as he pushed away from the puke-filled toilet and tried to open his eyes. He fought hard to keep them open against the undertow, but his will caved, followed by his consciousness.

# CHAPTER FOURTEEN

JOE FISCHER'S EVENING at work went pretty much like his first sexual encounter—too fast and too confusing. There was a throbbing behind his temples that he knew he'd better get used to.

*With my luck, it's probably the beginning of an ulcer.*

He chewed on aspirin between sips of Jameson. The whiskey felt good, but the pills, like this whole day, left a bitter taste in his mouth. He had two dead bodies and a shitload of questions that he wasn't sure he wanted the answers to.

After sitting at his desk for an hour, waiting on Seth Kimball's call about his three victims, he was ready to say to hell with it. He would just go talk to Nick Bruce first. The phone rang before he reached his office door.

"Hello, Seth. Help me out here. What did you find?"

"Hi, Joe. Okay, so let's start with the body from Christie Road. The damage is most definitely from an animal attack. Judging by the severity of the mutilation, it was something pretty big. Now, you said the driver-side window had been smashed and the victim's face was found outside of the vehicle, right?"

"Right."

"Well, we're talking about something powerful and violent. In order for it to have punched through the window and come away with the side of the guy's face and most of the jaw, hell, I don't know, it's surreal. I've thought about that all day, and to tell you the truth, I don't have the slightest guess as to what kind of animal would be capable of something this aggressive, let alone one that would even attempt this sort of calculated move."

"What are telling me, Seth? It was an animal, but it wasn't an animal? I'm confused."

"So am I. Animals just don't think or act this way. The encounter seems, somehow, more human. Hypothetically, even if a person was strong enough to carry out the assault, he would need to have used a weapon of some sort, but the wounds on the victim were clean. No traces of a blade or tool of any kind. That brings it back to having been perpetrated by an animal. The wounds are more congruent with those caused by that of a large mammal with claws."

"What does that leave us with? A bear, a mountain lion?" Joe said.

"A bear, a mountain lion, or maybe even a wolf, would be capable, though the beast does seem larger than the last two. But to go at a person who was sitting inside of a vehicle, in the kind of weather we had last night, it doesn't add up. The behavior itself is abnormal. Usually, the type of mammals capable of this sort of damage only attack humans to protect their babies. Sometimes, though rarely, they may attack for food."

"And in this case, there was neither. So, how about the second victim, is there anything more there?"

"The second victim's death was caused by the car crushing down upon him. The leg you found on the workbench, however, was definitely torn from him before he stopped breathing. Physically, it certainly matches what I found with the first victim." Seth continued, "The body I picked up today, like the first, also suffered severe facial trauma. His arm was torn from his body. Again, the strength and savagery in these attacks is perplexing. The mutilated chest cavity looks as though something nuzzled right into it. We're definitely looking at an animal, where this one is concerned, more than likely the same one that attacked the first."

"Thank you for your diligence, Seth. Call me if you find anything else."

"Will do, Sheriff," he said.

Joe did not want to sit alone with the information, any longer than he had to. He got up and headed out of the station.

Ted McKinney resided in a small apartment over Ken Jenks's garage. Joe pulled into the driveway behind Ted's motorcycle. He climbed the steps and raised a hand to knock.

The door opened. Ted welcomed him in.

"Evening, Ted."

"Sheriff." Ted pulled out a fresh pack of smokes and tapped the package against his palm. "Care if I light up?"

"It's your house."

"You want something to drink? I have beer or water."

"I'm good."

Ted unwrapped the cellophane from the cigarette box, opened the lid and drew one from the pack. He placed it between his lips and raised the lighter to it. "What do you need from me?"

Joe picked at a banana sticker clinging to the bare counter next to the sink. He saw the empty grave. He saw the ravaged bodies. Despite his friendship with Ted's brother, Jack, Joe had never really been close with Ted. He wasn't sure which side of the debate Ted's feelings on the supernatural lay—the sane wild-animal types or the crazy werewolf zealots.

"You didn't happen to see anyone or anything else at the park while you were there this morning, did you?" Joe said.

"You mean like a psycho killer or a black bear?"

"Right."

"Or something else?"

Joe stroked his fresh whiskers. He wasn't going to feed it to the man.

"No," Ted answered. "I didn't see anyone or anything there. I just saw...what was left."

Joe nodded. "And you were there because..."

"I don't know. I wish I hadn't been. It's just these killings...I sometimes cruise by the park and think, ya know?" Ted took a long drag, exhaled and continued, "All this shit and the storm and the moon last night...damn, I don't know. It just made me think of what happened to Michele and Jack and Kelly."

"Me too."

Ted looked up at him. "You really think this was just some wild animal passing through town or coming down from the hills?"

Joe stood up straight and fixed his Stetson. "Thanks, Ted." He tapped the counter and started for the door.

"Sheriff."

Joe waited at the door.

"Is that really what you think?" Ted said.

Joe saw the empty grave. "Ted, I don't know what to think. Just stay in tonight, okay?"

"Yeah."

"G'night."

Joe closed the door behind him. He stared up at the darkening sky. The moon was still round and bright. He hoped the legends were right. He needed some quiet tonight.

# BLOOD AND RAIN

At the station, Joe found his deputies standing a little closer to each other than he'd like to see. "Clarke! Glescoe!"

They both jumped like a couple of teenagers caught sitting too close in a room alone. He wasn't sure how serious their relationship was, but he knew they were screwing. Although that violated his personal policy for workplace etiquette, there was nothing on the books that prevented it. Besides, Shelly Glescoe was a looker, and the pickings around this town were slim for both the men and women. Regardless, he didn't want them fucking in his station.

"How did things go with Ted?" Dwayne said.

Shelly's face was flushed. "I can't believe he found a dead body. Is he okay?" she said.

Joe walked up to the reception desk across from his two frisky deputies and leaned his elbows upon the solid, worn wood. He stood there looking down at the dispatch radio, trying to swim through all the drama flowing through his head. After taking a moment to collect his thoughts, he looked up at the two of them.

"Nah, but he will be. Ain't easy seeing someone the way he did. Where's Earl?"

"In the bathroom. Maria made her meat loaf again."

"Hmm." Joe almost smiled. He made his way to the right of the reception desk, toward his office, before pausing. "Glescoe."

"Yeah, Boss?"

"I want you guys being extra cautious out there."

"Yeah, Dwayne already told me. We'll be armed and ready for...whatever."

Joe was happy to see Deputy Clarke had some of his priorities in order. "Exactly, keep your shotgun loaded and in the front seat of your cruiser at all times while you're patrolling." He paused for a moment before continuing. "Seth Kimball said it had to be a pretty big animal that did this. Very aggressive, very volatile. Keep your eyes and ears open. Be safe tonight. Call me if you see anything." He turned back in the direction of his office.

Deputy Glescoe spoke up, "Sir?"

Joe stopped and turned back around. "Yes, Glescoe?"

"What are you going to be doing? Shouldn't you go home to Sonya and get some rest?"

He knew she meant well, and that he must look tired as all hell, but he had research to do and another phone call to make before he could call it a night. "I've got a couple of old case files I need to take a peek at. Sonya is at her friend's for the night. I'll be sure to stay out of your hair. Go ahead and act like I'm not here."

"Okay, Boss, but I usually save all my singing for the midnight hour. I hope you don't mind a little Destiny's Child."

Joe turned back toward his office so as not to let them see him smirk. "I'm okay with them, but I'm not one for bad karaoke."

Glescoe made a face of mocked offense.

Clarke laughed.

Joe swung the door closed. It felt good to have a minute of frivolity. Both Glescoe and Clarke were in for some confounding discoveries. He wouldn't wish this knowledge on anyone. It was the sense of burdening these two young officers, and the impending corruption of their innocence, that caused the smile to disappear from his face as he sat down at his desk.

After making a quick check-in call to Sonya, and urging them all to continue to stay put, he dove head on into a nightmare he had thought was behind him.

# BLOOD AND RAIN

That night, lying passed out in his bed from half a bottle of scotch, Deputy Randy Hines twisted and turned in his sleep. In his dream, he was hunted through the dark woods behind Paulson Park by a massive beast that walked upright like a man, but howled like an animal at the blood-red moon high in the night sky. Randy saw himself running buck naked through trees that looked as though they had been dead for ages. Adorned with cuts and gashes from scraping into branches, his own blood decorated his hands. He had a thought within the dream—something about covering up the truth. A low growl sounded from directly behind him and, then, a monstrous howl.

Randy Hines woke up screaming, lying in his own piss.

# CHAPTER FIFTEEN

"**J**OEL, WAKE UP, man." Wes held the cup of Dunkin' Donuts to Joel's face.

"Huh, what? Oh, hey."

"I don't think Nick's gonna be much use to us, least not for a couple of days. We gotta strike while the iron's hot. Here."

Joel sat up, rubbed his eyes and accepted the coffee. "What's the plan?"

"I couldn't sleep last night...bad dreams...anyway, I'm going to see the good sheriff, and you, my friend, are going to Hollis Oaks General Hospital."

"What for?"

"That's where they took the bodies. The guy you're going to track down is Seth Kimball. Get whatever you can out of him."

Joel sipped his drink. "Cool. Meet back here?"

"Yep."

Joel watched Wes, keys in hand, head for the door. "Hey, if you got the car, how am I getting there?"

"It's down off Main Street. It's like a twenty-minute walk."

"Seth Kimball, please." Joel smirked at the look the receptionist was giving him. It wasn't every day that a guy with a dayglow-painted Mohawk and wearing a Circle Jerks T-shirt showed up asking for the coroner.

"And what is this regarding?"

"Oh, sorry. Joel O' Brien. I work for the *Insider*. I'm here to do an interview." He smiled.

"If you want to just have a seat, I'll let him know you're waiting."

"Cool. Thanks."

Twenty minutes later a man in dress slacks and a light-blue button-up shirt walked over to him.

"Hi, Mr. O'Brien?" he said as he stuck his hand out. "Seth Kimball."

Joel stood up and shook his hand. "I know we didn't set anything up. Thanks for seeing me."

"I'm not sure what this is about? You work for the *Insider*?"

"Yeah." Joel looked at the large woman two seats over. She held a Nora Roberts book, but had been eyeballing him since she sat down. "Can we talk outside?"

"I'm pretty swamped—"

"I heard."

"The *Insider*, huh?"

"*Crypto*."

Kimball's gaze darted from Joel to the lady next to him. "Make it quick. Come on."

The coroner led him out through a side entrance to the employee-parking area. He pulled out a cigarette and offered one to Joel.

"Don't smoke," Joel said. "Tobacco anyway."

Kimball lit his cigarette. He shifted his weight from one foot to the other. Then back again and dug at his forefinger with his thumb. "The *Crypto Insider*. What can I do for you?"

Joel pulled out his mini voice recorder and pressed the red button. "You handled the bodies from the attacks over in Gilson Creek this weekend?"

"Yes," Kimball said. His gaze dropped to the device.

"Did you happen to notice anything peculiar about them?"

"That's still part of an ongoing investigation. I'm not at liberty to discuss my findings."

"That's okay. I don't want you to get in trouble. It was an *animal* attack though, correct? I mean, that's what the sheriff told reporters."

Kimball sucked down another drag. Then flung the butt to the ground. "Looks like it, yes."

"Is there any possibility that it wasn't?"

"Excuse me?"

"Were you the coroner here in 1997?"

"No. Listen, Mr. O'Brien. I have a lot of things to get to—"

"Just one more question. Do you believe in werewolves?"

"I don't have time for this. If you want to chase monsters, Mr. O'Brien, why don't you try writing fiction? Have a good day."

Joel hit Stop on his recorder and watched the coroner speed-walk back inside. He wondered if Wes would have better luck.

Deputy Randy Hines tried to focus on the paperwork, but couldn't get past the impossible shadow left from last night's dream. He got up from his desk to grab another cup of coffee.

"Hey, Randy," Rita said. "You feeling okay?"

"Yeah," he lied. "Just trying to get through all of this paperwork."

"Did you hear any more on Theresa Turcott's boy?"

"No. Seth Kimball was supposed to talk to Joe last night. I haven't seen him yet this morning."

"Damn shame," Rita said. "Can't imagine what this is gonna do to her. She's had her struggles."

Randy knew about the Turcotts. A family in the bottle. Joe hadn't said much about Keith's death. Just that it could be related. Dwayne, on the other hand, told him about the kid's leg. Randy had seen the damage to the car's roof with his own eyes. It looked a hell of a lot like the car out on Christie Road.

The doors to the station opened. A guy in a T-shirt and jeans, sporting a lip ring and a ponytail, walked to Rita's desk.

"Hi. I was wondering if I might be able to speak with the sheriff."

"He's—" Rita said.

Randy joined them. "Sheriff's out at the moment. I'm Deputy Hines. What's this regarding?"

"I'm doing some research on this weekend's incidents. Just wanted to ask a few questions."

"We're still looking into things. Who are you affiliated with?"

"You'd probably laugh if I told you."

"Try me."

"Okay. I run a weekly publication called, the *Crypto Insider*—"

"I'm afraid I'm going to have to ask you to leave." Randy stepped around the counter and motioned toward the door.

"But I haven't done anything. I just want to inquire—"

Randy grabbed the guy's elbow. "Listen."

"Hey."

Randy pulled him to the doors. "Don't go stirring up any nonsense. These are good people in this town. We just lost three members of our community. The last thing we need is your trash rag drumming up articles on monsters and ghosts. We've had enough horror for the week."

Randy opened the door. The guy jerked his arm free and walked down the front steps and onto the sidewalk.

"You've got about twenty-eight days until the next full moon, Deputy. You're gonna have to spill the beans about this sooner or later."

Randy instinctively put his hand to the gun on his hip.

"Whoa. Hey, I'm leaving."

He watched the guy back away with his hands up. A cold rush of adrenaline pumped through his arms and chest. The hand on his shoulder startled him.

"Oh sorry, Randy. What was that all about?" Rita said.

His heart hammered. "Nothing."

"You okay? Your hand is shaking."

He still had his hand on his gun. He raised it and wiped his mouth. "Yeah, I think I'm going to take a stroll down to Mel's and grab something to eat."

"You sure you're okay?"

He didn't answer. He just kept rubbing his mouth and chin. "I'll be back."

§⦁⦁⸳⸳⦁

Wes exited Jenner's Grocery with a can of Mountain Dew and a copy of the *Coral County Sentinel*. The stories were separate. There was one for the guy out on Christie Road and another for local teen Keith Turcott on Bixby Drive. There was nothing about the incident at the park. Not today anyway. He wondered if he'd be able to get something out of the Turcott kid's parents. It was a shitty move, but he didn't drive all the way up here for nothing. He called the hotel.

"Hey," Joel said on the other end.

"Hey, did you get anything out of the coroner?"

"Nah, but he seemed real edgy. Hightailed it back inside after I mentioned the word *werewolf*."

"You what?"

"I knew he wasn't going to give me anything. It got a rise outta him."

"Yeah, well, that's just about what I got here too. Sheriff was out. Deputy Hines escorted me out of the building."

"Shitty."

"Yeah, but I'm calling because I need you to do me a favor."

Wes pulled his car into the Turcott's driveway. Joel had found the address on the internet for him.

The garage looked like something exploded inside. Most of the door was gone. Wes grabbed his digital camera from the front seat and snapped a few pictures. He glanced at the trailer next to it, checking the windows to see if anyone was watching him. Satisfied no one was, Wes checked the area in front of the garage for animal tracks. There had been no mention of the beast being involved, in the paper or on the newscast this morning, but he had a feeling.

"Can I help you?"

He spun around at the woman's voice and tucked his slim camera into his back pocket. He waved to the woman in the doorway. "Hi. Mrs. Turcott?"

"Yes?"

"Hi, my name's Wes Kaplan. I work for a paper out of New Hampshire. I know this isn't the ideal time to speak with you, but would you have a couple minutes to spare?"

"I...I already told the sheriff everything...I..."

"I just have a couple of quick questions, ma'am, and then I promise I'll be out of your way."

She looked dazed. He could smell the booze on her breath. He jumped at his chance before she could turn away or say no.

"What happened to the garage door?"

Her gaze floated to the garage and then out toward the forest over the small field that led away from it.

"Ma'am?"

"Do you..."

"Do I..."

"Do you believe in the supernatural?"

"Yes."

"Whatever did that was not from around here."

"Did you see it?"

"I heard his screams..." She disappeared in the memory. Wes waited for her to return.

"When I came to the door...I saw it bust through the garage and run out there..."

"What did it look like?"

"It killed my boy and then it ran out there." She pointed toward the woods.

"You saw it though. What did it look like?"

"It killed my boy." She was gone. Tears rolled down her red cheeks.

"Thank you, Mrs. Turcott. I'm sorry for your loss."

He left her in the doorway. She stayed there as he got in his car, staring out into the woods beyond. The goose bumps on his arms told him he had his story.

# Chapter Sixteen

By Thursday, life in Gilson Creek had returned to normal. The sound of birds chirping came just before the sun's golden glow crested the horizon and signaled the dawn. The Donavans' across the street followed shortly thereafter. Allan Donavan made his way across his creaky porch, in a worn-out housecoat, to see where the paperboy lazily had planted his copy of the morning *Coral County Sentinel*. The more genteel types—like his neighbor Marv Thompson—found copies of the *New York Times* on their stoops.

Joe nodded at both men. Mr. Donavan waved back. Marv the asshole did not.

Joe met the morning the same way he always did. He leaned against the support beams of his front porch that were in dire need of being repainted. He liked to breathe in the mornings, telling himself it gave him a sense of things to come. He wasn't sure how or why he did this exactly—it was just one of his daily rituals.

He heard car after car roll down his street, blaring the sounds of Wild Ted's Morning Meds as they passed by. Some people liked to get their mornings off and running with loud rock music, but Joe thought a cup of Folgers did the trick just fine.

Life hummed along as if nothing out of the ordinary had occurred, though if anyone had seen the bodies of

Brian Rowel, Keith Turcott or Mike Ouellette, they would have known better.

The *Coral County Sentinel* ran obituaries on Michael "Old Mike" Ouellette and Keith Turcott. For Old Mike's they went with the generic, but acceptable, mountain lion story. Despite the fact that there hadn't been any mountain lion sightings in Maine since Gilson Creek's last series in 1997, and in all of Maine since 1938, people went along with it. There was no mention of the severed arm, the gnawed-on chest cavity or the massive damage inflicted to the face of the deceased. Keith Turcott's obit simply stated that he died from injuries suffered in his garage.

School was done for the summer. The teens of Gilson Creek flocked to Emerson Lake en masse. Joe knew Sonya and her friends would spend most of their days there too. He'd give them the days in which to do so. The beach closed at dusk, but Joe was already planning to supply the lake with a deputy to make certain the water and sand were vacated by dark.

Summer was supposed to be full of promise and good times, but for Joe it looked like another season of silver bullets and dread. The next full moon was in twenty-six days.

For Nick Bruce, summer's promise and the idea that anything was possible made him want to stay anywhere but inside.

Wes called him that morning to make sure he was okay and to let him know that he and Joel had managed to scrape together a terrific article for Friday's edition of the Crypto Insider. His Full Moon Monster was going to be front-page news again. Wes said that if Nick was interested, he'd love to have him stay on the story.

# BLOOD AND RAIN

Nick hadn't returned Wes's phone calls. He'd only started to feel better this morning.

He cleaned the bite on his arm. The wound was no longer black (if it had ever been black), and it appeared to be healing quite well. The teeth hadn't sunk in as deep as he'd originally thought. He felt there was no need to go to the hospital. Whatever infection there might have been had run its course.

Nick entered the kitchen. His mom was sitting at the table, drinking a cup of coffee and thumbing through one of her entertainment-gossip magazines. She looked him over.

"Good morning. Feelin' better?"

"Yeah. This coffee fresh?"

"It was an hour ago."

"Good enough."

He poured a mug of her burnt Blueberry Cobbler and joined her at the table. He watched her gaze fall to the bandage on his arm.

"Did that happen in your car?"

"My car?"

"Yeah, AAA guy dropped it off Sunday morning. You get in an accident?"

"Not exactly." He remembered the blown tire. "I got a flat."

"What happened to your arm?"

"Some animal bit me while I was changing the tire."

"*Animal?*"

Her face went pale.

"What? I'm okay. It wasn't even that deep," he said.

"It was probably that mountain lion that killed Old Mike and that man on Christie Road."

"Mountain lion?"

"Yes. And that's where the AAA guy says he picked your car up." His mother scooted out of her seat and to his side.

109

She hugged his head the way she used to when he was little.

"You're lucky to be alive."

He shrugged out of her hold. "I'm fine, Mom."

"We better get you to the doctor." She made a move for her car keys on the kitchen counter.

"Jesus, Mom. I said I'm fine."

"Don't you talk to me like that. Now, come on. We're taking you to see—"

"No. We're not." Nick shot up to his feet. The chair slid across the floor and slammed into the cupboards. The little tree of mugs rattled.

His mother took a step back.

"I'm okay. I just need some air."

He left her standing in the kitchen, grasping her keys. Outside, he stopped at his car. He forgot to ask her where his keys were. He decided to walk it off. Whatever it was.

He'd never really raised his voice to his mother. That had been his father's thing. He, Daniel Bruce, had been the hard one. The big-mouthed macho loser. Until he turned into a ghost and vanished from both of their lives. Good riddance. Nick would never be like his father.

He reached the end of his street. Part of him wanted to go home and apologize to his mom. Let her take him to the hospital for her peace of mind. The woods across the street called to another part of him. Something deeper, primal. He sniffed the air—something musty lay beneath the scent of pine and dirt.

He stepped off the pavement and onto the path. For being laid up for the better part of a week, he felt spry, loose. He broke into a jog, and then into a sprint. He felt free...and hungry.

# CHAPTER SEVENTEEN

**M**ELANIE MURDOCK'S THURSDAY morning commenced as always with a packed house and *Wild Ted's* morning program playing over the speakers of her busy establishment. They were playing best of shows for the next couple weeks while his band went on the road.

This morning, Mel's Café was humming along with its full roster of regulars, the majority of which were devouring an order of the "Best Stack in Town" and unconsciously nodding along with or tapping a foot to an Aerosmith classic. Melanie listened to Kenny Larson, Pat Caron and Bob Dube, a three-man work crew for Elias Construction, snorting, chuckling and making juvenile comments about what they'd like to do to her or her young waitresses if they got the chance. They didn't think she could hear them. Two tables over, Allan and Dot Donavan were enjoying their orders of eggs and bacon. Allan took his sunny-side up, with a black coffee. Dot had hers scrambled, with a hot cup of Earl Grey tea. Both were well into the seventies and Mel found them completely adorable. They just sat quietly, eating the warm food before them, feeling comfortable and more than happy just to be sitting together sharing another beautiful morning. Alex McKinney sat alone in a corner booth, half-awake and waiting for his brother Josh. They would blast through a quick meal of bacon and hash, as they always did, before heading down the street to open the auto shop for the day's business.

Mel listened to the conversation between Kemp Peaslee, Timothy Harper and Kylie Potter, who were all perched on their regular stools, commenting to each other about the abnormal heat wave that was supposed to start today, but mostly they spoke of the horrible death of Old Mike. They shared stories of his nonsensical ramblings and about the many separate occasions when they had each picked him up, walking or stumbling along the side of the road, sometimes two towns over, not even sure where he was or what he was doing there. Mel even added her tale about the time she'd found him passed out in front of the café doors.

She knew, for some quaint communities, town drunks were seen as eyesores or blemishes on the face of their small-town charm. Mel was happy that her people went the opposite direction. Most of her customers spoke fondly of Old Mike—Sheriff Fischer had once referred to him as a town landmark. To Mel, he was just another of Gilson Creek's many colorful characters. He may have been eccentric, but he had always been harmless. His sudden passing was a notable and sad footnote to this early summer season.

Sitting alone at the counter, farthest from the loud discussion group was an old, haggard-looking man who could have easily been mistaken for a homeless person. Scraggly, long gray hair hung down to the middle of his back, matching an unmanaged beard that covered a face with numerous deep, leathery wrinkles and scars. Dark, distracted eyes stared through the breakfast before him. He was dressed in a long dark-green trench coat and wore a flannel shirt, stained work pants and a pair of combat boots. The fact that today was supposed to be in the high eighties to low nineties only accentuated his out-of-touch factor. He was picking at the breakfast she had set before him an hour ago—a piece of toast and a cup of black coffee.

The tattered-looking soul being ignored and left alone was none other than former Gilson Creek Sheriff Stan Springs.

Mel had learned plenty about the man over the years from various sources. He had accrued an interesting history of sorts since vacating his official post with the Gilson Creek Sheriff's Department. He had unexpectedly resigned from his position as sheriff near the end of the spring of 1997, dropping out of sight from the people he had sworn to protect. He had told the *Sentinel* that he knew the town would be in the more than capable hands of his number one deputy, Joe Fischer, and that was the sole comforting factor that had allowed him to make the move so abruptly. Also he had no doubts Joe was ready for the job.

Seemingly overnight, one of the town's most recognized and beloved public officials became a recluse. He spoke to no one, outside of the sheriff, following his resignation. Sheriff Fischer told her that Springs traveled down to Augusta and checked himself into the Augusta mental health facility.

Ever since he returned, he'd been different. Mel wondered where it had all gone wrong for the guy.

Stan Springs stared into his black coffee and replayed his history. He thought about his own unraveling. He thought about it every day.

He remembered the day he went into the loony bin.

He told Joe Fischer that for the better part of the previous year, he had not trusted his own instincts or his own sense of reality, and things had finally reached the point where he had to face the hard truth. The reality he admitted to Joe, and to himself, was that the loss of control and state of distrust evolving within him had been building with more intensity over the long, cold winter. He'd done his best to hide his struggles, though he was sure Joe had noticed, but he no longer felt fit to work, let alone to defend his town or its people.

He was on his own, even though Joe tried to be there for him, and he knew the amount of responsibilities that were involved in being the sheriff, even of a town as small as Gilson Creek. Plus, Fischer already had a little girl to raise on his own. The young man had enough on his plate to tend to, without dealing with an old, senile bastard like him. Going to the mental health facility made the most sense. Going of his own volition, he could leave when and if he felt well enough to do so. Like the rest of the patients, he was on lockdown after 8:00 p.m., but he'd traded his way around that one.

Prior to checking in, his mind had become his own prison, where he could barely even recognize himself or his own thoughts. He had been having terrible visions at the time. Things he could not rationalize. Some came while he slept, and others, the ones that really shook him up, came while he was wide-awake.

For instance, he could be staring out his back window, at the thick forest that stretched out infinitely, like an ocean of dark pine trees. He had always thought it to be a beautiful, breathtaking view. Only, now, he would see something darker. The once brilliant mass of pines would hold an aura of malevolence.

It didn't make sense. There was no reason for thinking such things, but he could not vanquish the dreary feeling. He would see the forest as an army of horrible dead things that were making their way, inch by inch, closer to his property, coming to drag him out to whatever evil waited beyond.

# BLOOD AND RAIN

At least, being in a facility, he wouldn't be alone. He'd be looked after by psychotherapists and nurses. He packed a suitcase of clothes and car magazines, told Joe, and only Joe, that he was leaving and drove himself to his new safe house.

His irrational fears abated for the first couple of weeks of his residency, allowing his thoughts to return to simpler things: classic cars, John Wayne movies and the Red Sox.

Then along came the dark spring and summer seasons, and with them, the dreams. He remembered night after night of tossing and turning, waking up stuck to his sheets, from being drenched in sweat. He couldn't tell if it was his own distraught mind causing these bad dreams, or the stories being recounted to him by Joe about the brutal deaths springing up back home.

Fischer came to him for counsel on the killings, and he felt obligated to listen, even though he didn't want to. The memories were too much, but he was a man of honor and loyalty, and he felt compelled to help in any way he could, especially since he considered himself responsible.

Joe tried to explain the extensive damage he and his deputies encountered in each apparent attack. It wasn't just the mutilation of the bodies, but also the damage to the car in the case of the McKinneys.

It was Stan who, with some reluctance, asked the sheriff if he believed in monsters. Ghosts, goblins, ghouls, werewolves—the things he had been seeing in his own tortured mind. Joe tried to laugh off such a foolish notion, but his laughter died with one look at the former sheriff's face. Stan was deathly serious, and as much as he knew Joe wanted not to admit it, he could see in the younger man's face that he too knew it was something supernatural. A werewolf.

Both dates of the first two attacks coincided with a full moon. Each set of victims was torn to pieces, a car had been battered off the road and onto its side, and trees had been knocked over as if from a hurricane or tornado.

Would Joe figure it out?

The two men immediately started researching the folklore of werewolves. Stan used whatever books Joe would sneak in to him—his therapist would frown upon such things, considering Stan's state of mind and reason for being in the facility in the first place. Stan battled his inner demons, writing down every bit of possibly pertinent information he could gather. In his dreams, he paid for every word. But at the time, he thought he could help destroy it. He thought he could rid himself of the curse, or at least help Joe to...

A voice broke the haggard ex-sheriff's trip down memory lane.

"You all right, man?" said the young gentleman behind him.

Stan's mind returned to the café. His coffee was staring back at him. The memories faded. Someone had placed a gentle hand on his shoulder and was looking at him with both apprehension and concern in his eyes. Stan recognized the youth as Alex McKinney.

"Get your fucking hand off me," he growled.

Josh grabbed his brother and pulled him toward the café's doors.

"Sorry, sir, he doesn't know any better," Josh said.

Mel watched as the former sheriff made his way out the door and around the corner of the building. He had paid, always did, and had been a quiet customer—a little weird, but harmless—but for the first time since he had made his cryptic return from his self-induced exile, she was afraid

116

of him. She wasn't sure if she wanted him coming back in. She would have to call Joe and talk to him first. He knew the guy best, if anyone really did.

*"Get your fucking hand off me."*

Alex looked as if the devil himself had just advised him to mind his own business.

"Big V," she said to her head cook. "I gotta make a call. If anyone needs something get one of the girls?"

"Sure thing, Mel."

She took the cordless and went to the breakroom.

Sheriff Fischer picked up on the third ring.

"Sheriff?"

"Mel, I told you to call me Joe."

"Sorry. Joe?"

"Go ahead."

She thought about how to say what she had to say. She closed her eyes and blurted it out praying he didn't think of her as just another pain in his ass. "Sheriff Springs was in this morning, and well...he sort of snapped."

"Snapped how?"

"Alex McKinney grabbed his shoulder and asked if he was all right. The sheriff's eyes just went angry. He turned and growled at Alex. Told the kid to keep his hands off him, but he was a tad more vulgar about it."

The line went quiet.

"Joe?"

"I'm here," he said. "I'm guessing he scared Alex shitless."

"Sure did. Me too. That's why I'm calling you. I'm not sure I want him back in here. The place is buzzing, everyone's on edge with what's happened lately..."

"I'll have a talk with him."

"It's just that I know you guys were close."

"Mel, please. Don't worry, okay?"

"Thanks, Sher—Joe."

# CHAPTER EIGHTEEN

**T**HE SUN HOVERED above, high and bright, adding to his misery. Stan Springs stopped at the road and stared at the McKinney brothers heading down the sidewalk. Part of him wanted to follow them—a deep, mean part of him. He stayed put, letting them go on their way for now. He dared a glance over his shoulder and could make out that big-titted bitch behind the counter, phone in hand, calling the sheriff, no doubt. Fuck her. Fuck them all.

His blood didn't just boil, it roared. It raced through his veins, his heart humming like the engine of his old '57 Black Widow. He was like an old stock car all right, but what he had under the hood couldn't be bought or sold. It was something only the cursed and the forgotten, the lonely and the tortured, endured. A price to pay doled out by some sadistic god above, or below. It didn't matter which deity or demon pulled his tendons from beneath his flesh like old strings, he no longer gave a shit.

He'd overheard that ignorant racist Pug Gettis mumbling through his false teeth about Old Mike, something about him sleeping on a park bench and then being ripped apart by a mountain lion. That's the thing about small towns—they're filled with half-truths and misinformation. Gilson Creek held a lot more secrets than its people knew.

Stan remembered the heated conversation he and Old Mike had just around the bend from here two months ago.

The drunk stumbled into him as they passed—Stan heading to Mel's and Old Mike heading wherever wasted quitters wandered off to—causing Stan's glasses to hit the ground and break. The eyes of the sloshed and brown-toothed vagrant, realizing whom he'd bumped, went dark. Storm clouds moved in over his brow. "I'd say sorry, but you don't deserve it. You quit on this town. You quit and let that monster have his way. You ran away and hid while that thing ate through us. Three kids, just in high school, torn up and strung up for the world to see. And you just hid away. Shame on you," that drunken son of a bitch said just before spitting in Stan's face.

There were no witnesses when Stan grabbed the smelly bastard and delivered a right cross worthy of a gold belt across the sunken, bristled cheek of his accuser. It felt so good he delivered two more for good measure. He left the unconscious fool in the dirt on the side of the road.

Old Mike never ratted him out. He probably couldn't remember whether the assault had been real or imagined. No matter, his accusations struck a chord Stan thought forgotten.

Something revved within—something dark, something powerful.

The drunkard hadn't been wrong, at least not completely. There were truths, half-truths, to his accusations of abandonment and resignation. That it was cowardice, on the other hand, was fucking laughable. A monster, he'd called it.

*That's funny*, Stan thought. Most people live with ghosts of their own pasts, some often referring to skeletons in their closets. Stan lived with something much larger, much more tangible.

Stan Springs made his way down the sidewalk, thinking of an old novel he'd read years ago by Guy Endore. Stan's thoughts were of the French and of monsters. He continued on under the hot sun high in the sky, headed for his fortress of solitude. Sweat barreled down his forehead, his thick chest, and his thighs.

He would wait and see if the sheriff paid him a visit. He doubted Joe Fischer would do much more than knock on his door. A heart-to-heart with his old friend was long overdue.

*Bonjour, Sheriff.*

# Chapter Nineteen

**S** ONYA WAS GLAD to be back in her own bed. She'd spent the last week at Kim's, and even though they had a blast whenever they were together, she needed the peace and quiet.

With Mrs. Donaldson working late every day, the girls were left to themselves and their vices of choice. Usually that was pot, but it could have been worse—they could have been pill poppers like some of the freakier girls at school.

Lying on her bed in the comfort of silence, she felt drained. Both her body and mind could use the rest. On top of all that, she'd not seen her dad since Saturday morning, and outside of a couple quick phone calls, she hadn't really talked to him either. Something wasn't right with him. She heard it in his voice. She knew when he was busy, but she also understood when he was avoiding her. This past week had been a combination of both. Whatever it was he was working on, he didn't want her to know about or be involved in. She hadn't seen much of Alex this week, either. He'd been busy working at the garage during the day and off running various errands in the afternoons. He was helping his brother out and making decent money. She was excited for him, but missed him like crazy. They hadn't slept together since the afternoon in Kim's guest room on Sunday, and though she wanted to be with him this very instant, she needed a night to herself even more.

When she had called him earlier, she told him tomorrow night would be their night. He promised to come over for dinner with her and her dad. Afterwards, they could go to the Cineplex in Hollis Oaks. She really wanted to see the new *Spider-Man* movie. She liked Tobey Maguire, but she *loved* James Franco.

Sonya took a nice, long shower and threw on a comfy pair of Hello Kitty pajama bottoms and an old KISS T-shirt she had dug out of her father's box of outdated clothes a couple months back. As she brushed her wet hair, she thought back on the night she had stumbled upon the box of her dad's old things in the basement while looking for a photo album. He must have been a rocker back in the '70s, though you'd never know it, with all the James Taylor he listened to nowadays. The box had been filled with bell-bottom jeans and old worn-out concert shirts. Bands like Led Zeppelin, Black Sabbath and Deep Purple were on the clothing. Truth be told, she was expecting to find a joint rolled up within the clothes.

She confiscated the KISS and Led Zeppelin shirts and absolutely loved wearing them to bed, as they were so soft from the past numerous washings. Her dad caught her with one of the shirts on a few nights after she'd taken them upstairs and told her he had forgotten all about them and the box. He said he had put all the clothing he was fond of in it, but that he knew her mom would throw it out, so he had hidden it deep down in the basement.

That was a great night. He talked about all the crazy stuff he and his pals had done as dumb kids, going to rock concerts and smoking grass—which is actually how he referred to it. He was so old. He also spent a good amount of time that night doing something he rarely did—talk about her mom.

She knew it was too hard on him to discuss her mother, but she and her father had laughed long and hard about her picking on him for wanting to keep his old shirts, and about how if her mother were alive today, she would make remarks about the cowboy hat that he wore every day.

He told Sonya the story about when he tried to grow a mustache. Her mother hated mustaches so much that the one time he decided to grow one she had refused to kiss him until he shaved it off. Needless to say, he didn't have it for more than a week. Her mom was particular when it came to her dad and his appearance—especially after he became a police officer. Her dad recounted how he had tried to sell her mom on the fact that the mustache went with the cop sunglasses, and they laughed until there were tears when he told her that her mother said he looked like one of the Village People.

Sonya didn't get the reference, but laughed right along with him. She loved seeing him that happy. He was usually upbeat when he wasn't being Mr. Cop, but she could count on one hand the number of times that she had seen him smile so wide or laugh as hard as he had on that night. It was one of her favorite memories, and wearing his old concert shirts to bed had become a part of her nightly sleep attire thereafter.

Her father picked her up from Kim's that afternoon, but took off right after dropping her in the driveway. He said he had to go see an old friend and after that he'd be home for the night. He had deliberately failed to mention a name, choosing to remain vague and using the anonymity of the generic term *old friend*. That struck her as weird because he always wanted her to know right where he was on his nights off, in case of an emergency.

She chalked it up to being a part of the enigmatic character he had taken on recently, and decided that wasting any more of her relaxation time worrying about it would be stupid. Her dad had always been fond of saying "worrying is like a rocking chair—it gives you something to do, but it doesn't get you anywhere". He was right, as usual.

Besides, she had some summer reading to get to—a pile of Stephen King and Bentley Little books stacked next to her bed, just waiting to give her the creeps. There was nothing like a little *Shining* while home alone. She had to admit, she liked being scared. The recent deaths in town only added to the ambiance.

She grabbed a glass of milk and headed to her bedroom. Before picking up her book, she wondered once more where her dad had gone and who the mystery friend could be.

She quickly reminded herself of the rocking-chair adage, shook it off and dove into the misadventures of a man named Jack Torrance.

# CHAPTER TWENTY

**S**TAN **S**PRINGS **STRETCHED** his legs, arched his back and felt the powerful, blessed blood course through his body. There was a time when the impending change had been a terrible burden. Oh, the guilt had tormented him. He'd even played along with the charade, helping Joe Fischer dig up every whisper, every rumor or piece of folklore they could find on the shape-shifting monstrosity. And as hard as Stan tried to keep the beast away, in those early days, the monster always came home.

He couldn't remember where or how he'd been cursed. He only knew when.

It was an early spring offer from Douglas Hendricks to come up-country and hunt on his cousin's land. *"The Allagash is the best bear huntin' this side of the country."* Doug's words drizzled somewhere in Stan's memory.

Stan normally only hunted during deer season, but after the death of his sister, Elaine, in January of that year left him the sole surviving member of his family, he decided a weekend away with an old friend in the North Country might be a good reprieve from the sudden isolation he felt.

The morning was quiet. He and Doug were up before dawn and tracking something massive. Doug insisted Stan take the tree stand. Stan refused. He didn't consider hiding in a tree and taking cheap shots at clueless creatures to be hunting. Doug took the stand; Stan stalked the ground. One minute there was a sound to his right; the next he was waking up at Doug's. Doug's wife, Missy, was tending to a deep wound on the back of his right leg. Stan remembered blood. He remembered Doug pacing the room and Missy trying to disinfect his wound with a bottle of homemade alcohol.

The next day they took him to a proper hospital where he was stricken with some sort of fever/infection. Three days later and thirty pounds lighter, Stan was released. By the end of the week, home and back to work, Stan's leg was nearly good as new. His mind, on the other hand, was far from it.

The low rumble of an all too familiar vehicle broke Stan from his reverie.

The drive to Stan Springs's house filled Joe Fischer with anxiety and trepidation. He didn't know if Stan would listen. Joe liked to think that he avoided Stan, giving him his space because he knew the man.

Who was he kidding? The truth was he stayed away from Stan for the same reason everyone else in town did. It wasn't a favor. No, they had lost touch. But even more than that, it was what he thought of every time he saw the man. It brought him right back to that horrible summer. All the books and all the time spent talking about full moons and monsters. Stan Springs was a constant reminder of the beast.

Stan's driveway came into sight. His old Ford pickup sat unused on the lawn. Joe swallowed hard and gritted his teeth. A mixture of emotions—abandonment, anger, guilt and fear—ran the gauntlet inside of his head.

# BLOOD AND RAIN

Joe stepped out of his truck, closed the door and stared at the bedroom window upstairs. The curtains fluttered and closed as the shadow behind them disappeared. Joe instantly regretted coming here.

Stan Springs watched the familiar green Range Rover pull into his gravel driveway, the loose pebbles crunching beneath its tires. He stared down through worn-out eyes. He brimmed with discontent, watching as Sheriff Fischer stepped out of the truck, wearing a look of uncertainty beneath his Stetson. Springs smiled at the sheriff's obvious discomfort.

He stretched and clawed a hand across his hairy, barrel chest. Snagging a tattered button up shirt from the end of his bed, he slipped his powerful arms through the thread-bare sleeves, not bothering with the buttons. His heavy feet thundered down the stairs as he made his way to meet his successor at the door. He wondered if Fischer's visit would happen to have anything to do with his little spat with the McKinney kid. He'd seen the fear in the eyes the McKinney brothers and every other patron in the diner. He couldn't really see either of the McKinney boys whining to the sheriff, they both had reputations to uphold. More likely, it was that big-titted bitch, Mel. Either way, Stan was eager to have a talk with his old friend.

*This should be fun.*

Joe couldn't shake the sudden feeling that this was a bad move. Springs wasn't the man he once was. Hell, who knows what kind of drugs they'd had him on all those years. He'd read somewhere that antidepressants and antianxiety medications could change the chemicals in a person's brain. He dismissed the thought. He was being stupid. He was nervous because he had been avoiding his former mentor. He was the jerk here and owned every right to the guilt that pulled at his stomach.

He climbed the half-rotten steps to the wide front porch. A single gray rocking chair sat ten feet from the door as the only object dressing the porch. He had shared many beers over the years out here on late evenings with his former friend. There used to be another rocking chair, a red one with a crooked rocker that made it wobble. Before, there was also an old red Craftsman toolbox in the corner, plus various rags, old hunting magazines and a metal Coors Light cooler between the chairs, which was always filled with Budweiser. Stan might have stored it all before heading down to the hospital, probably had, but Joe imagined that Stan would have at least brought some of the old things back out by now. The absence of "life" on the porch was unsettling. He steeled himself and stepped up to the large oak door, his knuckles poised.

Stan opened the door before he had even finished knocking. He looked worse than Joe remembered. His long, scraggly gray hair, combined with the way his unkempt beard stretched out around the bottom of his face as if it were trying to escape from the man wearing it, gave him the appearance of a lion. From the look in this tattered but still powerful-looking man's squinting, dark eyes and the scowl on Stan's face, Joe was half expecting a roar, rather than the quiet response he received.

"Sheriff, what brings you out my way?"

There was a trace of a smirk behind the beard. Joe wasn't sure he liked it. "Can we talk?"

"I've been wondering that since I got home," Stan said, the resentment in his eyes creeping into his voice.

"I know. We haven't had a chance to catch up sin—"

"What the fuck do you want?" Stan interrupted.

The sudden change in tone caught Joe off guard. He was here on behalf of Mel, but he was also here hoping to...hoping to what?

"Well, if that's it, Sheriff, I really must be getting back to my reading," Stan said. The large man stepped back to close the door.

"I have to talk to you about what happened today at Mel's."

Stan flung the door back open, stepped over the threshold and out onto the porch.

Joe took a step back and gave him space.

Stan folded his arms over his broad chest. "Is this about that little piece of shit, Alex McKinney? He put his hands on me. I just told the kid he should think twice before touching someone he doesn't know," Stan said as his voice began to rise.

Joe placed his hands on his hips. "From what Mel says, you scared the hell out of her and her customers. She's not comfortable with you being at the café. I'm going to need you to stay out of there for a little while. At least until Mel feels—"

"Fuck you," Stan said. "And fuck that big-titted whore." Stan's face went red as he stepped forward, forcing the sheriff down from the porch and onto the steps. "Get off my property right now. Get the fuck out of here."

Joe stepped down onto the loose gravel, being sure to stay out of the man's reach. He knew irrational when he saw it, and Stan was wearing it like battle armor because he didn't want anyone getting to him. He was scarred, he was wounded, he was pissed off— he was *unpredictable*.

"All right, all right, I don't want any problems. I'm leaving," Joe said in the calming tone he usually reserved for talking down hotheaded teenagers.

"Damn right you are. Get the fuck off my property," Stan said again.

Joe paused before getting into his truck. "I mean it though, Stan. If I see you at Mel's I'm going to have to—"

The lion of a man hopped down from his porch. "Don't worry. You won't fucking see me there. Now get the fuck out of here."

Joe got into the truck, started it up and pulled back out onto Old Gilson Creek Road. He watched for a second longer as Stan Springs stood at the foot of his porch, like a bear defending its den, fuming. His chest was heaving, his eyes burning like a wildfire. Joe couldn't help but wonder how the man had been released from the mental health facility—he was raging like a beast.

Joe was probably overreacting. Maybe Stan was just being highly emotional. After all, Joe had just told him that he was no longer welcome in the one place he liked to frequent, so of course he'd be upset.

He threw the truck in gear and pulled away, watching the shell of the man he used to adore turn and stamp up the steps back into his house.

He wondered if he had just poked the wrong hornet's nest.

# CHAPTER TWENTY-ONE

**N**ICK WAITED OUTSIDE Jenner's Grocery Friday morning.

*What will Wes and Joel's piece look like? Are they really going to use my Full Moon Monster?*

He thought about it so much last night after he returned from his romp through the woods that he had dreamt about it. In the dream, Wes and Joel had made *him* the monster. He had been the beast responsible for the killings. This morning, he'd woken up grinning. *If only.* He gazed at the bandage on his arm.

"Morning, Nick," Dave Jenner said.

"Hey, Mr. Jenner."

"You're here early."

"Yeah. I just needed to pick up a few things."

Mr. Jenner stepped aside and ushered him in. Nick went straight for the magazine rack in the closest checkout lane.

"Anything I can help you find?" Mr. Jenner said.

He didn't want to say. Nick knew that his original article had irritated a number of locals. He wasn't sure which side of the divide Dave Jenner was on.

There was only one copy of the *Crypto Insider* left. He grabbed it.

"That's last week's edition. New one should be coming in within the hour. Charlie and Nina usually get the weeklies out on the racks by nine or so."

*Damn.*

"You got something in there?"

"Not me. Not this time."

Mr. Jenner glanced around and then lowered his voice. "Truth be told, I thought you were on to something."

"Oh yeah?"

"Yeah, and I'd be lying if I said that what happened this past weekend didn't scare the shit outta me. Pardon my French." Mr. Jenner's gaze dropped to Nick's arm. "You okay?"

Nick put his arm behind his back. "Yeah, I caught a touch of something earlier this week..."

"I thought I saw your car out by the park the other morning."

"Oh that, yeah. I got a flat tire." Nick tried to gauge whether Mr. Jenner was fishing for something or if it was just his paranoia.

"You musta been caught out in that storm, huh?"

"I, yeah...lucky for me someone happened to come by and..." A white van pulled up to the front doors.

"Oh, there's your vendor now."

"Three Dead in Gilson Creek: Eyewitness Cries Return of Full Moon Monster"

"Thanks, Mr. Jenner."

"You just keep me in the loop. You hear anything else, I wanna know. Sheriff doesn't seem to be able to connect the dots. Either that, or he's afraid to. Old Mike was the only one in town, well, besides you, who knew what really did that to those poor people."

Nick promised and slipped outside. *Old Mike.* Nick wasn't so sure about that one. Everyone knew what Old Mike thought it was—a werewolf. Nick's assessment was much vaguer, at least he thought so. His Full Moon Monster was fictitious. His version could just as easily be a Bigfoot.

# BLOOD AND RAIN

As much as the supernatural fascinated him, Nick still had yet to lay eyes upon any spirits or beasts. Like with Jesus, Atlantis, and aliens, seeing was more than believing—it was confirmation. Were these things possible? Of course. Anything was possible, but he didn't believe that God watched from above or that there was a great missing city under the sea.

He'd never been abducted and right now, much to his own surprise, he was hoping that there wasn't a wolfman ripping apart the drones of his small-as-fuck hometown.

*Eyewitness.* The "credible" account came from Theresa Turcott, the mother of Keith Turcott. The article went on to say that the "eyewitness" saw the fur-covered beast explode from the garage, after hearing the screams of her boy. She said "it ran into the woods". *Hmm.* Nick wasn't sure what to make of it. Wes and Joel sure as hell believed. And they wanted him to "stay on the case". There was definitely *something* out there.

He tossed the paper in the trash can by the Dunkin' Donuts and decided to jog home. He was feeling great. He'd never been an exercise guy, not outside of Phys Ed anyway, but he had pent-up energy that demanded release. Much like this morning, he ducked onto a path through the woods just past Gilbride Avenue and hoofed it all the way home. He could have run forever.

Ted McKinney hung up the phone with his drummer, Rick. The Broken Exes were headed out on tour for two weeks. It was a shitty move to pull out last minute, but he knew Rick's brother, Bobby, could fill in. Hell, Bobby was a better technical player. What they would lack in stage presence—Ted's forte—they would more than make up with overall performance.

He also decided to still use his vacation time from the station. He needed to get away, but not too far away. He'd rented a room for the next couple of weeks at a little shithole place in a Hollis Oaks strip mall. It was called the Lobster Motorway Inn. Maybe he was batshit crazy, but he wasn't convinced that the sheriff believed the mountain lion story any more than he did. He didn't know how far Joe's acceptance for supernatural possibilities stretched, but he'd be willing to bet it was a lot farther than the man let on.

He packed his saddlebags—laptop, T-shirts, jeans, underwear, iPod—then jumped on his bike and headed out.

His room wasn't quite ready when he got to the inn. He decided to hit up the 7-Eleven for his beer and cigarette rations.

Near the checkout, a Maxim featuring Kirsten Dunst from the new *Spider-Man* flick caught his attention. She'd come a long way since *Interview with a Vampire*. Ted picked it up and noticed the headline on the cover of the paper next to it. The *Crypto Insider*. He added it to his purchases. *Beer, babes and the Return of the Full Moon Monster: Tonight at the Lobster Motorway Inn!* He laughed to himself and grabbed a carton of cigarettes at the counter.

The girl with the tattooed knuckles and atrocious breath who was ringing him up asked him if he'd seen the new Spidey movie yet. He hadn't, and wished she would stop smiling at him with her blackened teeth. Luckily, she didn't ID him. Being a quasi-celebrity, the last thing he needed was this girl knowing where he was staying. He thanked her and left to check in.

His room featured a little kitchenette, a minifridge, a recliner on which the upholstery dated it back to the early eighties and a double-sized bed. Not the Waldorf Astoria, but a decent, livable space.

He kicked his feet up in the recliner and read the article on Gilson Creek's Full Moon Monster. The article made it sound like it could be a frigging Bigfoot, as much as a werewolf.

Ted leaned toward the latter. The writers were on to something, but he wondered how much was for copy and how much was actually what they believed.

He pulled out his laptop, cracked a Bud and lit a smoke while he waited for the Inn's horrible connection to link him to the Internet. He typed "werewolf" in the search bar and hit Enter.

# CHAPTER TWENTY-TWO

"**H**ONEY," **JOE CALLED** up the stairs. "Alex is here."

"Be right down," Sonya said.

Joe lifted his Stetson from his desk and stared at the headline on the trash rag—"Eyewitness Cries Return of Full Moon Monster". He'd asked Dave Jenner to take them down from his racks, but the grocer was as defiant as he was superstitious. He outright refused. Joe scarfed up the copies in the first two aisles, but didn't have enough on him to snag the rest. So far, only Ann Shultz had asked about the wolfman. But he was sure more would speak up.

Tonight, though, he'd promised his daughter a return to normalcy. It was his night off and he wanted to spend it not thinking about the one thing he couldn't stop thinking about. Joe placed his hat back over the paper and opened the door.

"Hey, Sheriff," Alex said.

"Alex. Come on in. I hope you like baked pork chops and green bean casserole."

"Sounds good."

"It's the most gourmet thing I know how to make. Otherwise, it's spaghetti or hot dogs."

Sonya bounced down the stairs dressed in one of his old concert shirts and a knee-length red skirt, her blonde hair in a braid. She looked so much like Lucy, especially back in their younger days.

"Are you ready for Dad's 'Sheriff's Special'?"

"Starved."

Dinner flew by. Joe enjoyed talking with Alex about his father. Jack McKinney's son was a chip off the old block. Luckily his Uncle Ted's rock-jock, playboy lifestyle hadn't rubbed off on the boy. Joe would never fully approve of anyone courting his baby girl, but Alex McKinney was as close as he could imagine anyone would come. He was polite; whether from fear or respect, or both, Joe appreciated the courtesy. He was resilient and responsible.

Joe knew the kid probably had his negatives too, but he seemed to make Sonya happy.

"Alex is giving me a ride to Kim's."

"Oh, I thought we were going to watch a movie or something?"

"Sorry, Dad. Kim called earlier. She asked me to spend the night. Do you mind?"

"No. Go ahead, honey."

She kissed his cheek and said, "Thanks, Dad. Love you."

He watched her go. He would call Kim's mom to make sure the girls stayed indoors. Full moon or not, he didn't want them out after dark. As they drove away, Joe's mind turned back to the beast. For once he wished something else would happen in this town. A burglary, holdup, even a good, old-fashioned brawl down at Gil's.

He picked the Stetson up and reread Wes Kaplan's article. The bastard had actually had the balls to interview Theresa Turcott.

Joe tossed the paper and tried to distract his mind with a book.

Nick walked into the house to the sounds of his mother and her boyfriend fucking. Instead of going to his room and putting his headphones on, he plopped down on the living room sofa and cranked up the television.

After a minute, the moans ceased and someone mumbled. Jerry came out buttoning his jeans with a cigarette in his mouth. Nick's mom followed. Her afterglow made him ill.

"Hi, Nick," Jerry said. Jerry picked up a T-shirt from the coffee table and slipped it on.

"Did you have a good time fucking my mom?"

"Jesus, Nick. Watch your mouth."

"Sorry, Ma, but I could hear your moans halfway down the street."

"Well, *I'm* gonna get going," Jerry said. He gave Nick's mom a kiss before heading for the door.

Nick sat with his arms folded across his chest, and stared daggers at his mom. The front door shut. After a few seconds, Jerry's car roared to life.

Nick's mom broke the silence.

"What in the hell was that all about?"

"What? Listen, you don't hear me humping girls into hysterics. How about taking my living here into consideration?"

"Maybe you should be humping some girls."

Nick felt the heat flush his cheeks. His lips tightened. His hands clenched.

"You were out. You've been gone all morning. I didn't think the empty house would mind. Next time Jerry is here, you better apologize."

"Fuck Jerry."

"Excuse me?"

Nick shut the television off and went to the kitchen.

His mother grabbed his arm.

"Don't fucking touch me."

Her eyes went wide.

He opened the cupboard where she kept her booze and took the unopened bottle of tequila with him to his room. He left his mother near tears in the kitchen.

# CHAPTER TWENTY-THREE

**S**TAN **S**PRINGS **SAT** at the black-and blue-tile-covered bar of Gil's Tavern, nursing a Jack and Coke. The place seemed quiet for a Friday night, but what the hell did he know? Up until a few nights ago, he hadn't been in the place in over seven years. He hadn't even recognized the young kid with all the arm tattoos, tending bar. Billy Richman, Greg Richman's boy. *All grown up with nowhere to go. Guess tending bar beat out your father's hope that you would play in the big leagues.*

There were a few older fellas at the end of the bar, drinking Budweiser and talking about how right Bill O'Reilly always was, and how unfair it was of this treacherous country of ours to be disrespecting George W. over the war in Iraq. Stan even heard them refer to "all the democrats down in Portland" as "a bunch of queers".

*Small-town minds.*

Just like in his dreams, he would enjoy devouring as many of them as he could.

The dreams had intensified since his feedings a week ago. He couldn't sit at home in peace. The dark visions had crawled back into his days as well. The black forest, the skeletal limbs clawing at him, and the anger.

Joe Fischer and that café whore pushed him back into this madness. Who the hell did they think they were? He'd been avoiding both of them since Joe's big pop-in warning, but there was payback coming. He was going to make damn sure of that. Right now, the whiskey and the scumbags around him were fuel enough for his rage. And he welcomed it.

"Hey, Deputy, off tonight?" Billy Richman said.

Stan glanced over at Dwayne Clarke. One of Joe's boys.

"Yep. Can I get a Happy Meal?"

"Coming right up."

"What the hell's a Happy Meal?" Stan grumbled.

The young deputy looked surprised.

"Ah...it's a shot of whiskey and a tall boy."

Stan left the response in the air between them. He smirked at the boy and went back to his drink in silence.

"You're Sheriff Springs."

Stan held his glass just before his lips. "Not anymore." He finished the glass and slammed it down. "Another."

Billy mixed him another and placed it down on a fresh napkin.

"What's the line on last weekend?" Stan said.

"The line?"

"Don't play dumb with me, boy. What'd Joe tell you happened to those folks?"

"Looks like we got a wild animal on our hands."

"Is that so? Just like in '97?"

"Highly unlikely that the two are related, but, yeah, from what I know about the attacks that year, it looks a lot like it."

"You sure you ain't heard nothing else."

"You know something we don't?"

Stan pushed back from the counter, then stood.

Deputy Clarke was startled, but regained his composure.

Stan downed his drink, stopped behind the deputy and dropped a heavy paw on his shoulder. Clarke tensed beneath his palm. "Why don't you ask your sheriff what happened to the last young deputy who went chasing wild animals for him." He patted Clarke's shoulder and started for the door. Stan didn't wait for a reply. He didn't care what the kid had to say. If he stepped in his way, Dwayne Clarke would end up just like Brett Curry. Stan climbed into his pickup. He rarely used the vehicle. He preferred to walk, but he had plans for tonight.

Across town, Melanie Murdock tried hard not to fall asleep on her couch. The heat wave currently clinging to Gilson Creek sapped all her energy. She was lying on her way-too-comfortable sofa with a box fan pointed directly at her. Regardless of the artificial breeze, this heat had her sweating like crazy. Even lounging in only a tank top and bikini bottoms was too much to bear.

She was alone again on a Friday night. The story of her life. She was trying to make it through an AMC showing of the horror classic *Halloween*. They always played horror movies on AMC on Friday nights, and since breaking up with Hank four months ago, she hadn't missed one single movie that was part of their *Fear Friday* showcase.

She loved scary movies, always had. Hank had absolutely detested them. Telling her that the people who watched them were sick and got off on that crap. He was a westerns guy. It was Clint Eastwood and John Wayne, or bust. If she had to see another movie about a guy riding a horse into a town where nobody knew him, only to have him rescue its people from a mustache-wearing bad guy whom he had no business interfering with, it would be too fucking soon. She'd love to see John Wayne mosey up to Michael Myers and see how far that would get him. She was guessing he'd get grabbed by the throat, lifted off his feet and finished off with about five stabs to the chest. Now that she would watch.

She was startled when her phone rang.

"Hello?"

"Hey, Mel. It's Joe. I didn't wake you, did I?"

Her heart fluttered. Nervous and excited, not to mention surprised, she tried hard not to let any of those emotions through with her response. "No, I was just watching—"

"*Halloween* on AMC?"

"Yes! How did you know?"

"I was watching it myself and I remembered you talking at the café about this *Fear Friday* thing a couple weeks ago. Truth be told, I'm just glad they're not showing *The Howling*."

"What, you don't like werewolf movies? Don't tell me you bought into any of that crazy wolfman shit that Old Mike used to spout off about?"

There was silence from the other end of the line.

"Sheriff?" Melanie said. "Are you still there?"

"Joe," he finally said. "Remember? You can call me Joe. And, yeah, I'm still here. Truth is, or rather, the reason I was calling was to, uh..."

She found his vulnerability appealing.

"Mel," he continued, "I was wondering if you wouldn't mind having company. That is, if you might want someone to watch the movie with."

"Yeah, I think I'd love that," she said.

"Great. Should I come over? Or, do you want to swing over here?"

"Either way is fine with me," she said. "Is Sonya home?"

"No, she's over at her friend's for the night. Tell you what, how about I swing over to your place? I can grab us something from Anthony's on the way. If you're hungry, that is?"

"If you just want to grab some beers, I finished off the couple I had in my fridge a little earlier. I've got some chips and dip here."

"I'll stop at Anthony's, then head right over," he said.

"You'd better hurry. Michael just rolled into Haddonfield in that sweet station wagon. You don't want to miss any of the good stuff."

"I'll throw up the cherry top and be there before Laurie gets out of school," he said.

"See you in fifteen, then?"

"Make it ten."

Melanie hung up the phone. She couldn't believe what just happened.

*What was about to happen?*

Joe Fischer had just asked to come over. They had been flirting for years, but she never expected that he'd ever make a move. She'd always been attracted to him, and since she asked him to talk to Stan Springs, they had gotten a little closer, she thought. She felt like he was protecting her.

Lights appeared on the far wall, casting down from the ceiling. Someone was in her driveway.

*Who the hell could that be?*

Melanie hopped up. There was no way it was Joe. Not that fast. She was only wearing bikini bottoms. She ran to her bedroom and threw on the short red running shorts she'd been wearing earlier. Melanie considered putting on a T-shirt, but then thought better of it. She looked great in a tank top. She smiled to herself as she went to the front door.

Drawing back the curtain, the smile fell from her face.

Stan Springs was sitting in her driveway in a pickup truck; she didn't even know he had a vehicle. He was just out there, staring at her house with his dome light on so that she could see who it was. If he was trying to intimidate her, it was fucking working.

*Where are you, Joe?*

*He'll be here any minute,* she answered herself.

147

*What if that crazy son of a bitch gets out of his truck? What then?*

She crouched down behind her door. Then she was compelled to get back up and make sure Springs was still in his truck.

On the television, Michael Myers stood behind a row of tall bushes. He waited for the girls he would later torment. The irony was not lost on Melanie.

Just as she climbed to her feet, she heard the truck start. The engine roared repeatedly. All the while, the dome light remained on as she watched his wicked smile.

*Come on, Joe. Please.*

Grinning like the devil, the truck roared backwards, spun around, and squealed off into the night.

Melanie sighed, relieved, but completely petrified. What did he want? What was he going to do?

She was shaking when Joe's Range Rover pulled into the driveway almost five minutes later. Throwing open the front door, she ran to him.

Stan Springs got a hard-on observing the fear he caused Melanie Murdock. The crippling look on her face was priceless. Oh, and how she quivered, cupping her hands over her mouth, backing away from the window as he revved the engine. He felt like he was going to explode in his jeans. She'd get hers, but not tonight. No, tonight wasn't quite right. He was salivating as he drove through the darkness. He'd be back. Soon enough, the full moon would return. That should set the ambiance perfectly.

"Good night, bitch," he muttered, glancing into his rearview mirror.

He considered going into Hollis Oaks and finding some companionship to sate his urge. It was always harder to combat the primal impulses once he stopped fighting the curse. And hell, didn't he deserve a good fuck? Hollis Oaks wasn't a mecca for fine women, but even small cities offered a sample-size of whores on call. He couldn't even remember the last time he'd taken a woman, outside of his bestial form, that is. He'd fucked and slayed his fair share under the great eye in the sky.

*Fuck it. Why let the wolf have all the fun?*

He pressed the pedal and drove toward the town line.

# CHAPTER TWENTY-FOUR

**"I'M GONNA GO** do a loop around town, unless you want to do it?" said Deputy Shelly Glescoe to Deputy Hines. She needed a reason to vacate the too-sticky, too-quiet confines of the Gilson Creek Police Station. The humidity was horrible. She was sweating and felt like she needed a shower.

She'd been watching Randy try not to fall asleep at his desk. He looked awful. He hadn't been the same since last weekend. He seemed tense, quiet, moody. Rita told her he'd even pulled his gun earlier this week on a guy asking about the animal attacks Her only two-way conversations tonight had come from the part-time dispatcher, Earl Penny. Earl was on with them until four in the morning.

Earl, the part-time dispatcher wasn't much of a talker unless you got him going on about Elvis, but overall, he was nice. He was short and bald, wore thick glasses and smelled a little like molasses. He reminded Shelly of her papaw.

She waited a few seconds longer for Deputy Hines to respond, as her question just seemed to float out across the room under a cloak of invisibility. "Randy?"

He looked up, rubbed his temples and said, "Sorry, Glescoe. I've been battling a migraine for the last couple of hours. Yeah, go on out."

"All right, I'm heading out. Earl, you feel free to give me a shout if you need me."

Earl looked up from his Tom Clancy novel and responded with a simple, "Ay-yuh."

She took one last glance at Hines. He kept his face toward the work laid out before him. Shelly turned, grabbed the keys off her desk and headed to the doors. She wondered if it was a headache or if something else was bothering him. He was a private guy. Maybe his mother was ill or something. She would have to try to drag it out of him. Maybe when she got back.

"Shelly?" Deputy Hines called out.

She stopped in the doorway. "Yeah?"

"You have your shotgun, right?"

"Yes."

"Just making sure. Sheriff's orders. Holler if you need me."

She originally planned to swing through downtown first, to check on Gil's and the general store, but decided instead that she would go out to the quieter parts of town beforehand. She loved patrolling those quiet areas of town after dark. There was something comforting and almost serene about crawling down rural roads, past the homes of people she knew, and for the most part liked, making sure they were okay. She felt a bit like a mother keeping a watchful eye over her children.

Dwayne would make a great father someday. She was in love with him, though she had yet to say it aloud. She was sure he felt the same way, and she really wanted him to say it first. Childish? Maybe, but that's just how she felt about it. They had been seeing each other, a lot of each other, for the better part of the last four months.

They had thought they were being sly about it too, but the sheriff put that poor theory to bed a few weeks ago. He didn't say he knew they were an item, he didn't have to. It was the way he addressed them when they were together that implied they should behave themselves and remain professional. She knew the sheriff didn't exactly agree with the relationship. Hell, they both knew going into it that it could get very complicated, but so far, so good. She was supposed to give Dwayne a call tonight after her first patrol. She had assured him she could take care of herself, but it was nice to have him worry. She decided to turn back toward town and see about meeting up with Dwayne. There wouldn't be anything happening out here tonight— there never was. She turned around in the first driveway she came upon and headed for Brighton Circle.

Shelly pulled up in front of Gil's Tavern to a few hoots and whistles from the drunk and the dumb. "Thanks, guys. Any of you driving tonight?"

They all mumbled and moaned.

Dwayne slipped into the passenger seat. "Hey. How's the late shift going?"

She wanted to kiss him, but the drunken crew was still watching. "Good. Quiet. Just the way I like it."

"I thought you liked it rough?"

"Behave yourself. How much have you had to drink tonight?"

"Me? Couple of drinks."

"Did you hear about what happened down at Mel's?"

"Oh yeah, the thing with Sheriff Springs?"

"Yeah, I guess Mel called Joe, and then Joe went to have a talk with him."

"What? Why?"

"Told him to stay out of Mel's for a while."

"Weird." Dwayne said.

"What?"

"He was here when I got here tonight. I talked to him."

"Really? What did he say? What was he like?"

Shelly had been fascinated with the ex-sheriff since she found out about him. The hulking, scruffy-looking guy she saw walking in and out of town from time to time had once been Joe's idol. She'd seen the portrait of Springs when he was clean-cut, standing next to a younger Joe and Deputy Hines. It was still hanging in Joe's office. If no one said anything, she wouldn't believe it was the same guy for all of Donald Trump's money.

"He was...kind of dark, cryptic." Dwayne said. "You know, like some villain in a movie. He was asking about the animal attacks. Asked what Joe's line was?"

"Joe's line?"

"Yeah, something to do with the mountain lion attacks back in '97."

"Hmm. That is weird." She figured it might just be the insanity scratching its way back into his brain. If the attacks in '97 triggered his problems, these recent incidents sure as hell weren't going to do him any favors.

She watched Dwayne stumble a bit as he waved to Kemp Peaslee.

"A couple of drinks, huh?" she said.

"Hey, I didn't say they weren't strong."

He smiled his goofy grin.

"Why don't you let me give you a ride home?" she said.

"Sure. Let me run in and take care of my tab."

She watched him go inside and thought about the ex-sheriff. She wondered if last weekend's full moon had made everybody in town crazy.

# CHAPTER TWENTY-FIVE

**D**EPUTY **HINES COULDN'T** get through his pile of paperwork. His head was killing him. Migraines ran in his family. They'd gotten worse since last weekend. No matter how much he tried he couldn't stop seeing the bodies. Old Mike's half-eaten chest, the poor Rowel guy's face. Joe hadn't broached the subject yet, but he knew. Just like in his dreams, just like in the crappy paper—the beast had returned.

"You okay?" Earl said. "You look a little pale."

"Just need some Advil or something."

"I got some Aleve up here. Why don't you take a couple and go lie down on the cot out back? I'll come get ya if Shelly calls."

"I think I might take you up on that, Earl. Thanks." Randy didn't think he'd be able to sleep. He hadn't been able to the last few nights without alcohol, but the drugs might work on the migraine. The beast, not so much.

❧

He tried to rest on the cheap cot out back. Earl's Aleve hadn't kicked in yet, but it didn't matter. He didn't really think he'd be able to sleep anyway.

After a few minutes of pretending it might work, he gave up and returned to his desk. The station phone blared to life as soon as his ass hit the chair.

"Deputy Hines," Earl bellowed from the dispatch desk. "Sheriff's on the phone."

"Hines."

"Randy, I need you to come out to Mel Murdock's place. It seems Stan Springs paid her a visit."

Hines ran his fingers through his short blond hair. "Can't you get Glescoe? She's out patrolling right now."

"If I wanted Shelly over here, I would have called her. I called you, Randy."

Randy rubbed his temples and responded, "I'll be right over." He hung up the phone, grabbed his keys from the desk and nodded to Earl on his way out.

**❦**

Within minutes, Deputy Hines pulled his cruiser up alongside the sheriff's Range Rover. Hines, with his window rolled down, waited behind the wheel as the sheriff approached.

"Sheriff," he said.

"Randy, I need you to head over to Stan's place and see if he's there."

"Do you want me to bring him in?"

"No, just go out and see if his truck is there. Don't step foot on his property, you hear me? If the truck is there, hang back and watch for a little while."

"Sheriff, I'm not scared of that old bastard. Let me go talk to him."

"Trust me, Randy, you should be. I'm not sure what's going on with him lately, maybe it's all this..."

Mel was sitting on the porch steps listening.

"Like I said, you are not to set foot on his property unless instructed to do so, you hear me?"

"Yes, Sheriff."

"Good. Call me on my cell once you confirm whether he's there or not." Joe lowered his voice. "Mel's asked me to stay with her. She's pretty shaken up and I don't blame her."

"Okay, Sheriff."

Randy backed out of Melanie Murdock's driveway and headed out toward Old Gilson Creek Road.

He left off the gas as he reached his destination. Stan Springs' driveway was empty, the house set in total darkness. Staring at the place, four tall, dark pines reaching up like claws just behind it, Randy shivered. The place, here in the dark, no one home, gave him the creeps. He couldn't say why. Just seemed odd for a man with no family to be living in such a large place alone.

"Probably should've just stayed at the nuthouse," he said.

Headlights bloomed from the curve farther down the road.

He'd let it pass, and then double back. He'd have to hang around for a while to satisfy the sheriff's orders. Hopefully, Springs would return—

The truck blew by him.

"Speak of the devil."

He watched in his rearview as brake lights came to life and the truck pulled into the drive.

He continued down the road a piece before pulling in and turning around at Pug Gettis's place. When he rolled by Springs's house again, the truck was parked, but the house lights were still out.

Randy shut his headlights off, did a U-turn, and eased his cruiser to the shoulder twenty yards down from the end of the driveway. If the old man left the property, he would see him.

*Hell, I could've pulled him over for speeding back there.*

Sitting in the stillness, the shade from the trees next to him helping the night achieve a deeper black, didn't help his anxiety. He didn't like being out on Old Gilson Creek Road or Christie Road this late at night. The body of Brian Rowel passed through his mind and sent a chill up his spine. Since the night of Deputy Brett Curry's demise, Randy had made it his business to know what nights the full moon fell on and the next one was only a couple weeks away.

Whenever he was stuck on third shift, like he was tonight, he'd sit outside of Gil's Tavern, parked in one of the darker corners of the parking lot, listening to sports talk radio rather than driving out here. He'd never told anyone that he was afraid or uncomfortable with patrolling either of the outer roads. It was a secret he chose to keep to himself. He only drew about two night shifts a month anyway. He didn't see the sense in going out to the edge of a usually quiet town, or the harm in pretending that he had.

And now, here he was. Joe was supposed to be the closest connection to Stan in this town. Randy had seen the man he used to call sheriff many times since his return from the loony bin a couple years back. He was a grizzled mess. How does that happen to a man?

*Will it happen to me?*

A coyote howled.

In his mind, Randy saw Old Mike's severed arm, all the blood and the half-devoured chest.

*It's only a coyote...*

A branch snapped in the woods.

"You know what? Forget this."

Despite the heat still clinging to the night, he rolled up his window and turned the ignition. Even though he'd been staked out in front of Stan Springs's house for all of five minutes, he pulled onto the road and headed back toward the station.

Stan Springs crouched just out of sight behind an old decrepit tree near the rear of Deputy Hines's cruiser. His teeth lit up with the red of the brake lights, making his off-kilter grin look as though it were filled with blood. He stood up as he watched the car pull away.

He couldn't wait to return to the house of Melanie Murdock. That bitch was going to wish that she had kept to minding her own goddamn business. And maybe that useless little shit, Alex McKinney, would be next. They would all be wishing they'd left him alone.

Stan walked down his driveway, made his way around the far corner of his home and headed out into his backyard. He looked into the blackness of the forest before him, remembering the fear he had once felt while looking out upon this dead piece of earth.

He laughed to himself. It was a dead, joyless laugh. He stepped onto the soft soil with his bare feet and walked into the forest and its nocturnal bliss.

# CHAPTER TWENTY-SIX

**THE FOURTH OF** July came and went without a hitch. In the two and a half weeks since the last full moon, Joe's head was pulled in a million different directions. His mandated 9:00 p.m. curfew caused a few sparks to fly among the twenty-somethings and a few of the parents in town, but most of his community understood. No one wanted to be the next Old Mike.

Sonya split her time with either Alex or Kim. They'd barely had the opportunity to speak. He'd loosened the reins. He knew she wasn't going to be happy about being locked down later this week, but there was no way he was going to allow her out with what was coming.

Stan Springs's odd drive-by at Mel's house seemed to be a one-time thing. He hadn't been by her home or the café since, though Gil had mentioned that he'd been drinking and talking to himself at the tavern most nights. So long as he wasn't bothering other people, Joe didn't mind. Gil agreed.

The relationship between Mel and him was another complicating piece to the puzzle. The timing was far from ideal, but without her company on his free nights, he probably would have already cracked. Part of him still struggled with sleeping with her. He knew it was dumb, but he felt like he was cheating on Lucy.

Sonya had walked in on them kissing during one of her stops home for money. She'd smiled and winked at him. His daughter's acceptance meant a lot to him, and to Mel.

The biggest pains in Joe's ass over the past few weeks had been the bored shitheads at the *Crypto Insider*. They continued to try and get him to feed them something over the phone for their rag. Rita explained what Randy had done when they showed up that first day while he was out. Joe was certain they wouldn't dare come back to the station, but, still, the phone calls were relentless.

And it wasn't just the two pseudoreporters. Their articles had stirred up a handful of his most level-headed townspeople. Pug Gettis, a God-fearing, every-Sunday front-rower at Saving Grace Baptist, had inherited Old Mike's role as wolfman alarmist. Christine Morris and Tina Bazinet had called the station at least every other night reporting anything that moved in the dark. Deputy Clarke had broken up more than one beach party of local teens down at Emerson Lake after curfew. The last party, he reported two nights ago, had a wolfman theme. Two of the boys, Troy Butler and Brad Bennington, had been escorted home dressed up like it was Halloween and howling in the cruiser, drunk as a couple of Gil's best customers. The *Crypto Insider* was doing him no good.

Even with all this madness, Joe managed to prepare, hopefully better than seven years ago, for whatever would unleash itself on his town this weekend. Today, a trip to Barlow Olson's gun shop was in order.

He arrived at Olson's at 3:00 p.m. A Closed sign hung in the front door.

*You've got to be kidding me.*

Then he noticed movement inside of the shop. From behind the counter, a large, bearded man waved him in. Joe shut the truck engine off and left it parked at the curb. He got out and met Olson at the door.

# BLOOD AND RAIN

The man was the size of an NBA center. He stood at least six foot seven, probably about 280, maybe 290, pounds. He was dressed in a pair of green work pants and a black T-shirt bearing a blood-spattered skull with a knife sticking through it—*Kill 'Em All, Let God Sort 'Em Out* scrawled across the top in blood. He wore his mane of gray hair, pulled back in a ponytail. His beard, which had been dark brown the last time Joe stopped by to visit him, had also gone the way of silver. He looked much older than his fifty-two years.

He shook Joe's hand—he certainly hadn't lost an ounce of strength—and welcomed him into the shop.

"My apologies about the sign, Sheriff. You just sounded like you had something heavy on your mind. I figured we might need the privacy." Olson meandered back toward his regular perch behind the glass counter at the center of his little shop.

The place looked much the same as it always had. Guns of all shapes and sizes were proudly displayed on racks and hooks on the wall behind the long glass case containing every kind of knife you could imagine. A line of shotguns followed a row of rifles. Beside them was an arrangement of handguns displayed in the shape of a heart.

Barlow Olson was an odd duck. That was never in doubt.

There was a fancy-looking new banner above the guns that read *Convert Threats to Carpet Stains.*

"Nice banner," Joe muttered as he fiddled with an unlit cigarette.

"Thanks, my friend Paul came up with that. Catchy, huh?" Olson glanced at the sleeping smoke Joe twirled between his thumb and index finger.

"It's...an interesting slogan," Joe replied. He tried on a smile, but in his current state, could only muster a weak smirk.

Olson turned around, appearing to admire the flashy black-and-yellow banner, and then smiled back at Joe. "I like it."

Joe gave a small laugh. "Well, it's definitely you."

He followed Olson's gaze as it returned to the unlit cigarette in his hand. "What can I do for you today, Sheriff?"

Joe wasn't sure how or where to start. He decided to be straightforward with his old friend. "Barlow, it would appear Gilson Creek has a...a werewolf problem."

"No shit, Sheriff. What can I do to help?"

Joe was semi-stunned by Olson's response. Olson must have seen it on his face.

"Sheriff, I've been around these parts for a long time. I worked this shop when I was sixteen. I stood right here next to my daddy back when it was his. There was one thing my father used to always say. 'Barlow, my boy, there ain't nothin' impossible.' A lot of parents say that to encourage their children, give 'em a little boost, but my daddy was talkin' about something else."

"Is that right?" Joe placed the cigarette between his lips.

"Why don't you come out back with me? I'll join you for one of those."

Joe pulled the pack from his front pocket and drew one out for Olson.

"Come on." Olson accepted the cigarette, stepped out from behind the counter and nodded toward the back of the store.

Joe followed the mountain past a wall of swords straight out of a samurai movie. The big man pushed open the back door. Natural light spilled warmth into the room.

Olson slapped a Zippo against his thigh and lit his cigarette. He straightened his arm and sparked Joe's.

Joe took a drag and exhaled. "You were saying about your daddy?"

"My daddy was friends with a hunter by the name of Silas Wyatt. Big game, mostly. Black bears, moose. One day Silas comes into the shop, stone-cold sober, and says, 'Olson, I need you to do me a favor.' Daddy says, 'What's that?' Silas says, 'Need me some silver bullets.' Daddy turns to me and asks me to get him some aspirins from out back."

Olson takes a couple of puffs from his cigarette and continues, "I stop at the curtain that used to divide the back area from the front of the shop and listen. Daddy says, 'Only one thing needs silver bullets.' Silas says, 'I know. That's why I'm comin' to you.'"

Olson takes another drag and stares up at the sun burning bright above the trees to the east. For such an intimidating presence, the man has the softest green eyes Joe's ever seen. Warm, welcoming.

"My daddy knew about 'em even then. Not that I had a clue about any of it. Them bullets I gave you back in '97? Leftovers from a previous order."

Joe dropped his butt to the tar and crushed it beneath his boot. "That so? From what?"

"You ever hear of them slayings up in Jackman? Was the year before your troubles."

"Don't think so. Jackman's a heck of a way up there. What's the connection?"

"A boy comes down. Says his cousin sent him. Cousin's name is Megill, I know the name. Old Silas married a Nancy Megill from Allagash. So the boy asks for the silver slugs, same as you. I got 'em for him. After giving the rest to you I decided to follow up on the area I know Megill's from, and uncover all these stories of mutilated bodies and such."

"Same as me."

"Same as you."

"We got anything left in the old silver line?"

"Funny you should ask." Olson opens the back door and gestures for Joe to head in. Back at the counter, Olson pulled out a big yellow box. "You ain't the first one to come in here this week asking for these."

Joe tipped his Stetson up and raised his brow. "Anyone you know?"

"Nope. He was a real nervous fella. About six one, black hair, kind of grown out a bit, and sideburns. Real intense looking."

"Give you a name?"

"Yep." Olson heads out back and returns with a pink sheet of paper in hand.

"Ted McKinney."

"And when was this?"

"Few days ago. Sold him a piece."

*Great, just what I need.*

"Told him I didn't have the bullets though. Told him he watched too many movies. Didn't know him from Adam, y'know. Least you came with a reference."

Joe thought of Stan.

"Another guy called on the phone. Didn't give me a name. Said 'dude' a couple of times. I just figured it was some kids caught up in that cartoon monster you got people writing about."

*Couple of annoying punks from New Hampshire.*

"Yep, probably just a couple of dumb kids. Listen, Barlow, I need to know more. Obviously, after last time, I didn't expect to be back here under these circumstances. Your father ever pass down anything you might think can help make sure I'm not back in a couple years?"

"You filled it with the bullets I gave ya last time?"

"Yep. Every last one."

Olson leaned back and scratched his beard. "Daddy never involved himself any further than stocking and selling the bullets. Said knowing something was out there and doing his part to aid in its demise was good enough. Me, I ran the same way, until it hit so close to home."

Olson bent down and came back with a black sheath featuring three gold inlays. He held it out to Joe.

Joe took the weapon in his hands.

"Is this what I think it is?"

"You can't just shoot these things. The silver will fuck the shit out of 'em. Drop 'em out of commission for a long-ass time, but it's not enough."

Joe unsheathed the blade. The steel came free with a quiet *sssss*.

"That there is a Masahiro Yanagi Katana blade."

Joe set the sheath down on the counter and held the beautiful sword in his hands. He felt both in awe and out of place holding the weapon. He placed a finger to the sharp side of the blade. When he pulled his finger away, he noticed the thin red line where he had made contact. "And this should work?"

Barlow leaned back and stroked his beard. "I've done a little more research since checking on the Jackman stories. According to what I found, only way to keep a werewolf down for good is to take off its goddamn head."

# CHAPTER TWENTY-SEVEN

**T**ED MCKINNEY MANAGED to secure himself a gun—a Glock just like Dwayne's. The bastard at the gun shop denied ever having sold silver bullets. Told Ted he watched too many monster movies. *Fucking asshole.*

A little research after the fact led Ted to SBBulletForgers.com, an online company in the Southwest that made and sold real silver bullets. Wolf killers is what they called them.

The tracking said his package was due tomorrow. He hoped it wasn't a scam. He'd spent two hundred dollars on the box of ammo. The bullets had used the last of the tour money he'd saved. His time at the Lobster Motorway Inn was over.

In his time at the Lobster, he'd learned more than where to buy wolf killers. He'd entered chat room after chat room on different sites: WolfenAround.com, WerewolvesandVampires.net, unrealreality.net and, the most useful, Monstersamongus.com.

The Monsters Among Us site focused on myths and folklore in the States. Areas like New Mexico and South Texas where chupacabra sightings were heavy. Also, they talked a lot about a valley of the undead in Alaska, where a clan of vampires supposedly lived. There were also the Mothman myths of the Southeast, and Helltown in Ohio. It all sounded like the work of some very creative minds, but the werewolf story he found reported in Northern Maine from 1996 was too close to home to ignore.

In early 1996 a Jackman resident, Norman Megill, an avid black-bear hunter, disappeared while hunting in the town of Allagash. Friends reported finding him at his home several weeks later. They said he was aggressive, not his normal hearty self. His cousin, Jason Collins, reported that Norman confessed to being attacked and bitten by a monster wolf that walked upright like a man. Said that it happened while he waited out the bear he'd been tracking. Collins claimed Megill bore no wounds or scars consistent with his supposed attack and grew hostile when asked about the missing marks. A year later, a series of deaths in and around Jackman were reported. Collins and Megill both went missing shortly afterwards.

Ted found that the mutilations described in the bodies they found matched both what he'd seen in the *Crypto Insider* picture taken by Nick Bruce in '97 and what he'd seen left of Old Mike in Paulson Park. The only difference, as far as Ted was concerned, was that a large animal attack in that part of the state was much more plausible. Still, locals reported all sorts of "wolfman-like" activities. No more bodies were found past the first set, but the number of missing persons increased. The site reported that the disappearances coincided with the full moons.

At the bottom of the Jackman stories, there was a list of misconceptions about werewolves. There was no name attached to this list, but Ted copied it all down anyway. The one that caught his eye was that silver bullets caused serious damage, but acted more like a poison. In order to kill the beast you must behead the monster. The last one on the list scared him the most—the werewolf could change into its bestial form at any time during a full moon, whether the moon was high in the sky, shining bright, or still waiting for the sun to give way. Pretty much, the monster could stalk its prey in the light of day just as easily as it could at night. Ted hadn't heard any of this before, but that's what made them stand out.

And he wasn't about to take any chances. He'd grab a whole box of ammo and the nice shiny ax he had at home. If you're going to do a job right, you better have all the right tools.

Nick Bruce walked through the aisles of Jenner's Grocery picking up vegetables and side items he had no intention of consuming. The main course was what it was all about. He'd always been a steak guy, but in recent days he'd taken the love for red meat to the next level. His latest self-prepared meals had mostly consisted of warmed-up hamburgers. A slight brown to the outside, pink throughout. But they didn't suit his craving.

Two days ago, his mother purchased two nice big steaks from Nelson's Meat Market for her and Jerry's one-year anniversary dinner. She left to visit one of her old high school friends that afternoon. Nick stumbled upon the juicy treats in the fridge. A pull, like a recovering alcoholic left alone with a bottle of whiskey, overcame him. He took the plate to his room and devoured the raw meat.

When his mom got home and found the steaks missing, she came to his door, but not one foot closer. She hadn't dared to tell him what to do since that day in the kitchen. She cried.

That night, he woke from another fever dream of black death and torn flesh. He was nearly crippled by the pains that racked his body. He'd vomited blood before, but this was darker, like something out of his dreams.

Since then, he'd been consuming nothing but steak and raw hamburger. The sickness hit him each and every night, but the pull was too strong to deny.

"Picking up some more steaks?" Alan Cormier said.

"Yeah, three of the fattest and freshest you've got."

"Man, you're eating like a king. What have you been doing for work? I've seen that Full Moon shit in the *Insider*. You working that old scene again?"

"Sure," he lied.

"You must be making bank. That shit is hot right now. Tomorrow night's the big one, huh?"

"Yep."

"Hold up, I'll get you some cuts from the back."

"Eating like a man, huh?"

The gruff voice startled him. The hulking form of Gilson Creek's former loony-bin sheriff, Stan Springs, stood like a mountain at his side.

"Yeah, they're for my mom and her boyfriend's anniversary." He didn't know why he offered up an excuse, but like the draw to the meat, he just felt the need.

"How's your arm these days?"

"My arm?"

"Sorry. I saw you a couple weeks ago with it bandaged up."

"Oh that. I…"

"Here you go, Nick. Three of my best," Alan said. "Oh, hey. What can I get for you, sir?"

Nick grabbed the white packages from Alan's hand.

"Nothing for me. I was just looking." Springs nodded to Alan. "I've got to leave some room in these old guts." He turned his head to Nick. "Preparing for a feast this weekend."

The former sheriff walked away. Alan shrugged at Nick.

A hunger pain struck his insides. Without a word, Nick strolled to the front of the store. He tucked the meat packages into his waistband, paid for his other groceries and hurried around to the back of the store. He tossed the carrots and the box of rice to the ground and ripped out one of the stolen steaks.

As he tore through the blood-drenched delicacy, he couldn't help but feel like he was being watched.

Stan stood behind the trees, with a clear view of the young man eating bloody meat behind the grocery store. He could smell the raw sustenance. His stomach growled. He'd been keeping tabs on the kid since their roadside rendezvous, but hadn't decided whether or not to have a real talk with him. The change would hit him soon, and young Nick Bruce would make a fine killer, he was certain of it.

While Stan wanted to see what kind of monster he would make, he currently had his own hungers to feed.

After this next cycle, Gilson Creek would never be the same.

# CHAPTER TWENTY-EIGHT

"**B**ACK IN **BUMFUCK,** Maine—hell yes," Joel said. "Where are we staying this time?"

"Motel 6 again. It's cheap and we can smoke our brains out."

"Damn, I wanted to stay at the Bruton Inn. That place has some old ghost stories, man."

Wes was sketching pictures of hairy men with pointed ears and sharp teeth. "We're not here for ghosts. We've come to cover the Full Moon Monster, and don't you forget it."

"Nah, I know, man. But we gotta take a trip just to explore that next time. I freaking love ghosts."

"You've never seen a ghost and you know it."

"But if I did, I'd be fuckin' stoked."

Wes held up his finished masterpiece. "What do you think?"

"Dude, that's awful. Have you not drawn since fifth grade art class?"

"Fuck you, Joel. Our exit's coming up. Junction to Route 5."

"I'm just fucking with you, man. It looks cute."

"You're a dick."

They both laughed as Joel careened the vehicle off to the exit on their right.

The drive up Route 5 to Hollis Oaks was spent cranking the Specials and the Misfits.

Joel pulled into the Motel 6 parking lot. "Home, sweet home."

"I'll go see if I can check us in early," Wes said. "You grab the gear."

"What the fuck is all this shit anyway?"

"Stuff I got from Harry Pierce. He owed me a favor."

Wes got their keys and helped Joel lug in the cameras and sensory devices he'd borrowed from his old roommate Harry. They got the equipment inside and cracked the six-pack of PBR Tall Boys.

"So tell me, what's the plan?" Joel lit a smoke and offered one to Wes.

He eyed the equipment on the bed. "We really shouldn't be smoking around Harry's shit, but what the fuck." He grabbed the proffered smoke and lit up. "From what I gather, we have a couple of hot spots. Paulson Park is obvious, but I'm thinking somewhere around Old Gilson Creek Road seems perfect too."

"So, what, we set up cameras and this shit at the park and somewhere along the side of the road?" Joel said.

"I found a pretty sweet spot for us to spend the day. Emerson Lake."

"Okay?"

"When's the last time you got laid?"

"What? Since Stacy, I guess."

"Well, just off Old Gilson Creek is Emerson Lake," Wes said. "I don't see any reason why we can't set the shit up just off the beach."

"Outta curiosity, why the lake?"

"Email I got a couple days ago. Might be nothing, might be something. One of the locals emailed me that she saw something watching her from the trees just off of the sand."

"She saw it? But the moon isn't full yet? I'm callin' fraud."

"Maybe, probably, but if there's a werewolf in this town, and I think we can both agree that there is, somebody is hiding their full-moon identity."

"Okay."

"What if that somebody is scoping out their territory?"

"I like it. I like it."

"So...we set up in the spot the girl says she saw this figure, then we hit the beach for a couple hours of sun and bikini watching."

"Genius. Cheers."

Wes clanged his can to Joel's. "Drink up, bud. Tonight, on Full Moon Eve, we drink to the monster that's gonna make us a million bucks."

Deputy Clarke saw Ted's Honda Rebel in the driveway. The black bike, still dressed with saddlebag, told Dwayne Ted was back. He stopped and ran up to say hello.

"Hey, Ted, what the hell? When did you get back?"

Ted opened the door and walked back to the couch. He was watching *An American Werewolf in London*.

"Got back today."

"And you're watching werewolf movies. Of course."

"Studying."

*Oh God.*

"Well, how was the tour?"

"Don't know. Didn't go."

"What? What are you talking about? You left. The show's been on best of shit for the last two weeks."

"I needed to get away for a bit."

"Well...where the hell were you?"

"Dwayne, you're my best friend. We need to talk."

"Oh for Christ sakes, Ted, what is it? More monster nonsense?"

"Listen, I need to show you some things."

Ted got up from the couch and crossed to the little desk next to the TV.

"Holy shit, Ted. Where the hell did you get that?" His friend held a Glock 9mm identical to his own.

"Bought it at the gun shop in Hollis Oaks." He set the gun down and lifted a brown box.

"And these are silver bullets."

"Silver bullets," Ted said.

"Wolf Killers, actually."

"Jesus, Ted, listen to yourself. I've kept my mouth shut for a long time, but this...You have to get your shit together. I mean, *silver bullets*? Are you fucking losing it or what? What were you doing for the last two weeks?"

"They're *my* fucking bullets, this is *my* fucking gun, and I'm not going crazy, Dwayne. Has Joe said anything about Friday night? Huh?"

"No, because Joe's not fucking crazy. The craziest thing he's doing this weekend is closing Emerson Lake at five instead of eight."

"I know it's hard to believe—"

"It's fucking stupid."

"But I've seen firsthand what this thing can do. What this thing will do again if we're not ready."

"I don't have time for this." Dwayne went to the door. "Why don't you go talk to Joe? Maybe he'll put you up for the next night or two at the station so you don't have a chance to fucking accidentally shoot yourself or somebody else."

"Uncle Ted."

Alex McKinney and the sheriff's daughter, Sonya, came through the doorway.

"Hi, Dwayne," Sonya said.

"Hey, Sonya." Dwayne turned back to Ted. "Don't go filling these kids up with all of this. Joe will kill you."

"Night, Alex. Night, Sonya."

"Night, Dwayne," Sonya said.

"What was that all about?" Alex said.

Sonya gave Ted a hug. "How was the tour?"

"I...I wasn't on tour."

"What do you mean you weren't on tour?" Alex said.

"Sit down, you two." Ted placed himself between the kids and the gun lying on his desk.

Sonya followed Alex to the sofa.

"I needed to work out a few things. I told the band to take Bobby in my place."

"But your bike was gone, and you weren't at—"

"I know. I was looking into something."

"Are you still in the band?" Sonya asked.

"Sure, maybe, I don't know."

"Well what about this weekend? We're supposed to see you guys at the Nail?"

"Alex, I don't think anyone should be going anywhere this weekend." Ted didn't want to tell them any more than he had to. Who knows what Joe would do if his daughter came home talking about werewolves. "This is..." he turned to Sonya. "Your father knows there's something out there."

"Yeah, but we haven't had any attacks since that one night," she said. "Whatever it was is gone."

"Unless you think it's a—"

"Alex, I'm not saying it's anything. Call me superstitious, but I know I'd feel better if you kids weren't out there running the roads Friday night. There are coincidences that just make it seem...maybe this animal feeds in certain areas in cycles. I don't know,

179

I'm not an expert, but I'm sure your father would agree with me, regardless."

"So we need to find something else to do Friday," Alex said.

"You need to just stay in, stay home and watch a movie, hang out with your friends."

Alex got up. "You can't tell me what to do. You're not my father."

"Alex," Sonya said.

"I'm not your father, but I don't really want to find you mauled on the side of the road, either."

"Come on, Sonya."

"Alex, it's..."

Ted let him leave. He didn't know what else to say without shouting "don't fucking go out unless you want to get torn apart by a fucking werewolf".

Then Sonya waved and shut the door behind them.

Ted picked up the Glock and gripped the weapon in his hand. He thought it would fill him with a sense of strength and security. Instead, it felt incredibly small.

"So where was he?" Shelly said.

"He didn't say." Dwayne sat on the edge of Glescoe's desk.

"That's weird."

"Has Randy said anything?"

"About what?" she said.

"I don't know. It sounds stupid."

"What is it?"

"Ted's convinced the wolfman stories are true. He asked me what Joe's plans were. Same as Stan Springs."

"You starting to believe in monsters?" Glescoe smiled.

"I've always believed in monsters, just the human kind."

"So what are you thinking?"

"I don't know. I don't want Joe to laugh in my face. Do you know where Randy is?"

"He was scheduled to have off today, but Joe called him in."

"What for?"

"I didn't hear. I think he went to meet him somewhere."

Dwayne tapped his fist against his knee and then scooted off the desk. "Call me on my cell if you see Randy. I want to talk to him."

❧

Randy Hines pulled up next to the sheriff's Range Rover. They were parked down the block from Mel's.

"Sheriff?"

"We need to talk."

He knew what this was in regards to. He'd been dreaming about it for the last three weeks. Randy stepped out of his car and joined Joe at the front of the truck.

"Cigarette?" Joe offered.

"No thanks, I don't touch the things."

"I shouldn't either." Joe exhaled. "I know this isn't easy for you."

*That's putting it mildly.*

"But I also know how much you love this town. You saw those bodies. You know what we're dealing with."

"But how?" Randy said. "I mean, after what you did to it?"

Joe took a drag and stared at the forest beyond the end of the street. The sun sinking below the treetops burned a fiery, dark shade of red. "Appears I didn't do my job well enough."

"Is it...the same one? Is it possible there's another...?"

"I checked the grave. It's empty."

181

Randy paced between the vehicles and bit his thumbnail.

"I've already been out to see Olson. He's done a little looking into this problem of ours. I want to show you something."

Randy followed Joe around to the back of the truck. Joe reached in and pulled out a metal case shaped like a sword.

"What are we going to do?"

Joe flicked the cigarette butt into the dirt and unsheathed the gleaming blade. A flash of the setting sun's bloody hue caused Randy to squint. "We're going to finish it."

Nick Bruce was sicker than he could ever remember being in his life. Death had knocked on his door a dozen times since he finished the second steak from Jenner's. Relief came in minute spurts when he would faint from the pain, but as if the physical pain weren't enough, his nightmares were even worse. His mind had shown him things over the last six or seven hours that he could never have even come close to imagining on his own.

In his fever dreams, he was chased, hunted and haunted by an animal with very sharp teeth and razor-blade claws. He'd been killed. He'd been slaughtered, and then forced to watch the large animal chew through his dead carcass. Sometimes he was spared the ability to feel the beast gnawing on him, but in most of the nightmare blasts, he felt every bite and every lick.

In his last dream, it all changed. He became the one doing the hunting. Though, it wasn't the creature he hunted, but the citizens of Gilson Creek. He chased down the radio jockey Ted McKinney. He cornered Deputy Dwayne Clarke. He stalked Sheriff Fischer and his daughter. He murdered them all. He didn't just take their pathetic lives, but tore them each apart, limb from limb. And as if that weren't enough, he devoured every last scrap of torn flesh and lapped up each minuscule drop of blood and fluid. He wasn't sure of what he'd become in his dreams, but he knew he was no longer just a man. Not even close.

His eyes itched when he opened them, like the time he had conjunctivitis. There was even a sticky discharge. He wiped the thick wetness from the corners of his eyes.

His room—silent and black—felt too small, constricting. He swung his legs from the bed and stumbled to the door. The muscles in his thighs and calves were knotted. His entire frame ached from top to bottom. Even his face hurt. And it wasn't the surface, but what lay beneath. All he could think was that it felt as if his cheekbones and his forehead were swollen.

The kitchen was dark, save for the light above the stove. His mother wasn't here. He couldn't smell her. He wondered how he knew this, but the strange pain in his bones wouldn't allow him to dwell on it. He needed to get outside. Needed the fresh air. He needed to run.

# CHAPTER TWENTY-NINE

**N**ICK OPENED HIS eyes against an impossibly bright light and felt a warm breeze dance across his body. He was stark naked, lying in his backyard, and hadn't a clue how he had ended up this way. Had he lost a whole night? He picked himself up off the lawn, noticing an instant change in his well-being.

Not only did he not feel like death, but quite the contrary—he felt outstanding. He heard every chirp from the creatures in the woods beyond his mother's broken fence, which her boyfriend Jerry promised to fix two months ago. He glanced around at the grass and could see every crimp and curve in each blade that surrounded him. He held his hands out to his sides and flexed. His muscles were hard, taut and strong.

Nick rose to his feet and noticed his nosy neighbor, Tina Bazinet, staring at him from behind a transparent curtain in one of her back bedrooms. He looked down at his own nakedness and leered back at her. Her mouth dropped, and he could have sworn that he'd also heard the gasp as it escaped past her false teeth. He waved. She screamed and ran from the window, disappearing out of sight. She would probably call the police, but what the fuck did he care. Let her. He would be gone by the time they managed to mosey on over here. He had better things to do. The sun was shining high up in the sky, and he felt that he should be out enjoying its warmth and beauty.

Nick stepped through the back door and found Jerry at the counter, pouring a cup of coffee.

"Ah...sorry, Nick," Jerry said. He shielded his eyes and scurried out of the room. "I guess you didn't know I was here."

Nick followed him to the doorway.

Jerry sat on the couch. "Your mom had to go to help her friend Cindy with some errands. She should be back around noon," he said.

Nick felt his mouth tighten; then his teeth, protruding from his gums, began to fall to the floor with a series of tiny taps. The taste of blood on his lips elicited an electric charge within him. His labored breaths were loud to his ears.

"You okay...?" Jerry craned his neck away from the morning show on the television.

"Jesus, Nick. Your mouth..." Jerry's eyes went wide, his skin transparent. His heart beat like a conga drum in Nick's ears.

"What the fuck is going on?" Jerry stepped and stumbled over the glass-covered coffee table. His mug hit the rug below him with a whispered thud that to Nick sounded like the thump of a book on concrete.

Jerry fell on his elbow before the television stand. He held his hand up to ward off Nick. The hand quivered. "You, you, you..." he stammered.

Nick was on top of him in seconds. Jerry's shriek was interrupted as Nick's bloody mouth—his jaws now extended, his new teeth dripping crimson—chomped down over the man's maw. Jerry's body jerked, his hands and feet flailed in spasms. Nick savored the crunch of his mother's boyfriend's teeth and bones in his mouth before he spat them to the floor. He stood and noticed the black daggers at the ends of his fingers.

# BLOOD AND RAIN

There was a mirror in the bathroom.

His swollen forehead appeared heavy over eyes that were yellowing from the edges inward. The bloody fangs in his large mouth were stained pink. The coppery taste on his tongue only made him crave more. His knuckles were also swollen, shaping his hands into claws. Whatever he was becoming wasn't waiting for the moon to replace the morning sun. This beast was not chained to the night.

Nick stepped out into the morning, his changing form naked for the world, or his neighbors, to see. He'd never been so alive. He clenched and unclenched his hands. His body and mind were exploding with cravings, the majority of which were nasty, even vile. He ran across the road and into the woods. He headed toward Emerson Lake, with images of sun, sex and blood playing before his jaundiced eyes.

Tina Bazinet sat anxiously holding a cigarette in one shaking hand, a loaded shotgun in the other, and awaited the arrival of the Gilson Creek Sheriff's Department. She had watched out her kitchen window as that pervert next door, Nick Bruce, stood naked in his driveway flexing his hands.

As she watched him, she realized he didn't look right. The smile on his face seemed somehow unnatural to her. And his face, especially his mouth, looked funny. Like a kid with fake vampire teeth in his mouth. Complete with fake blood. She felt a malevolent weight to the air suddenly press down on her.

He crossed the road and disappeared into the woods. That man was going to do something very bad. She wasn't sure where that ominous thought had come from, just that it was right. She lit another cigarette and continued to wait.

Deputy Clarke arrived ten minutes later.

# Chapter Thirty

**T**OO MUCH BOOZE spilled around inside of Joel's head like poisoned sludge. He was grateful at least to find Wes up and at it. The car was loaded. Wes slammed the passenger door and grinned.

"Coffee, bud?" Joel said.

"There's some in the lobby."

"That shit?"

"Hey," Wes said. "It's free."

"And it will make me crap like I just ate a bunch of dead people."

Wes walked in past him. "We can hit the Dunkin' Donuts on our way out. You gonna shower?"

"Nah, figure my stink will help attract our specimen."

"Ha, more like scare it away. Well, man, if you're ready, grab your shit and let's get goin'."

Joel grabbed his Chucks from the end of his bed and threw them on. "Ready. We are coming back tonight, right?"

"Yeah, unless you get eaten."

"Shithead."

They rode in silence. Joel's excitement from last night crashed into a wall of anxiety. He wasn't afraid, exactly, but all of the other emotions seemed to be hitching along. Wes's creased brow and clenched jaw told Joel that his friend was feeling it as well.

189

"Is this it?" Joel said. Two four-foot-high blocks of concrete marked the dirt road that appeared to descend into the mouth of the woods.

Wes turned the car onto the gravel. The faded sign came into sight.

*Emerson Lake Open Sunrise to Sunset. Lifeguard on Duty. Swim Safe.*

A freshly painted sign just below it read:

*TONIGHT ONLY: BEACH CLOSES AT 5p.m. NO EXCEPTIONS.*

"Arooo." Joel laughed.

Wes stopped the car and reached in the backseat.

"What are you doin'?"

Wes aimed one of his cameras at the signs and snapped a photo. "In case we get enough to dedicate the whole issue to our little wolfy."

"Right on."

Surprisingly, they weren't the first ones there. About ten other cars and Jeeps were parked in the grass parking lot.

"Pig, dude." Joel pointed at the cruiser on the far right.

"Okay, here's what we'll do. We'll go set up the park first, and then come back here when the place is packed. We'll blend in a lot better with a crowd."

Sonya checked the window. Heath's Jetta was parked in the driveway.

"Come on, hot stuff," Kim shouted from the passenger side.

"Be right down."

Sonya pushed the sunscreen lotion into her backpack, threw on her sunglasses and strolled out her bedroom door. She hopped down the stairs and saw the yellow notepad on the couch.

*Hey, honey,*

*I know this is a lot to ask, but I really need you to stay home today. Alex and the gang can come over if they want. I left thirty bucks on the counter if you guys want to order in. There's supposed to be a wicked storm later. I just want you kids off the road tonight.*

*Love you,*

*Dad*

Bullshit. She already had plans. Like she'd told Alex's Uncle Ted, there hadn't been one single animal attack in nearly a month. She grabbed a bottle of water from the fridge and went to meet her friends.

"Hey, lady," Kim said. "What took you so long?"

She climbed into the backseat. "My dad left me a note. I'm supposed to stay home."

"What? Why?"

"I don't know, but I did hear him on the phone last night saying that he's closing down the lake at five. He did say you guys can hang out here?"

Heath met her gaze in the rearview. "Under the sheriff's watchful eye? I don't think so. Besides, we agreed—beach and then movies. I'm seeing the new *Spider-Man* movie today. Everyone has seen it but me."

"Shut up," Kim said. She slapped his arm. "We can still do both, right, Sonya?"

"I don't know? Why don't we just get to the beach and we'll take it from there?"

"I'm down for staying here tonight," Kim said.

Heath sighed. "Well, the movie starts at four. I'm goin' to the movie."

Kim looked back at her.

"We'll hit the beach, catch some sun, grab some lunch, head to the movies and be back here by dark," Sonya said. "Me and Alex have seen it already, but it's definitely worth seeing twice." She didn't want to worry her dad, but she knew it was really the night that he was stressing about. "Okay, that's the plan. For now."

"Good, are we ready? Can we get this show on the road?" Heath said.

Kim looked at Sonya. They both burst out laughing.

"Okay, you guys have your fun. Payback's coming at the beach." Heath reached over and squeezed Kim's knee. She laughed and slapped his hand away. He grinned and backed the car into the road.

Sonya saw Mr. Donavan out on his porch, smoking his pipe. She waved. He nodded in return.

"So what time is Alex off?" Kim said.

"He said Josh only needed him for one job this morning, but that it involved lifting an engine, so it could take a while. Said he'll call when they're just about done."

"That's cool. We can have some girl time while he's slaving in this heat."

"What the hell am I supposed to do?"

"Oh calm down," Kim said. "You brought your cooler full of 'iced tea'. You can drink and swim."

"That sounds safe. How about we have a three-way instead?"

Kim smacked his arm again. "You wish, jerk."

"C'mon, babe, you know I'm joking. I would never touch another girl." Heath's eyes glanced to Sonya in the rearview mirror. "No offense, Sonya."

She waved him off. "None taken."

"You'll be fine," Kim said. She leaned across the center console and kissed his cheek. She turned to Sonya. "So the beach closes at five today?"

"Yep. Dad's orders."

"Lame. Oh well, we'll probably leave around two or so. Otherwise we'll burn up like a couple of lobsters."

# BLOOD AND RAIN

Sonya waited for Heath's wolfman comment. He didn't offer one. Curious. "Oh, I almost forgot." She pawed through the front of her bag. "Here, can you put this in?"

Kim took the CD from her hand. "Full Moon Fever?"

"Trust me. Just put it in."

The opening chords to a Tom Petty classic wafted through the car.

"I love this song!" Kim said. She turned it up.

*Perfect summer song for a perfect summer day.*

Sonya leaned back and watched her town whiz by the window.

Joe got an early jump on the day. He'd driven up and down both Christie Road and Old Gilson Creek Road twice already. "Calm before the storm" was a cliché, but damn if it wasn't true of this morning. This town was beautiful. He'd lived here his entire life. Met Lucy here, had Sonya. For all the heartache in the last decade, he wouldn't change a thing.

He was grateful to have Randy on board and seemingly ready for what the night might bring. They had decided to break the truth to Clarke and Glescoe. They were good kids, but they didn't have the pedigree or the experience of Somers or Paulson. They were raw, innocent. Hell, they might even think he was fucking with them.

*Werewolf.*

They'd think he was as crazy as Old Mike. Whatever the case, his back was now firmly pinned against the proverbial wall. He decided to let Hines and Glescoe catch a little more shut-eye before hauling them in for the meeting. Though, he was sure Randy's sleep was probably as useful as his had been.

It was hard to close your eyes and not see the blood. Joe didn't like the bad feeling that seemed to slowly be conquering his confidence, either. That awful dread, that this time things weren't going to go down as easily.

Daylight was burning fast. It was nearly noon already. He'd spent part of the morning reassuring people that the Full Moon Monster was just a bunch of rubbish concocted by a couple of punks trying to sell copies of their trash rag. Hazel Betts called in and said she saw something lurking around her garage. Something just like Theresa Turcott described.

*Damn those* Crypto Insider *jerks.*

Dwayne had to leave his spot at the lake to find out what the hell Tina Bazinet was freaking out about. Something about a naked man in her backyard.

Joe had hoped his town would keep it together a little better than this, but the combination of boredom and supernatural hype was apparently too much to handle for some small-town minds.

"Sheriff?"

"Go ahead, Rita."

"Pug Gettis just called. He wants you to come out to his property. Says something has his dogs howling and growling. Says he's convinced there's something in the woods that's causing them to go crazy."

*Here we go again.*

"I'm out that way now, Rita. I'll swing by."

Nick Bruce slipped through the forest, quick and agile as any ninja he'd ever seen in a movie, hell, more like a cheetah in the Sahara. He stopped at the site of Christie Road. He was near the spot where the sheriff had turned him around the night that out-of-towner's body was found mangled and mutilated. A glimmer from the ditch before him caught his attention. He reached down and picked up a rearview mirror. Checking his stinging eyes in the reflection, he saw the thick mix of orange and yellow around his larger-than-normal pupils. His mouth, still smeared with blood, jutted forward a good four inches from where it normally was.

He knew what was happening. Belief was not a choice.

*He* was the Full Moon Monster. He was the wolfman. He wondered what the final result might be. Would he remember it? Would he have control?

He turned his hungry eyes to the other side of road and dropped the mirror. His destination was on the opposite side of town out by Old Gilson Creek Road. He bolted across the empty street and headed toward Emerson Lake.

# CHAPTER THIRTY-ONE

"**T**HANKS FOR COMING, Sheriff."

Pug Gettis was a small guy in his late fifties and had black, scraggly hair with a few gray streaks that told his age as much as the wrinkles around his old blue eyes. His ranch-style house was out on Old Gilson Creek Road and it neighbored Stan Springs's place.

"Sheeba, that's the mama German shepherd, has been yelping and growling all morning. Them two, the pups, been doing the same when they're not whimpering in the corner like they are now."

Sheeba was intently focused on the woods. There was definitely something out there causing her stress.

"You say they started acting up this morning?" Joe had to shout over the barks.

"No, just about half hour or so ago."

Joe could hear another dog barking in the distance. "You have another dog somewhere?"

"Kipper. He's the big daddy. He started all the fussin' and broke his chain. I got another one on him and had to put him down in the cellar. He damn near bit me twice on the way."

Joe looked through the trees. Animals could sense these kinds of things. He shivered.

"You hear or see anything out here so far?"

"Nope, but I got old Betty ready if that monster comes rushing out at my girls."

Joe eyed the rifle leaning against Pug's old Chevy. He clapped Pug on the back. "Why don't you go grab your rifle? We'll go have a look-see."

Pug nodded, grabbed the gun and joined Joe. "You got anything bigger than that?"

Joe gripped his Magnum. "Worked for Dirty Harry."

"Ain't no bank-robbin' nigger in there."

Joe's jaw tightened at the racial epithet. He let it slide and thought of the silver ammo in his gun. "Either way, she'll put a nice hole in whatever it is."

The dogs continued to bark as he and Pug crept toward the tree line. Joe kept his gun aimed at the dirt, and peered in. The hairs on his body rose up like bodies from the dead. The blazing sunlight at their backs wasn't as comforting as he wanted it to be. Something was making those dogs lose it.

A shuffling sound just beyond them stopped Joe in his tracks. He held out a hand. Pug stopped next to him, rifle aimed and ready. Joe noticed the barrel wavered under the guy's shaky hands.

*BANG*

The sudden blast of Pug's rifle knocked Joe off-balance. His ear screamed.

"Shit, Desi," Pug shouted. "Sorry about that, Sheriff. Becky's damn cat, Desi."

Joe fingered his ear and waited for the ringing to cease. He glanced through the trees once more before motioning for Pug to head back.

"Definitely something out there. They can sense it. Might be our mountain lion," Joe said. "Desi might be down a few lives, coming out of there intact without taking your bullet."

"Sorry, Sheriff."

"Becky home today?"

"She's got church stuff. She usually comes back around four on Fridays."

"Well, why don't you take that rifle and hole up inside 'til she gets home. Just in case."

"Sure, sure, Sheriff."

"I'll go swing by Sheriff Springs's place and see if he's noticed anything this morning."

"That old loon?"

"Good day, Pug."

Stan Springs awoke to the knocking on his door. Sheriff Fischer. He could smell the mix of cigarette smoke and Old Spice.

He grabbed a housecoat to cover his naked form but hesitated as he reached for the doorknob. His eyes. He knew the thick, sludgy feeling. Knew what it meant. Joe probably wasn't ready to see them just yet, and Stan wasn't willing to spoil the surprise he had in store for later. He put on the pair of black sunglasses from the bookshelf by the light switch and answered the door.

Sheriff Fischer raised his cowboy hat and nodded.

"Stan."

"Sheriff."

"Just stopping by to see if you noticed anything poking around your yard this morning?"

"Like what? A mountain lion?" He couldn't hold back the smirk.

"Pug Gettis's dogs, as you can hear, are all stirred up. Just wondering if you saw anything."

"I haven't seen shit. I was sleeping sound as a pound before you came knockin' on my door."

"All right, Stan. Sorry about that. If you see anything, can you just give Rita a call?"

"Sure, Sheriff." He let Joe get to the steps. "Sheriff?"

Joe stopped a step from the ground.

"How's Mel doing?"

"What did you say?"

"You heard me."

Joe came back up the steps and straight to the door. Eyes intense, chest puffed out like the big hero.

Stan shoved him hard enough to knock him across the porch.

The sheriff's right hand went to his gun, his left came up between them. "Stan, you lay your hands on me again, I'm going to have to take you in."

He let out a gruff laugh. "You try that and you know there's going to be a fight."

Joe's nostrils flared, his cheeks reddened. Stan took a deep breath. The sheriff's heartbeat hammered. The emotional stimulus was intoxicating.

"That was you at Mel's house a couple weeks ago."

"You mean the night you stuck your little faggot deputy outside my driveway?"

"I don't know what you're going through, but I sure as hell wish you'd—"

"Good luck with your fucking wolfman, Sheriff. You're gonna need it."

He slammed the door shut and ran his fingers through his coarse hair. This town was in for a bloodbath.

Joe was stuck somewhere between wanting to take the old man up on his challenge and hoping he never had another reason to set foot on that property. He climbed into his truck and turned it back toward town. Joe slammed his fist against the steering wheel and reached for the pack of Camel Lights on the dash. He took a drag and tried to let the nicotine do its trick.

*Shorthanded—we're not going to be enough.*

Stan would have made a great ally. His knowledge, his experience. Too bad the man was batshit crazy on top of being an asshole.

Joe turned the radio on. He needed a reprieve. Unfortunately, he got another reminder.

"...just remember, Emerson Lake closes at 5 p.m., so keep the parties inside, people. With the storm that's coming this afternoon, you won't wanna be out there anyway. This is Wild Ted signing off. Keep us cranked up, keep it safe, and when you look up at the sky tonight, take Ozzy's advice. Here's a little "Bark at the Moon". See ya!"

*Ted McKinney.*

Joe could do a lot worse. At least he knew Jack and Ted had hunted these woods with their father when they were younger. He still had a few hours to mull it over. He could use all of the local help he could get, and Ted was already armed and certain of what was coming.

Ted headed for the station's back door. He'd had to bullshit his station manager and

Tonya, the overnight girl, about the tour he never went on. He wasn't up for Freddy Daniels—Fab Freddie, as he called himself on air. Fab was always looking for the Mötley Crüe stories. Rock, coke and hos. Not today.

Fab waved and said "Hey, Ted" just as the door shut.

Ted hopped on his Rebel and cruised out onto the street, kicking up dust.

He hadn't been scheduled to return to the air until Sunday, but he woke up at 3:00 a.m. and couldn't get back to sleep. He figured he could distract his mind at work, and also use the platform to do his part in warning his listeners about tonight. He wasn't quite ready to shout out werewolf alerts, but he did reiterate the sheriff's curfew a number of times, along with the fact that Emerson Lake closed at five tonight instead of eight.

The problem was that Sheriff Fischer was apparently banking on the idea that the monster wouldn't show until nighttime. Ted's guts told him that what he'd read on the Monsters Among Us website was correct. He had read that the beast could stalk in the day as easily as it could by dark. He hoped he was wrong about that, but of all the things he'd read in the last few weeks, that's the one that stuck out like a broken spoke.

Ted pulled into his driveway. Upstairs, he grabbed his Glock and his silver ammo. He stuffed them in a duffel bag, along with a couple of beers, two extra packs of smokes and his hatchet. He imagined himself chopping at the wolf's head like Tommy Jarvis in *Friday the 13th: The Final Chapter*.

*Die, Die, Die*

He shook the vision away and hurried for the door.

He zoomed out on the road dead set on staking out the lake.

Sheriff Fischer's Range Rover slowed in the opposite lane.

Ted stared straight ahead. Lights lit up behind him, accompanied by the loud squawk of a siren.

*Shit.*

He pulled his bike to the side of the road and waited.

"Ted."

"Sheriff."

"Where you off to?"

"I was thinking about catching some rays." He looked Joe in the eye. "You?"

"Ted, I want to talk to you about something we discussed a few weeks ago."

*Hmm. What is this?*

"Is this about the real reason you're closing the lake early tonight?" Ted said.

Joe crossed his arms over his chest and nodded. "I was hoping you might be willing to come down to the station with me and show a little support."

"Oh, Sheriff." Ted shook his head. "I'm sorry, Joe, but I already made plans today."

"The beach?"

"Yeah, the beach. Is there anything else?"

Joe sighed. "No. Would you reconsider?"

"Can't do it, man, but can I ask you something?"

"Shoot."

"How certain are you that this thing can only hunt at night?"

Joe slapped Ted on the back. "Do me a favor? Don't shoot at any of my townspeople. Oh, and don't go getting yourself killed."

Ted laughed. "Yeah, right back atcha."

Sheriff Fischer walked away.

Ted started his bike and kicked up a little more dust. He had a date with a nightmare.

# CHAPTER THIRTY-TWO

**S**ONYA SAT, LEGS crossed, on her spread-out Mickey Mouse beach towel, sweating to death under the hot summer sun at Emerson Lake. She was getting irritated waiting for Alex to finish up at his brother's shop. She watched Kim and Heath chase and splash each other in the water and wished that Alex were here so that they could be doing the same thing.

He stopped by this morning and surprised her with coffee and jelly doughnuts from Dunkin' Donuts—her favorite. He had driven over to Hollis Oaks to get them for her. She thought it was a sweet gesture. He told her he had wanted to do something special for her, because she was so amazing and because he was grateful to have her in his life. He didn't stay very long after that—his brother needed him for a couple hours at the shop to do a job. They had all made plans to head over to the lake today, so he promised he'd meet them there right after he finished up.

She'd arrived with Kim and Heath just before noon. It was now two o'clock, and still no sign of Alex—not one single call. She picked up her phone to make sure she didn't have it on Silent. The glare of the sun on the display screen made it impossible to read. She had to find some shade.

She got up, looked around and spied the only shade anywhere, which was on the other side of the beach, by the trees. She grabbed her T-shirt from the top of the cooler they had brought with them, threw it on over her hot-pink bikini top and headed over to the shaded tree line.

Nick Bruce salivated as he watched all the hot, oiled-up bodies laid out along the only place Gilson Creek had to offer for summer fun. He scanned the crowded beach from the little look-out hidden by the trees at the end of the beach. He tried to decide which of the pretty, young things to bring up to this shaded spot with him. He hadn't decided whether he would fuck them, kill them or eat them. Maybe all the above. Would he have control? Either way, his body was starved. He could feel the blood pummeling through his veins. A sense of power, an energy like nothing he'd felt in his life surging within him.

He spotted a long-haired blonde headed straight toward his spot. He recognized her and grinned—Sonya Fischer.

*Oh man. If only.*

Sonya stood in the shade of the trees that skirted the far side of Emerson Lake. Her cell phone rang just as she got ready to flip it open.

"What's taking you so long?" she whined.

"I'm leaving right now. Are you guys at the lake?" Alex said.

"Yeah, we've been here for a while. So hurry up and come hang out with me."

"I'm on my way," he replied. "I'm fucking sweating my balls off here."

Relieved and reinvigorated with excitement, Sonya said, "Okay, hurry up."

"See you in a bit."

Sonya jumped, dropping her phone into the sand just as someone grabbed her shoulder from behind.

"Hey, what are you doing? You okay?"

"Jesus, Kim. You just scared the shit out of me," she said with her hand held over her suddenly pounding heart.

"I saw you taking off and thought you were pissed at me."

"Pissed at you? Why would I be pissed?"

"Because Heath and I have been off in our own world since we got here. Was that Alex on the phone?"

"Yeah, he got stuck at work, but he's on his way now. And I'm not mad at you guys. I told you, I get it. He's leaving for college soon. You two should be enjoying every second together. I know if it were me and Alex in you guys' shoes, I wouldn't let go of him until the day he left. I'm fine, you guys just never mind about me. Have fun."

It had bugged her that her best friend had been so tied up this summer, but what she said was true. She did understand, and probably, under similar circumstances, would have been doing the same thing.

Kim hugged her and said, "You're the best. I love you so much."

"Yeah, yeah, yeah." Sonya hugged her back. They held hands as they stepped across the hot and rocky beach, back to their spot by the water.

*Damn it.*

Nick clenched his fists. That dumb, ugly bitch had to come over and ruin everything.

He was watching them walk away when he recognized another person headed his way.

"Joel fucking O'Brien." Oh, this could be perfect. Nick didn't see Wes Kaplan anywhere. Either Joel was going it alone, or Wes was elsewhere. Either way, Nick's thirst for blood would be sated.

Wes was right. If the officer was still here and Joel didn't see him, he was probably too busy bird watching to notice the little Mohawked dude tromping across the beach with the dark-blue duffel bag. Joel found the spot referenced in Wes's email. There was a lookout-type area at the corner of the beach. Joel couldn't see anyone up there.

He smiled at the two girls—a short, dark-haired girl and a blonde cutey in a KISS t-shirt and hot pink bikini bottoms—as they passed by him. The dark-haired girl giggled and whispered something to the blonde. Joel's smile spoiled.

*Fuck you too, bitches.*

He reached the incline that led up to the designated spot for their Full Moon Monster photo session. A strange, musty animal scent hit his nose. "Okay, that seems perfect." He set the bag down on a flat, soil-rich patch between the two trees that looked out over the beach and lake. He unzipped the bag and began to haul out the equipment.

Wes had dropped him off to get this site set up like what they had just finished down at the park. He abandoned Joel here temporarily while he went into town to grab them some food. A fat, juicy burger sounded pretty damn good right about now.

Joel had three of the small black sensors set up when something heavy thumped down behind him. He slowly turned his head.

"Holy fucking Christ." He jumped up and backed away slowly.

*Not happening.*

Joel hit the tree at his back, and his bladder released. The urine puddled at his sneakered feet. The man-thing crouched on the ground before him, and licked a thick black tongue over its horrible mouth of teeth. The thing's eyes—a sickly yellow-orange blaze—were hungry. Its hands were on the ground, its fingers burrowed in the dirt. The jet-black hair upon its head stood on end; its unkempt beard seemed to do the same thing. The bestial man—the Full Moon Monster—unleashed a low, deep, guttural growl.

# CHAPTER THIRTY-THREE

**M**ELANIE MURDOCK ENTERED through the back door to her café. She couldn't stay cooped up in her house alone any longer. Joe had begged and pleaded for her to hide away with her movie monsters for the night. He'd succeeded in creeping her out. She found herself jumping at every shadow, at every scrape of a branch of the big apple tree out back, against her den window, and at every minuscule creak of the floorboards.

She kept seeing Stan Springs sitting in her driveway, wearing that awful smile. She thought she saw him standing at the shaded end of the hallway, clawing at her den window and creeping around in the other room.

Joe had promised to have his deputies doing periodic drive-bys to make sure she was okay, but it wasn't enough to ease her paranoia. She waved down Deputy Clarke on his last run by and told him she needed to go in to work. He offered to drive her.

Stan Springs hadn't set foot in the café since Joe had spoken with him. She'd not even seen the man since the night in her driveway. Her friend Heather said she'd seen him down at Gil's once or twice. She said he sat there drinking alone and talking to himself. Mel didn't care, so long as he stayed away from her business.

Upon dropping her off at the back entrance to the café, Deputy Clarke assured her that he would be in the area when she was ready for her escort home.

Katie Brooks entered the tiny breakroom as Mel was looking through the minifridge.

"Hey, Mel, I didn't know you were working tonight," Katie said.

Mel noticed the barely seventeen-year-old waitress slyly trying to slip her pack of Camels into her purse. "Where else would a girl rather be on a Friday night?"

"Yeah right, I know where I'd be," Katie said. She grabbed her name tag from the small, brown tray on the table in the center of the room.

"Oh yeah, where's that? Jeremy's house?" Melanie had stepped away from the lone break-room window as she egged her young employee on. "Out on a hot date?"

Katie blushed. "No! I'm not that kind of girl."

"Oh really? Where exactly would an innocent princess such as yourself be found on a Friday evening? If she wasn't working at the greatest café on earth, that is?" Melanie said.

"At the beach, of course," Katie said.

"Of course. Well, my dear, why don't you go get your sunscreen and your beach towel, and go live out your dreams."

Katie's mouth dropped. "What? Are you serious? But I just got here."

"It's up to you, darlin'. I have nothing better to do tonight. If you want a free night—" Melanie began.

Katie hugged her. "Thank you, thank you, thank you..."

"Don't go thinking this is going to be some kind of regular thing. I want to have some Friday nights on the town too, you know." Melanie smiled at the prospect of getting to spend those nights with Joe.

"Thank you, Mel. You are the most awesome boss on the planet." Katie fished her purple cell phone out of her purse.

"Yeah, yeah, now get outta here before I decide that I'm the one who needs to go swimming." She watched Katie hurry to the time clock, her phone already to her ear.

Katie punched out, mouthed thank you to Mel, waved and headed out the door.

Nick Bruce dragged the broken body of Joel O'Brien behind a large rock just beyond the electronics the man had been working on. A trail of the blood from Joel's shredded throat traced their path.

"Yo, Joel?"

*Wes Kaplan. Two birds...*

Nick slunk down in the shade of the trees.

"Joel? Where the fuck are you, man? Don't tell me you actually convinced one of these country bumpkins to play with your dick? What the hell?"

Wes dropped the fast food bag and cup holder of Cokes to the ground. His eyes locked on to the crimson path.

"Hi, Wes." Nick's voice was unrecognizable to his own ears. It squeezed through his throat like his voice box was constricted.

"Nick?"

"In the...flesh," he said. Nick stepped from behind the tree. Joel's blood covered his hairy, thick-muscled forearms.

"Are...what...you're..." Wes said.

Nick laughed—or at least he offered something that still passed as a laugh—as Wes's face turned white. Nick was enjoying the ghostly effect his new look was having on everyone.

"Shhrr."

Wes turned to run.

Nick flung his new body forward and threw his right claw into the back of the fleeing *Crypto Insider* editor.

Wes Kaplan whimpered.

Nick's clawed hand slammed through the meat on the back of his former boss and wrapped around his spine. Blood gushed over his widening wrist. The dark hair on his arms extended. Nick could see his blackened lips protruding past his wet nose. He pulled Wes to his broadened chest. "*I'm* your headline now."

Wes's eyes stared off into the ether. His dying breath escaped his pale lips.

Nick tightened his claws over the spine until he heard the bones crack. He flung Wes's body backwards. The carcass slammed into the tree he'd hidden behind and crumpled to the dirt.

The monstrous version of Nick began to devour his kills.

The phone startled Randy Hines from another bad dream. He'd dozed off at his desk.

He hadn't caught a single wink of sleep last night. He picked up the receiver. "Hello?"

It was the sheriff. "Randy, I need you to grab Dwayne and have Rita call Shelly in. We need to prep them for tonight."

Randy's hands grew clammy at the thought of tonight. "Will do, Joe."

He hung up the hefty black receiver, wiped his palms on the tops of his knees and took in a deep breath. He'd struggled to come to grips with the beast of their past, but he had to admit, knowing they, or Joe rather, had stood face-to-face with the creature before and taken it down, made it a little bit easier to let that sliver of hope shine into his heart of hearts.

Shelly Glescoe picked up her cell phone on the second ring. "Hi, Rita, what's up?"

"Hey, Shelly, Joe wants you down at the station by three. Some kind of meeting, I guess."

"What is it?" she said.

"Didn't say, just told me what to tell you."

*What the hell?*

"Okay, Rita. I'll be there."

She had no idea what this urgent meeting could be about. Had she missed something?

She called Dwayne, but got his voice mail.

*Fuck it, I'm not waiting until three.*

Shelly Glescoe put on her uniform, grabbed her gun and headed down to the station.

Ted pulled his bike up behind his nephew's black-and-gold Camaro.

*Goddammit.*

He'd haul Alex home by his ears if he had to. He stuck his helmet in the saddlebag and hefted his other bag of wolf-killing goodies over his shoulder.

He spotted Alex and Sonya not far from the steps to the beach.

"Alex. Sonya."

"Did you bring the beach toys?" Alex said.

"Yeah. Listen, you're going to think I'm a dick, but today I don't give a fuck. You guys need to go home."

"What are you talking about? I just got here."

"Yeah, and there's a pretty ugly storm coming. Look at the clouds over there."

The weather report he'd read all morning was spot on. Black clouds were gathering west of the lake. Maybe there were twenty minutes left before the rain would start to fall.

Sonya stayed quiet at his side.

"Your father know you're out here? I'd bet not."

"Leave her alone. Did you come out here just to bust my balls? Oh shit, wait...is this about the full moon?"

Ted watched his nephew roll on the beach.

"Oh my God. You've got to be fucking kidding me?"

"Alex."

"You're out here trying to get me to go home because the wolfman is coming tonight."

"Alex, shut up and listen to me. I'm trying to do the responsible thing here."

"No, no." Alex got up. His five-nine frame stood its ground. A number of onlookers were glued to the boiling scene. "What the hell is wrong with you, man? This last month, you...you've been out there. You skipped out on your band, you skipped out on your job. Like you give a fuck about responsibility. You're fucking losing it and now you're acting like an asshole."

Ted dropped his bag to the sand and socked the boy in the mouth. Alex toppled over backwards and landed on Sonya. Voices murmured all around them.

Alex held his jaw and glared through Ted. "C'mon." He took Sonya's hand. They gathered their things and joined Heath Jorgensen and Sonya's friend Kim, closer to the water.

"What the hell are you all looking at?" Ted said. He planted himself in the spot vacated by his fired-up nephew and watched the heated conversation he was having with his friends.

Ted shook off his leather coat and pulled his smokes from the inner pocket. He lit up and waited to see if his jerk mode had been enough.

Joe Fischer arrived home hoping to touch base with Sonya before his long night began.

"Honey?"

The house was too quiet. He climbed the stairs. "Honey?" Nothing.

*Fuck.* She'd disobeyed him.

He walked into her room and over to the window. The promised rain had arrived. He watched the rain fall in fat droplets dotting the street. His only solace was knowing the night was still far away. He had time to find her.

*"How certain are you that this thing can only hunt at night?"*

Ted McKinney's question whispered through his mind like a ghost. A chill ran up his spine. Where had Ted read that? In all of Joe's studies with Springs, they'd never run across that one. The image of Stan Springs this morning, standing at the door in his housecoat and sunglasses— Sunglasses? Something itched a murky spot in the corners of Joe's brain. His headache was back in spades.

He tromped down the stairs and poured a tumbler of whiskey. He stared at the gold liquid and said a silent prayer. He downed the fiery swallow and stepped out into the oncoming storm.

Sitting in his truck, holding an unlit cigarette, his thoughts switched back to the interesting conversation he'd had earlier this week with Barlow Olson as the large man handed him the custom-made boxes of silver ammunition that were now sitting next to him on the passenger seat.

*"You can't just shoot these things. The silver will fuck the shit out of 'em. Drop 'em out of commission for a long-ass time, but it's not enough.*

Now, with the blade in the back of his Range Rover, Joe headed toward the station, prepared to address his troops.

He prayed to Lucy that Sonya was just out grabbing something to eat and that she'd be on her way home soon.

Dwayne Clarke was the last to arrive at the station. Joe watched him walk in and stand next to Deputy Glescoe, who looked like she was going to gnaw her fingernails clean off. No one was talking.

Joe leaned against Glescoe's desk. His arms were folded across his chest. He turned to the rest of his squad, looking each of them in the eye, one after the other. He didn't want to do this. He could see the confusion and concern on both Clarke's and Glescoe's faces. Rita was here too, and she also looked worried. The only surprise was Hines.

The man had been all over the place for the last month, making everyone concerned for his well-being. The version of Randy Hines before him now was standing up straight and looking focused. He looked ready. This was the Randy he had come to admire over the last eight years or so. This is the man who diligently served his town and had, in that space of time, been Joe's right-hand man. For the first time since Somers and Paulson left Gilson Creek–Somers for the military, Paulson for a position in Arizona–Joe felt the weight of their absence lessen. Joe and Randy locked eyes and exchanged a quiet understanding between them. Hines nodded. He was ready.

Joe began the meeting.

"Okay, so we have everyone here." He pulled out an overstuffed folder from behind him. "What I'm about to tell you never leaves this room."

# CHAPTER THIRTY-FOUR

**D**EPUTIES **DWAYNE CLARKE** and Shelly Glescoe sat beside each other in utter disbelief. Joe's words kept playing repeatedly in Dwayne's mind.

*"We're dealing with a beast that I have seen with my own eyes. I have shot and killed this...this thing before. It's not some random wild animal. It's not a maniac serial killer. It is a werewolf."*

Joe Fischer was not one to give in to an overactive imagination. He was an honest, God-fearing man. He was the sense in this town. He was the rock they all leaned on. If he was telling them that werewolves were real—they were.

Shelly broke the silence. "Do you think that's why Hines has been acting so strange?"

Her voice snapped him from his trance. "What?"

"Do you think Randy has been acting so strange because of all of this? I mean, Joe said he was with him that night, and that Randy saw it too. That's the kind of shit that could really mess you up. Hell, this kind of changes everything, doesn't it?"

She was right. This did change everything. It's not like they were fighting a deranged man or hunting a rabid fox. This wasn't even a goddamn mountain lion. They were searching for a monster.

"Yeah, I think Randy's acting strange has everything to do with this. If it had been me—" He suddenly envisioned himself standing before the beast, in his daydream the monster looked like the version from that old horror movie *An American Werewolf in London*. He saw himself standing before it, gun drawn and aimed at its elongated snout, the beast drooling, staring him down with its yellowy eyes—

"Dwayne?"

"If we see this thing, if we come face-to-face with this…" He couldn't bring himself to say it aloud. "Well, I just don't know how you come out of a confrontation with something that's not supposed to exist and go back to acting like it was just another two-bit criminal," he finally finished. He dropped his gaze to the floor.

"Do you think the sheriff trusts us?" she said.

"Why do you say that?"

"Didn't you see the way he looked at us when he told us to stay here until he called? I don't know…he just looked concerned. I think he's worried about us."

Dwayne stood, walked over to the coffee machine and poured himself another Styrofoam cup. He definitely did not need anything to stimulate his already shot nerves, but he couldn't sit still.

He thought of former deputy Paulson. He'd only worked with the man briefly before Paulson took a job out of state. When did Joe let him in on his werewolf theory? Had he told him and the other deputies immediately? Or had he waited until the night of the full moon to tell them as well? He was guessing it was the latter. The sheriff was a man with very broad shoulders. He looked out for all of his deputies. He had probably kept this whole damn thing to himself, to carry alone the weight of its psychological impact. Or maybe Shelly's right. Maybe he thought they were too young, too inexperienced to handle this whole situation. Regardless, they were involved. They would be out there, under the full moon, searching every dark corner of Gilson Creek, alongside Sheriff Fischer and

Deputy Hines. Dwayne looked past Rita's desk, toward the graying sky beyond the station's front windows. A storm was coming.

After a moment's thought Dwayne offered, "Maybe he is looking out for us, but I don't think that necessarily means he doesn't have faith in us as being able to do our jobs."

"Maybe I was just projecting my own sense of deficiencies on him. I mean, aren't you scared?" she said, once again gnawing at her near-nonexistent nails.

"Hell yeah, I'm scared. You saw those bodies. This thing is capable of tearing us to pieces." He regretted the words as soon as they left his mouth. He watched the woman he loved break down in tears. He went to her and pulled her into his arms, feeling the wetness on his shoulder. "Do you want to take a quick walk around the station? This is all pretty heavy stuff. Maybe some fresh air would help?" he offered.

She agreed, and they went out onto the front steps of the station.

***

Sonya convinced Alex to stop at her house before they went to Hollis Oaks. He needed to cool off a bit more after his bust up with his uncle, and she knew just how to help him relax, plus she figured after doing it, maybe Alex would change his mind about going to the movie and they could just hang there.

"You wanna take that off upstairs?" Sonya gave Alex her best come-hither look.

"You don't have to ask me twice."

He lifted her up; her legs coiled around him. They kissed their way up the stairs and into her bedroom.

Something fell out of his jacket as he flung the leather coat to the floor.

"What's that?" Sonya said.

"That?" He glanced at the object on the floor. "Oh, my switchblade."

"Switchblade? What are you, some kind of greaser now?"

"I always keep it on me, just in case," he said. "What about your dad? He's not gonna come busting in is he?"

"I don't think he's coming home tonight. He did tell me that he wanted me to stay home. He said you guys could all crash here. He doesn't want us out."

"Really? Like that night he made us stay at Kim's?"

"No, he wasn't that bad. I'm thinking it has something to do with Stan Springs."

"Why? Did he mention him?"

"No, but that guy seems to be getting under my dad's skin pretty good. I think he's making a bigger deal out of it than he should."

"Well, when he talked to me the way he did, it creeped me out. Has he seen him recently? I know I haven't."

"I don't know, I don't care," Sonya said. "Can we just forget about all that business for a little while? I want to have fun tonight."

"You just wanna get all hot and bothered watching your boyfriend, James Franco."

"I'm hot and bothered right now. So shut up and do something about it."

After they were finished and dressed, they headed back down the stairs and toward the door.

"Hold up a minute. I want to write my dad a note, in case he does show up before we make it back."

She grabbed the yellow notepad from the couch and flipped it over.

"Are you sure you wanna go to the movie tonight? Maybe we should just stay here so you don't get in trouble."

# BLOOD AND RAIN

There was her out. Still, there really hadn't been any attacks in a month. Hell with it. The movie was only a couple of hours long. They'd be back before nightfall.

"Yeah, we told Kim and Heath we'd meet them there. Besides, we'll be back before dark."

"What about your dad?"

"You let me worry about him."

"Easy for you to say."

"I'm just gonna leave him a note and let him know we're all together and that we'll probably all be coming back here after the movie."

It was dark outside. Not night, but the storm clouds looked like something out of a Tim Burton film. Dark, dreary, ominous. The wind and rain hammered at them as they ran to Alex's car. Sonya saw Mr. Donavan standing under the cover of his porch across the street.

*He's probably out smoking his pipe before supper.*

She gave him a quick wave and ducked into the car.

Allan Donavan smoked his pipe and watched as the car pulled away into the storm. He had an intense sense of foreboding as he watched the young lovebirds disappear.

*You'd never catch me out in this kind of weather.*

He was standing out on his porch under the protection of its gable roof. He was trying to enjoy the taste and aroma of the Cherry Cordial tobacco coming from his favorite pipe. It had always been his preferred after-dinner tobacco. Dot liked to have a couple of after-dinner mints; he always had his Cherry Cordial. There was this bitterness in his mouth tonight, though, that wasn't normally present.

They'd decided to eat supper early and hit the sack right after. He knew what kind of moon was coming tonight. He would finish his pipe and settle in for the night. Nothing

223

good ever came out of a night with a full moon, especially not in this town. He'd lived in Gilson Creek longer than most, and he knew that town had a bad history that was irrevocably tied to what he himself referred to as Gilson Creek's blood moon. He snuffed his pipe out, placed it back in his shirt pocket, stepped back inside his house and locked the heavy door behind him.

# CHAPTER THIRTY-FIVE

**S**TAN **S**PRINGS **THREW** his housecoat to the grass, took a deep breath and dropped to the ground. Long gone were the days when he tried to cage the beast, the days of attempting to fight the change. Long gone were the times of giving a shit about safety or compassion.

He allowed the first of the changes through. Control of the transformation was almost as thrilling as the kills. Black hairs rose from the epidermis of his arms, chest and legs. Muscles tensed and tore. His better half's teeth shoved the old enamel crowns from their home. He had to concentrate to halt the change at that.

Satisfied, he vanished into the sea of trees. He was hungry and it was time to feed. His first feast of the night wasn't more than a yard away.

**⁊ₒ⸱⸳⸴**

"Can't you shut those mutts up?"

Pug Gettis cursed his wife under his breath. "You know a way to make whatever's out there disappear? Dogs ain't doin' nothin' but warnin' us 'bout trouble."

"Well, they been yappin' since I got home. I want peace and quiet."

Peace and quiet. He wished for the day Becky'd learn to keep quiet. Unlike his wife, Pug considered his dogs to be the finest bitches in town.

"Well?"

"I'm goin', I'm goin'."

Pug grabbed the flashlight from the shelf on the porch in case he needed to check the treeline. Even though night hadn't fallen yet, the black storm clouds had a stranglehold on what remained of the daylight. He slipped out the door and into the heavy wind.

*Damn storms seem to follow that full moon.*

Pug wasn't a scaredy-cat like some of the people in town. Dave Jenner had closed the grocery store early today. Becky hadn't been able to get her chicken salad or her potato bread. That was the first thing she'd bitched about this afternoon.

He wasn't surprised in the least to hear Jenner closed early. Dave was a full-fledged wolfman believer. Must have been the only one in town who thought Old Mike was a God-tapped messenger sent to "save us all"—even when the sheriff's boys, or that cute female deputy, came to grab Old Mike from the store during one of his rants. Dave only called after so many complaints.

The dogs' growls and barks simply ceased. The howling wind acted as their replacement. Pug stopped. He thought he saw movement in the woods. A thwapping noise startled him. He looked and saw a branch from the old oak tree hammer down on the shed's roof. The girls' silence spooked his soul more than any of Old Mike's grisly tales. Pug inched closer, sweating through his work shirt. A few light rain drops had begun to fall.

*Thwap, thwap, thwap.*

*Now don't go getting' all superstitious out here.*

Pug put his foot down. His ankle rolled and he fell to the ground. "Uhh." His elbow jammed into his ribs. Something inside cracked.

A rash of snaps and deep crunches erupted off to the right of the dog shed where he thought he'd seen something.

Pug, his eyes not being what they used to, struggled to see what was there.

"Becky..." he wheezed.

The dogs began to whimper and whine.

"Beck...Beckeeee..."

The growl he heard caused his sphincter to constrict. He dug his elbow into the mud—it sunk like a stone—and tried to pull his injured body away from the awful noise. The pain in his ribs exploded. His whimpers joined his girls'.

"Bec...Beck...Bec..."

The shadowy tree line birthed a mountain of a beast. Pug Gettis shrunk in the face of the eyes gazing at him.

"Oh...oh...oh..." his mind skipped over and over.

The half man, half beast—Dave Jenner's wolfman—raced forward and ripped him into the air by the throat. Pug heard the high whines of his girls one last time and the crack of his own neck. The world faded to black as he was dragged into the woods.

The beast barely had finished lapping the blood and gore of Pug Gettis from its mouth when it arrived at the property of Mel Murdock. The monster stepped through the trees and found the house sitting in silence. It watched as the patrol car crept past the front of the home. Deputy Randy Hines was behind the wheel.

*Hello, Randy, you piece of shit.*

Stan Springs never had thought much of Hines, when he was running things in this shithole town. Randy had been just another weak, kiss-ass kid who wanted to feel empowered and have the security that a gun on your hip provided.

Stan had seen plenty of them during his seventeen years as the acting sheriff of Gilson Creek. Peter Sullivan, Mitch

Brennan, Kelly Hobson, Glen Richards—the list went on and on. They were all nice guys, none of whom would have lasted two seconds had they actually been placed in a critical situation. They were representatives of the law in a town like Gilson Creek for a reason. None of them would have so much as sniffed active duty in a big city.

Randy Hines, who was a Gilson Creek lifer, had been abused by his father growing up. Stan himself had to make numerous trips to the Hines home to question his parents over school reports of the multiple bruises Randy wore to class.

His mother, Lillian, was also a victim of Randy Sr. She had just been better at covering it up. Stan remembered her having fat lips, black eyes, finger imprints around her throat, and also the fact that she had a hundred obvious, made-up excuses for each wound's appearance. Randy Sr., of course, had denied having anything to do with the visual injuries apparent on his wife and son. With neither of them willing to come forth with anything remotely resembling an accusation, Stan's hands had pretty much been tied. A head-on collision with a drunk driver killed Randy Sr. one Sunday morning during Jr.'s senior year. There was a closed-casket funeral for him that no one attended.

Stan recalled Randy joining the force shortly after graduating from college. He was a pussy then and a pussy now—nothing more than a scared kid hiding behind a badge and a gun.

The patrol car left Stan's field of vision.

*Now let's see what little Miss Big Tits is up to.*

Joe Fischer was pulling his Range Rover into the parking lot of Mel's Café when the voice of Deputy Hines broke across his radio, "Sheriff?"

He picked up the two-way. "Go ahead, Randy."

"All's clear out by Mel's. Where do you want me to head now?"

"Take a ride out to the lake. Looks like the storm's coming in. It's almost five. I want you to make sure everybody's out. And if you see Sonya there, I want you to take her back to my house. Understood?"

"Yes, sir. What if she's not there?"

"Then you send everybody else home and head over to the town line and back."

"Roger that, Sheriff."

Joe stepped out of his truck, put his hat on his head and headed for the doors to the café. Deputy Clarke informed him that he had given Mel a ride in to work. He said she was too nervous to stay at home.

The thought of the beach made him nervous. It was a popular place for young adults to hang out, just about the only place in Gilson Creek. With the rain coming down, maybe they would all head for cover. Still, he was worried; even the rain did not possess the power to completely dampen teenage hormones. There were bound to be a few stragglers. Emerson Lake was secluded, surrounded by woods and a little too close to Old Gilson Creek Road. He should have left Clarke out there earlier, or just had the balls to close the beach for the whole damn day.

# Chapter Thirty-Six

**S**TAN SPRINGS—HALF man, half monster—stood in the living room of Melanie Murdock's home. Beer bottles on the glass coffee table. He counted seven empties in all. He hadn't pegged her as someone who would get drunk by herself. He sniffed the air. Cigarettes and Old Spice. So, the sheriff really was shacking up with her.

He followed the faint scent of sex to the bedroom. The flannel sheets were tossed about. A torn condom wrapper sat just below the edge of the bed. Stan took a step forward. Something sharp jammed his bare foot. He looked and discovered a gold pin stabbed into it. Not just any gold pin. A grin broke out upon his face. The gold pin was of an eagle with its wings stretched out in flight. It had been his before he had passed it on to Joe Fischer upon resigning from active duty. He knew that his former deputy was sentimental, but to still be carrying this around with him after all this time?

*How pathetic. This is going to be easier than I thought.*

Stan dropped down on all fours and let the hulk within come out. Maybe her escort would ride her home upon his white horse. There would be plenty of punishment to go around.

He bowed his head as his body cracked, stretched and shifted into its full monthly form.

Deputy Hines stepped onto the beach. He glanced upward at the darkening clouds. Lightning flashed out over the deserted waters of Emerson Lake. It had begun to sprinkle on and off over the last thirty minutes. It wouldn't be long before they got blasted by the full brunt of the storm. Young and old couples alike were already packing up and heading out. He continued to scan the few clumps of groups that remained for Sonya, and Alex McKinney. He watched from the bottom of the steps that led up to the dirt parking lot behind him. There was only the one entrance/exit. If the kids were still here, they would have to pass by him to leave.

He saw plenty of blondes, but no Sonya. None of the boys quite fit Alex's build, either. He looked beyond the dwindling crowd and saw the patch of woods known as the Lookout. There were a few kids gathered around the outskirts. He decided he'd better go have a closer look. Hines noticed the *oh shit* looks cross each of their faces. He smelled the weed as he stepped to the nearest member of the group, a short, blonde-haired girl maybe fifteen.

"Any of you kids know Alex McKinney or Sonya Fischer?"

A tall, lanky boy with brown hair—Randy couldn't believe how much the guy looked like Shaggy from Scooby-Doo—spoke up, "Yeah, man, I know them. They in some kinda trouble?"

"No, no, it's nothing like that. We're just trying to figure out their current whereabouts."

The short blonde next to Shaggy turned to Hines. "That's the sheriff's daughter. Shouldn't you guys know where she is at all times?"

Randy sidestepped the remark. "So have you guys seen them out here today?"

"Oh hell yeah, I saw Sonya here earlier. She was wearing this smoking hot-pink bikini. She was with Alex. They left after some guy punched Alex."

"Someone struck Alex?"

"Yeah, it was the guy from the radio, Wild Ted. And then Alex and Sonya left," the short blonde said.

"Thanks, kids. I need you to head home, as well. Sheriff's orders."

"Can we go back to your place?" another tall guy with a Red Sox hat said to Shaggy.

"No, my ma's home today. We should probably go over to Leslie's."

The short blonde agreed, "Yeah, we just have to put up with my brother..."

Their voices drifted into the background as Hines made his way up the incline to the Lookout. He stopped short of shaded area. The space, shrouded by its forest canopy, sat dark and still. Goosebumps sprung to life on his arms. He did not care to go any farther. The sky above opened and unleashed the rain. He looked back toward the lake. The last few stragglers, towels held up over their heads, hurried for the exit. Randy turned back to the Lookout. Thunder cracked. Hines jumped halfway out of his skin. He gave a weak chuckle and then swallowed it like a glass of syrup. There was no one here. He skidded down to the beach and jogged toward the exit. The jog became a run. He did not look back until he reached his cruiser. Ted McKinney's Honda Rebel sat all by its lonesome at the rear of the dirt lot.

"One of us will be out here to escort you home. Just call the station when you're ready to head out."

Mel followed Joe through the front doors of her café. She caught him under the small awning, above the café's entrance, that sheltered them from the unwelcomed downpour.

She reached for his arm. "Are you okay, Joe?"

He was pretty far from okay at this point. His stomach felt like there was a knife resting in it. His head hurt like a son of a gun, and his hormones were all out of whack. He smiled anyway. "I'm fine, Mel, really."

"Sonya's got a decent head on her shoulders. Alex too. I bet they're back at your house right now."

"She's not answering her phone."

"I can think of a couple reasons two teenagers wouldn't answer a phone."

He shook his head.

"Joe?"

He gazed into her brown eyes. She took both of his hands in hers, leaned into him and met his lips.

"Be safe, tonight."

He nodded, kissed the back of her left hand and headed toward his truck.

Joe picked up his two-way radio. "Randy, any luck finding them?"

"No. Sorry, Sheriff. I talked to some kids who had seen them, but no one knows where they went, but there was something of interest."

"What's that?"

"They said they saw Ted McKinney slug Alex."

"Ted hit Alex?" Joe cursed himself for not making Ted come with him.

"Yeah, his bike is still here at the beach, but I don't see him anywhere. Might have grabbed a ride home with this storm an' all."

"I don't know. It's not like him to leave his bike behind. Strikes me as the type who'd brave the weather. You sure he's not there?"

234

"Beach is clear."

Joe thought about what Olson had told him. That Ted had been looking for silver bullets.

"Randy, did you check that spot the kids call the Lookout?"

"I gave it a once over. Nothing."

"You're probably right. He probably got a ride home. Why don't you drive to the town line and back. Keep your eyes open. You see McKinney, Sonya or Alex, you radio me and then keep them with you."

"Will do, Sheriff."

Randy Hines took a deep breath, then, much to his own surprise, realized he was fine. The thought of being out on Old Gilson Creek Road alone scared him shitless, but he was tired of being afraid.

Fear had crippled him his entire life—when his dad whipped him bloody with his leather belt, when his dad threw fist after fist after fist into his ribs, when his teachers questioned him about the unexplainable cuts and bruises and when he heard his mother's pleas for forgiveness. It had gripped him when he tried to enter the funeral home where his father's body lay stuffed into a sealed casket. He'd halted outside the doorway, afraid the man would burst out and whoop him one last time.

Then, it got the best of him the night he laid his eyes on the monstrosity that killed Deputy Brett Curry, nearly decapitating him in the process. He had fallen down and watched the rest of the impossible scene play out as if it were some terrible nightmare. He just sat there and watched as Joe shot the beast down from behind. He just sat there and watched as Joe burned the remains of the thing into a charcoaled mass of disgusting-smelling death.

*Not tonight. No.*

He wasn't going to let any more people down. As he had his mother, young Brett Curry, Joe and himself, far too many times to count. Tonight, he would be there, standing side by side with Joe, defending his town along with his honor and his pride.

# CHAPTER THIRTY-SEVEN

**T**ED SLUNG HIS bag of tricks over his shoulder. He stepped around the boulder he'd ducked behind when Deputy Hines came up to the edge of the Lookout. A nasty, musty smell permeated the space, stronger even than the ozone accompanying the rain. He stepped forward, crouched down by one of the trees, smoked a cigarette, and watched Hines disappear toward the parking lot.

He lit up another smoke and took a look into the growing darkness surrounding him. He thought of that old Nietzsche saying about the abyss. The eeriness caused his skin to crawl with maggots of fear. All of the hurt and hatred he felt for the thing responsible for so much pain in his life suddenly didn't seem like enough.

He took the army bag from his shoulder, unzipped it and pulled out the handgun. The cigarette between his lips burned. The smoke wafted into his eyes as he fumbled with the box of wolf killers and hand-loaded the magazine.

He slid the last bullet in and paused. He squinted his eyes and leaned forward. It was hard to tell for sure in the growing gloom, but it looked like there was blood splattered across the foliage around him. There was more in the dirt behind him. He stood and searched more of the bushes close by. The thin, dark trail began at his feet and led in two separate directions. To his right, a large gray rock sat behind crimson-spattered ferns. The other line of blood disappeared. He followed its projected trajectory and found the red-painted front of a pine tree.

Branches snapped to his right. He followed the loud sounds as they moved to his left with alarming speed. Ted crouched. He was no Houdini, but it was his first instinct.

The movements ceased. The Earth seemed to stop cold. His heart hammered against his heaving chest.

Something was bulldozing through the trees toward him. Ted jumped to his feet and wished for a trapdoor to open below him.

The shape emerged from the abyss. The beast's yellow eyes glared at him. The cigarette and loaded magazine in his hands slipped to the ground.

*Jesus H. Christ Almighty.*

Black lips pulled taut over a series of jagged, meat-shredding teeth. Midnight fur covered the hulking figure. And those eyes. The beast made its move.

Ted dropped down, snatched the magazine, slammed it into the Glock and rolled to the right in one fluid motion. He brought the gun up with his right hand and squeezed the trigger. The *bang* was snuffed out by the beast's roar.

Ted registered the burning sensation at the end of his arm as the wolfman descended upon him and knocked him to the ground. Its massive arms swung once, twice, three times before it rose up and howled to the raging storm beyond the canopy of trees above.

The taste of blood, coppery and thick, was on Ted's lips. His palsied head rotated in the damp soil, his vision landed upon the severed arm— *Christ, that's my arm*, he thought—still holding the Glock he'd purchased to destroy the abomination. His last thought was of the Monsters Among Us website.

*Daylight...daylight...*

Ted McKinney's world went black.

# BLOOD AND RAIN

After a quick, uneventful spin down Christie Road, Deputy Randy Hines cut down

Jillison Lane and over to Park Street. He pulled up to the crossroads of Park Street and Old Gilson Creek Road. He could barely see anything through the rain pelting against the cruiser's windshield. He watched as the trees around him swayed wildly against the whipping winds thrashing them from side to side. He watched as the leaves that were being blown off the trees danced across the wet blacktop. It was all very mesmerizing, and far too much like one of the scenes from the nightmares that had plagued his recent dreams.

He took a deep breath and turned for another drive up Old Gilson Creek Road. He drove about half a mile down the road and pulled into the spot they used for speed traps. He killed the headlights, letting the darkness swallow him whole. He felt like a sitting duck, but the sheriff had assured him that he would be out to swap off with him after checking on his daughter. Hines just hoped that would be a lot sooner than later.

Joe pulled into the driveway of his well-lit home. He left the truck idling as he ran to the front door.

"Sonya?"

It was too quiet. Alex's car hadn't been out front. He stepped to the bottom of the stairs, and yelled up, "Sonya?"

Still no answer. He turned to face the living room again and noticed the yellow legal pad by his computer desk.

Dad,
Don't be too mad. I know you told me to stay home, but Alex and I went to the cineplex to catch a matinee. Kim and Heath will be there too. We're all together. We'll be back tonight before dark.
Love you, Sonya

He couldn't believe she had deliberately disobeyed him. My daughter, the rebel. And of course she picks tonight of all nights to play the female version of Jim Stark. The Cineplex was in Hollis Oaks. They would have to take Christie Road or Old Gilson Creek. He didn't like the idea of either. He put the notepad down and headed out the door.

Across the street, he saw a light on at the Donavans'. He crossed the road, walked up the beautiful cobblestone driveway and stepped onto the porch. He caught the pleasant odor of Allan's smoking pipe. *Cherry Tree, Cherry Court?* He couldn't remember the exact name of the tobacco Alan had preferred as part of his after-dinner routine, but he had always loved that scent. He stepped up to the front door and knocked.

Allan Donavan opened the door, wearing a red robe; the pocket held his pipe. "Hello, Allan. I hope I'm not disturbing you."

"Why, not at all, Sheriff. Just winding down the evening with a little television. What can I do for you?"

"Well, I was just wondering if you may have seen Sonya leave this afternoon. She probably would have left in a black and gold Camaro with her boyfriend."

"Oh, ah-yuh. I happened to see 'em headin' out while I was out here having my supper smoke. Why anyone would wanna go out on a night like this beats the sense outta me, sir."

"Did you happen to see which direction they left in?"

"Ay-yuh." He stepped forward and pointed away from the town.

Joe's heart sank.

"Thanks a lot, Mr. Donavan. Be sure and tell the missus I said hello," he said, turning to walk away, but then stopped to add, "Oh, and, Allan—you and Dot stay in tonight, okay?"

"Oh yes-ah. As you can see, I've already got my 'jamas and slippers on. Dot's already nestled in, and I was just getting' ready to call it a night myself."

"Sorry again if I disturbed you, Mr. Donavan."

Allan walked the sheriff to the edge of the porch. "Nah, don't be foolish, Sheriff. You caught me just in the nick of time. We always go to bed a little earlier underneath that moon." He looked up toward the slight illumination behind the clouds.

Joe followed his gaze. Then turned to meet the man's eyes. "Not a bad rule to follow. Well, you have yourself a good night, Mr. Donavan."

"Good night, Sheriff."

With that, Joe stepped back down onto the cobblestone and headed back to his house. He paused as he reached his truck. He sheltered his eyes and searched the nasty sky above for his nemesis. It was there, hidden behind the clouds. Shivers ran down his spine.

He didn't like this damn weather. He didn't like that his daughter had defied him, and he didn't like that she was out there, prey to whatever wickedness this night had to offer.

He needed to radio Hines and see if they had passed him yet. He'd drag her back here kicking and screaming if he had to.

* * *

The night sky had fully overtaken the storm-covered daylight as the werewolf finished devouring the flesh and blood of Ted McKinney. It was time to hit the town.

The creature that had been Nick Bruce sprinted through the forest, driven by a newfound lust for destruction. Every muscle rippled with new strength and fluidity. The blood that coursed through its veins and through its stomach brought with it an air of invincibility. The shot from McKinney's pistol had skimmed its shoulder. The wound burned, but it was nothing. Just like the four souls he'd already consumed. Nothing.

The trees thinned as the soaked blacktop came into sight. The beast launched into the air and landed on the faded yellow lines. It placed one clawed foot before the other and lurched down the center of Old Gilson Creek Road, begging for an encounter. It would revel in being spotted, just so it could have another chance to show off its prowess. Its power. Its hunger.

The beast continued down the road in search of its next tasty thrill.

# CHAPTER THIRTY-EIGHT

**R**ANDY HINES HAD been lost in an inner battle for his sanity, and he felt like he was getting his ass kicked. He hated himself for being so weak, so pathetic, so inept, especially at such a critical time. He saw his father's belt swinging down, felt the sharp snap of the old leather, heard his mother being pummeled then left crying. Later, he left his helpless mother to drown in a bottle while he ran away to college, and then returned to Gilson Creek, only to just about shit himself while watching the werewolf murder Deputy Curry.

Now, here he was, the scared little boy versus the cop trying to stand up and do the right thing, both struggling to win out. He stared blindly into the wicked night past his windshield. The ghost of Deputy Curry—his throat torn out, his blood-covered uniform—fell to the ground on a mental loop.

Thinking of that night, Randy gripped the wheel.

A dark car passed by. Alex McKinney's Camaro.

***

"I can't believe that they didn't ride with us," Sonya said. "I mean, I know Heath's leaving, and that they will probably break up when he does, but Kim's been...I'm sorry, I should just be happy we're hanging out tonight, huh?"

"No, I think you have a valid complaint," Alex said. "I mean, it's not like they don't spend eighty percent of their time locked away in her room, or making out during movies. Then again, I'd hate it if it were us in that position."

"You would?"

"Well yeah, but in our case it'd be you going off to college, leaving me with my brother and this boring fucking shithole town."

"Aww."

"It's true. It'd break my heart," Alex said.

Sonya's eyes welled up as she reached over and took his free hand. "You know what?"

"What?"

"I think we'll be fine without them," she said, a tear rolling down her cheek.

"Yeah?"

She leaned toward him and kissed him on his cheek. "I love you."

Alex had never felt his heart yearn for someone more than it did at this very moment.

"I love you t—"

Something was standing in the middle of the road.

"What the fuck is that?" Sonya said.

"Hold on!" Alex said.

He slammed on the brakes. The vehicle skidded closer and closer to the animal standing on the center line.

His heart begged to stop. His mind reeled as if trying to catch its balance, standing at the precipice of irrational possibilities.

"Alex!"

Sonya had her hands braced upon the dashboard as they approached the thing.

The creature launched itself into the air. The backside of the Camaro fishtailed and spun to the shoulder of the road before coming to a complete stop. They watched as the creature, which had landed a good distance away, spun around.

"What the fuck is that?" Sonya said.

Alex focused his line of vision on the hulking beast. It had to be at least seven feet tall. It was covered in black fur and had an elongated snout that flashed a set of deadly looking teeth in their direction. The thing looked as though it were harboring the body of Arnold Schwarzenegger beneath its fur.

Sonya's petrified voice interrupted his examination of the beast, "Alex?"

Alex could only manage four words in response, "That's a fucking werewolf."

"Dwayne?"

"Yeah, Rita."

"Melanie Murdock's on line one for you."

"Thanks, Rita."

Dwayne Clarke smiled over at Deputy Shelly Glescoe and picked up the phone.

"Hey, Mel, you ready to head home?"

"Yeah, ready as I'll ever be, I guess. Vinnie's closing up tonight. I'm just in the way over here."

"Home it is."

"Well...could you take me to the sheriff's house?"

"The sheriff's?"

"He told me last night that his daughter would be home if I needed someone to stay with."

Shelly brought her hands up and mouthed, "What?"

Dwayne put his hand up and motioned for her to wait a minute.

"Yeah, okay. Just let me call it in to him. Then I'll come get you. Okay?"

"That would be great. I just don't feel comfortable, being alone and all."

"No worries, Mel. Let me take care of it. I'll be over in a couple minutes."

"Thanks, Dwayne."

He hung up the phone and slapped his hands down on his upper thighs. "Well, well, well..."

"What?" Shelly said.

Dwayne stood, picking his hat off the desk and placing it upon his head. He walked over and sat on the corner of her desk. "Looks like the sheriff might have a little muffin of his own on the side."

Shelly looked at him with confusion in her eyes. She shook her head. "What? For Christ's sake, Dwayne, what are you talking about?"

He smiled at her and leaned down to her ear so that Rita wouldn't overhear him. "I think Joe's got something going on with Mel."

Shelly pulled back from him. "No."

"Yep, she sounded hesitant to go home, and who can blame her? She asked if I could take her to the sheriff's house."

"I guess if he was going to be with anyone, it would have to be Mel. I mean, they seem perfect for each other."

"Maybe I'll have to unofficially question her about her love life." Dwayne smiled.

"Dwayne."

"I better get going."

Dwayne pushed through the station door. Thunder rolled across the sky. All thoughts of love and life were squashed. His insides dropped a level. The sheriff's voice in his head reminded him: *"A werewolf."*

"Randy," Joe said.

"Go ahead, Sheriff."

"Are you out on Old Gilson Creek?"

"Yes, sir. I think—"

"Have you seen Alex McKinney's Camaro pass by yet?"

"Actually, that's what I was just about to mention. I thought I saw it pass by me a minute ago."

"Randy, you go stop those two fools right now!"

"Sir?"

"Do it right fucking now, Randy. That's an order! My little girl's in that car. I don't want them out on that road."

"Right away, Sheriff."

"I'm on my way. I'll be right behind you."

Joe's stomach felt as if it were at the bottom of the deepest, darkest sea. He turned on his siren and lights, and shoved the gas pedal to the floor.

# CHAPTER THIRTY-NINE

**T**HE **MONSTROUS CREATURE** stood in the headlights illuminating the road before them. Raindrops pelted the windshield. In the lights, Alex could see it perfectly. He wished he could forget it. It was just standing there, staring, breathing and daring them to make a move. Alex's car was still running. He looked into the yellow eyes of the creature, meeting its challenge, and pushed the pedal to the floor.

"Alex? What the hell are you doing? Are you fucking crazy?" Sonya gripped the dashboard.

The car shot forward until it was aimed directly at the beast in the road. The monster jumped, disappearing from sight. Before Alex could stop, there was a loud thump at the back of the vehicle. The car's front wheels lost contact with the asphalt. It was as if a gigantic stone had fallen from the night sky and landed directly on the back of his car. The front end of the vehicle went up in the air as the car came to a dead stop.

"Oh shit, oh shit..." Sonya was scrambling around in her seat, trying to find the monster.

The car sailed off the road. Alex tried to get it moving again, but just as he did, the werewolf landed on the hood. The front of the car crumpled beneath its weight. The car stalled.

Alex stared in disbelief.

*As fucking if.*

The werewolf lowered its face down to the windshield, staring him down. Its yellow eyes bled with a devious hunger that paralyzed Alex. The beast unleashed a long howl into the night. The depth and suddenness of the sound curdled Alex's blood.

Sonya screamed.

The beast turned its full attention to her. Pulling back its black lips until taut, it revealed a large set of dagger-like teeth. It furrowed its brow and growled. The beast hauled its massive arm back and threw it toward Sonya. Its clawed hand smashed through the glass windshield.

She twisted to the passenger door just in time, the claws of the creature scraped the side of her head, drawing blood and taking a chunk of her long blonde hair with it.

Alex pulled out the switchblade he kept in his jacket pocket and jammed the blade into the creature's forearm.

The werewolf let out a half howl, half cry. It yanked its bleeding arm back, pulling the entire windshield with it. It struck the knife that lay embedded in its muscle, sending it spinning to the ground.

Alex's jeans were soaked with from the rain coming through the newly vacated window. It was his turn to scream as the beast reached for him through the open space.

Its powerful, clawed hands grabbed ahold of the wide notch lapels of Alex's leather jacket and shoved him back, pinning him into the driver's seat, knocking the air out from his lungs. He felt something snap in his chest, but managed to latch on to the hair of the beast's arms and pull with all the strength he had left. The werewolf ignored his futile resistance and yanked him through the opening, throwing him toward the middle of the road.

Alex came down hard, smashing his chin on the road. Stars burst to life. He wheezed, trying to breathe. As the rain pounded back up from the blacktop, the lightning flashed just as the monster landed on his back, crushing him beneath its weight.

Sonya managed to climb into the back of the dead car, duck behind the seats and watch in horror at the nightmare unfolding before her. She stared as the beast brought its right arm up and slashed it down across Alex's face. She heard Alex cry out and saw the blood where the wolf's claws had scraped across his cheek. The monster raised its other arm, repeating the strike.

*It's toying with him.*

Sonya watched as the beast threw its head back, and heard Alex cry out, "No, God no!"

The beast drove its mouth full of daggers down into Alex's throat. Sonya couldn't see, over its massive shoulders, exactly what it was doing to her boyfriend, but she could hear it. She heard the monster growling and grunting. She heard the wet, gnawing sounds as the thing ripped her boyfriend's throat apart.

Deputy Randy Hines could make out a vehicle up ahead. He reached for his radio. "Sheriff, Sheriff."

"Go ahead, Randy."

"I'm closing in quick on some taillights off the side of the road. Looks like the Camaro."

Then he saw the thing stand up in the center of the road. "Holy shit, holy shit..."

"Hines, what is it? What the hell is it?"

"It's...it's the...the..." He dropped the radio from his hand and let off the gas.

Joe Fischer knew all too well what it was. "I'm coming, honey. Hold on. Daddy's coming."

"Clarke? Glescoe?"

"Go ahead, Sheriff."

"Dwayne, where are you?"

"On my way to pick Mel up from the café. She wants me to take her to your house, is that okay?"

"Forget about that right now. Have Glescoe pick her up. She can take Mel to my house, that's fine. We have a major situation. I need you to haul ass out to Old Gilson Creek Road right now."

"Sir?"

"Never mind, Dwayne, just get your ass out there! And make sure you've got your guns loaded with tonight's ammo."

"Is it the, the...?"

"I don't know. All I know is my daughter's out there being stupid. I don't have time to explain, just get out there."

"Right away, Sheriff," Dwayne said.

Joe stomped the gas pedal to the floorboards.

Hines slammed on the brakes.

The wolf turned toward the lights and sounds of the patrol car.

Randy Hines wanted to disappear. Even the policeman within his mind sought to run back home like a little boy. He reached for the 12-gauge shotgun sitting on the seat next to him, held it in both hands and stared at the adversary in all its illuminated glory in the headlights of the cruiser. It was bigger and angrier than he remembered.

*Not this time.*

He threw open the driver-side door, stepped out of the cruiser and aimed the shotgun at the beast. Randy Hines caught a glimpse of the bloody carcass lying at its feet. He saw Deputy Brett Curry lying there, instead of the body of Alex McKinney.

"Fuck you!" he said.

He aimed at the beast as it came snarling at him. He managed to squeeze off one shot at the blur of wet fur and muscle as it leaped through the air and smashed into him. His feet came free from the earth that had always bound them. The wind was knocked from his lungs before he even hit the ground.

He felt the full weight and power of the beast from his nightmares. He smelled its wet fur. The stench was sickening. He looked up into its face and saw nothing but rage. There was a human-like animosity within its ugly yellow eyes.

The creature that had been Nick Bruce latched hold of the deputy's arm that held the weapon and ripped the appendage completely free of the body. As the man screamed, the beast slammed a clawed hand down into his face, crushing the skull onto the road beneath.

Sirens and lights came blaring from farther down the road. The beast rose, arched its back and howled into the pouring rain. It welcomed the confrontation as another opportunity to explore. The approaching vehicles were still a ways away. There was enough time to have a little more fun.

It returned its attention to the stalled and battered car sitting at the roadside, and the girl inside.

Sonya could see that the shot fired had connected with the beast's shoulder. There was a huge chunk of meat and fur missing. The flashing lights seemed too far away. Tears barreled down her cheeks.

The monster bounded back toward her. She ducked her head down to the floor, praying to God for something, someone to save her.

The werewolf landed on the roof of the Camaro. She watched the ceiling close in above her.

Joe saw the werewolf leap onto the roof of the stalled car. He surveyed the scene laid out before him. In an instant, he saw Hines's cruiser and the two tattered bodies lying motionless in the road. Tears filled his eyes at the thought that one of them could be Sonya.

He slammed on the brakes of the Range Rover, jumped out of the truck and opened fire at the atrocity standing atop Alex McKinney's car.

The bullets whizzed by the beast as it managed to duck and swerve, evading the first series fired. The monster spun around to retreat. It was slammed in the back with the heat of the last two bullets. These two shots hurt more than the shotgun blast that had nearly ripped its shoulder off. Something wasn't right. It knew it had to escape. The beast leapt from the roof of the car and tore off running into the safety of the woods behind it.

# CHAPTER FORTY

**D**EPUTY **DWAYNE CLARKE** pulled up behind the sheriff's Range Rover, able to make out the sight of the sheriff grabbing hold of his daughter. She looked to be okay.

He grabbed the shotgun off the passenger floor, donned his hat and stepped purposefully out into the storm.

The sight of the two motionless bodies stopped him in his tracks. The first was Deputy Randy Hines. He couldn't make a positive ID on the second body from where he stood, but considering that Alex McKinney's Camaro sat off the side of the road, battered to hell, he assumed the torn-up body was the boy.

The thing that had done this to them could still be around. He gripped the shotgun a little tighter and stepped toward Joe. "What can I do, Sheriff?"

Joe Fischer held his daughter tight. The thought that he had come so close to losing her made him grip her as if the storm could pull her away at any moment. He'd be damned if he'd ever let that happen.

Sonya clutched him just as tightly. Her all-out cries had turned to nonstop sobs, quiet but deep enough that her entire body seemed to hitch with each one. She was scarred by something he could never take away. She'd seen the monster haunting this small town. It was no longer merely a drunkard's tall tale or some stupid rumor passed about during a junior high school Halloween dance. She was now cognizant of the unfathomable evil he'd tried so hard to keep from her.

He knew Deputy Clarke was standing behind him and that he had just asked him something. "Clarke?"

"Sheriff?"

"It's gone."

"Gone?"

"I got it, but it still made off into the trees. I'm not sure how bad it's hurt, or how far it can get, but I landed two silver bullets right into its back."

"Should I go—"

"No. I don't know what shape it's in. If it's still strong, I don't want you in there alone with it, and I'm sure as hell not about to leave my daughter out here. Call Glescoe and tell her to come pick up Sonya."

"You got it, sir." Clarke ran back to his car.

Joe pulled his daughter toward his truck. He felt her resist at first, but then go flaccid as she figured out what he was doing.

She felt the heaviness of her wet clothes, the nearly unbearable weight of something she had no way of comprehending. She couldn't quite put together how or why one minute Alex had been driving her from Hollis Oaks, then the next he was dead.

She wanted to be out of the rain. She let her father guide her to his truck, watched as he opened the passenger door and then climbed in. She looked out through the windshield and saw Alex's mutilated body. The tears came again.

Joe stepped up behind Clarke. "Where is she?"

"At your house. She's still got Mel with her. I guess the door is locked."

"The spare key's under the welcome mat. Tell her to let Mel in, tell her—hell, give me that." He grabbed the radio from Clarke.

"Glescoe?"

"Hey, Sheriff, you boys okay?"

Joe knew that Mel was probably sitting there right beside her, listening. "Yeah, we'll be all right. Tell Mel the spare key's under the welcome mat; tell her to make herself at home and to stay put. I need you to come out here and pick up Sonya."

"You got it, Sheriff."

After making sure Melanie Murdock made it inside the sheriff's house all right, Shelly backed out of the driveway and radioed Deputy Clarke.

"Clarke?"

"Go ahead."

"Dwayne, are you and Joe okay? Is Sonya all right? Where's Randy?"

"I'm fine, the sheriff's okay, Sonya's going to be all right, but...Randy and Alex McKinney...they're both dead."

Melanie Murdock found the sheriff's home a lot cozier than she had imagined it would be, although Sonya, who he'd said would be here, was not.

*Maybe she's in her room?*

Mel didn't feel like yelling up the stairs, but figured she should. "Hello? Anyone home? Hello? Sonya?"

The place was dead quiet. She decided to have a closer look around.

She expected to see the head of a 30-point buck stuffed and hanging over the fireplace. Instead, there was a print of Winslow Homer's *The Gulf Stream*. Her heart ached at the sight and tender surprise of the painting. The portrait's depiction of a man on a small boat, all alone, surrounded by a massive storm on a raging sea, was enough to break her heart. Is this how he felt? Losing a wife and raising a young girl alone?

She stared at the painting, lost in an overwhelming sadness brought about by the lonely scene. She stood there, looking at it for a long time, longer than she realized. She broke herself away from the painting and moved on to the computer desk. Across the lone shelf that sat over the monitor, there was a Boston Red Sox bobblehead of Manny Ramírez, a picture of Joe and Sonya at the beach, a copy of *Irish Thunder: The Hard Life and Times of Micky Ward*, another picture of Joe with a much younger Sonya at a Portland Sea Dogs game and a paperback copy of a book called *The Encyclopedia of Vampires, Werewolves, and Other Monsters*.

*Must be Sonya's. Kids these days, with their* Harry Potter *and their* Vampire Diaries, *and their* Dawn of the Dead.

She saw a note. It was from Sonya, who had apparently gone out to Heath's...Must be Heath Jorgensen. He was going with her friend Kim. They'd all been at the café together at least a hundred times over the last five or six months.

She walked over to the flat-screen television, turned it on and sat down on the end of the royal-blue suede couch.

The couch was as comfortable as it looked. *NCIS* was on. Mark Harmon was a good-looking man. Joe kind of looked like him. She smiled at the sudden realization.

The note said that Sonya would be back before dark. She was late. Mel decided to veg out until one of them came home. She hoped it would be Joe. She'd feel awkward if Sonya came in to find her lounging in their living room like this.

⁂

The rain had stopped, but the wind was now swirling hard enough to bend the trees over the road. Shelly could feel it trying to push her patrol car around.

She slowed to a stop behind Dwayne's. She could see him standing with the sheriff as they conversed over something lying covered on the wet ground—

*Oh no.*

She got out and went straight to Joe's truck.

Sonya stared blankly at the dash. Shelly decided to leave her be for the moment and walked over to where the two men stood.

"No time to fill you in, Shelly," Joe said. "Sorry, but I need you to get Sonya home right now. I don't want her out here."

She looked from Joe to Dwayne.

"It's out there," Dwayne nodded toward the woods behind the crumpled Camaro. "We need you to take her so we can see what happened to it."

"What happened to it?"

"No time, Glescoe. Get Sonya home," Joe said.

"Yes, sir."

Joe watched as she walked over to the truck, helped Sonya out and led her over to the cruiser. She turned the car around and headed back toward town.

Joe turned to Dwayne. "I hope you're ready for this."

"To be honest with you, Sheriff, I'm scared shitless."

Joe shifted his gaze back to the clump of trees he'd seen the beast run off into after he'd shot it full of silver. He watched for a moment as the tall pines swayed wildly with the storm.

He turned back to Deputy Clarke and said, "To be honest with you, Deputy, you should be."

# Chapter Forty-One

S TAN SPRINGS STALKED the night in bestial form. He thought of the first set of kills this summer. Of those, the man in the car was pretty fun, but shutting up that old drunk in the park thrilled him to the core. Before the start of this killing season, it felt like an eternity since the beast had been at full strength and able to hunt humans. Even when it had last attacked, over seven years ago, the kills had never been as exhilarating as these.

The beast felt stronger, smarter, better at perpetrating its acts of violence. It stopped and howled at the full moon as it appeared, disappeared then reappeared from behind the clouds above. This night had only gotten started.

It wondered how its neophyte was fairing? Becoming the beast had filled Stan Springs with anxiety and shame, but its lust for blood was insatiable and far too strong to be ignored. Perhaps they would meet tonight.

The beast's priorities turned to Mel Murdock and Sheriff Fischer. It howled into the fierce wind blowing against its thick fur. The werewolf crouched back down on all fours and continued on to its next destination— the home of Sheriff Joe Fischer.

Shelly rubbed Sonya's arm in a feeble attempt to comfort the poor girl who had just witnessed the brutal death of her boyfriend. She appeared to be asleep.

*Probably the mind's way of saving itself from going completely off the deep end.*

Even as she tried to pass on some compassion to the fractured girl, her thoughts were of her own boyfriend and his safety. At this very moment, Dwayne was heading into the dark forest, pursuing the beast responsible for all of this.

"Please, God, watch over Dwayne and Joe and help them destroy this creature. Don't let us lose anyone else," she said.

Shelly didn't pray very often—mostly as a last resort against impossible odds—but as she turned off Old Gilson Creek Road and onto Park Street, she was praying harder than she ever had before. She feared the horrors of this night were far from over.

She hoped and prayed that she was wrong.

The rain began to fall again. Dwayne Clarke heard its pitter-patter as the heavy droplets hit the canopy of leaves above his head. He and the sheriff made their way through the black forest, one soft step at a time.

"I can't see a fucking thing," Dwayne whispered. He was ready to have a panic attack.

*Who is actually crazy enough to go looking for something like this?*

*You, dumb ass, that's who.*

Joe's arm halted his forward progress. The sheriff put a finger to his lips and forced him to crouch to the ground.

Dwayne strained to focus his eyes. A large shape came into view. It was less than twenty feet from them.

If it could have attacked them, it would have by now. Surely the monster would catch their scent on the air before they were able to find it. It lay slouched against a pine and did not move.

Joe reached for the Maglite on his belt, aimed it toward the beast and flicked it on. He watched the rise and fall of the beast's massive chest. Then he reached for his Glock G22, unholstered the weapon, drew it up and aimed it directly at the beast's head.

Dwayne saw the thing that should not be lying in front of him. It was massive, covered with a thick black fur. It was lying on its back as the rain poured down upon it. The sheriff had his gun aimed at the creature. Clarke raised the shotgun he'd carried out with him, moving into position next to Joe.

"Is it—"

"I don't think so. Not yet, anyway."

Together, they began to creep forward. They stopped ten feet from the thing.

Dwayne couldn't believe his eyes. This was something from a Stephen King novel. Yet there it was, fighting for breath, dying before them—a werewolf. A real, honest-to-God, fucking werewolf.

"It's dead, Sheriff."

Joe aimed his gun between the creature's closed eyes.

Dwayne looked at him. "I think it's dead, Sheriff." He reached out with his right leg to kick the massive body.

"Get back, Dwayne."

Despite Joe's direct order, Dwayne stepped forward and kicked the beast. "See, it's dead."

The beast clutched on to his calf.

Dwayne screeched.

Joe stepped past his deputy, placed the gun directly to the monster's forehead—its yellow eyes opening as he did so—and pulled the trigger. He emptied all ten rounds of .40-caliber silver bullets into the head of the beast.

The loud explosions barked then died against the soundtrack of the storm raging against the forest. Deputy Clarke lay on the ground curled into a fetal position, his hands over his ears.

Joe's normally steady hand trembled. There were a series of clicks as he kept pulling the trigger of the empty weapon. He couldn't believe he had killed this wicked thing again.

His thoughts were interrupted by the voice of Barlow Olson, *"You can't just shoot these things. The silver will fuck the shit out of 'em. Drop 'em out of commission for a long-ass time, but it's not enough..."* Joe's authentic Masahiro Yanagi Katana sword was laying in the backseat of his truck.

He looked down at Deputy Clarke, who was only now uncurling himself. Joe waited until the Deputy got back to his feet and handed him his keys. "Go to my truck. In the backseat is a samurai sword. I need you to grab it and bring it back here as quick as possible."

Dwayne was looking at the crimson-splattered area the creature's face had once occupied. It was like looking down at a mess of bloody hamburger.

"Dwayne. Go. Now."

Dwayne pulled his eyes from the gory sight. "Right. A sword. In your truck? I can do that."

"Well, stop fucking staring at this pile of shit and go."

"Yes sir, Sheriff. Are you sure you want to stay out here...alone?"

"I'll be fine as long as you get your ass in gear."

"Yes, sir."

Joe stared down at the body of the werewolf. It seemed an odd thought, but for some reason, as big as this thing was, he couldn't shake the feeling that it had been even bigger before. He guessed it could have been altered in its rejuvenation period, between when he buried it and when it rose from the dirt grave, but that didn't feel right. It wasn't possible that this could be a different werewolf...was it?

A deep cold spiraled through his soul and spun a knot in his ulcer-ridden stomach.

Shelly pulled into the sheriff's driveway and she caught sight of something out of the corner of her eye. Some kind of large animal disappeared around the corner of the house. She thought of the werewolf. Her hands shook as she reached for the radio.

"Sheriff? Dwayne?"

"Shelly?"

It was Dwayne. She tried to keep her voice low and steady. "Dwayne, I think it's here."

"What's there? Where are you?"

"I'm sitting in the sheriff's driveway. Something huge just darted behind the house. I think it's the werewolf."

"Uh, I don't think so. I just watched Joe blow its head into oblivion. We found it half-dead, laying a little ways in the woods here. You probably just saw a dog. I think Joe's neighbor has a—"

"Listen to me, Dwayne Steven Clarke. I know what I just saw go behind this house was too fucking big to be a goddamned dog. Hell, it was too big to be a fucking bear. The werewolf is here. It's here. What the fuck do I do, Dwayne?"

"Back the fuck out of there and go wait for us at the end of Park. Just get yourself and Sonya out of there. I don't know what the fuck is going on, but just get out."

"But Mel...Mel is in there, alone."

"Get Sonya out of there, and then go back for Mel...or wait...fuck...just get Sonya out of there. I'm on my way."

Shelly put the car in Reverse as the guilt of leaving Mel in the house alone nibbled at her guts. She sped down Hilton Street backward, stopping at the end of the block. Sonya was out cold. She grabbed her shotgun from the floor by Sonya's legs, got out of the cruiser, locked the doors and started back to the sheriff's—back toward the werewolf.

"Sheriff!"

Joe heard Deputy Clarke yell. Another chill swept over him. "What is it?"

"Shelly just radioed. She says the werewolf is behind your house. I've got to go. You'll have to come get your sword."

"Dwayne?"

"Sorry, Joe, it's Shelly. I have to go..." His voice trailed away.

Joe knew there was another one. That's why this one looked different— it was.

He knew he should finish the job with the one lying at his feet, knew that if he didn't he ran the risk of it not being here when he returned, but the overwhelming fear for his daughter's safety overrode every sensible thought on the subject. He broke into a run. He'd have to hope blowing half of the damn thing's head off would do the trick.

Less than a minute later, he was burning down the wet road after Deputy Clarke, racing to protect his daughter from a real-life monster. It would take him at least ten minutes to get to his house from here. He hoped that wouldn't be too long.

# CHAPTER FORTY-TWO

**M**ELANIE MURDOCK AWOKE in darkness. She could hear the storm outside, the wind howling as the rain whipped against the windows. She remembered that she was at Joe's.

*I must have fallen asleep watching TV.*

She searched the blackness around her. She scanned the dark room for the red LED lights of a digital clock, something to give her an idea of how long she'd been asleep. She found nothing. She remembered the cable box. It should be on the shelf underneath the TV, showing the time. She sat forward, trying in vain to find the red digital numerals.

*Of course, the storm must have knocked out the power.*

She stood up, placed her hands on the couch and used it to guide herself back toward the computer desk. She couldn't remember if she'd seen a candle there or not. She thought that she had.

She crept along, not knowing the layout of the room. She bumped her shin on the edge of the coffee table, and made her way around it. She reached out, her fingers connecting with the leather back of the chair that sat at the computer desk. She reached to where she remembered the monitor being, found its edge and wiggled her fingers behind it, to where she thought she may or may not have seen the candle. Her mind told her something was going to grab on to her hand and bite it. It was a childish fear, but that didn't stop her from cringing as she fluttered her fingers behind the monitor.

Thunder rumbled.

She yanked her hand back, startled in the dark by the suddenness of the roar. She felt the house tremble. Her heart rate was sky-high. There was no candle on the desk. She decided to check the drawers.

After a minute of contacting paper, pens, paper clips and what felt like a chessboard, she came up empty-handed.

*Where the hell is everyone?*

Shelly crept down the street, crouched over, holding her pistol out before her with both hands. She was drenched from the rain that whipped across her face. The whole way down the street, she kept repeating to herself, "Please, please, please, please don't be the werewolf."

She passed the sheriff's closest neighbor's mailbox, bent down on one knee and tried her best to scan the perimeter for signs of any movement. The lights in the sheriff's house were no longer on. The porch light was dark, as well.

"Where to next?" Heath said.

"Can we go to Sonya's? I know you want to drink, but I feel like we should be there with her and Alex."

"You're just gonna be pissed at me all night if I say no, right?"

"Something like that."

"You're the boss." Heath put the car in Drive and hit the road. Kim dialed Sonya's house.

"Hello. Fischer residence."

"Ah, hi, is Sonya there?"

The line went dead.

"Hello? Hello?" Kim tried the number again. Nothing.

"Weird."

"What is it?" he said.

"Someone, not Sonya, but a woman, picked up, and then the line went dead."

# CHAPTER FORTY-THREE

**D**EPUTY **S**HELLY **G**LESCOE bit her bottom lip as she thought about Mel Murdock sitting alone in that blackened house. She was apprehensive about approaching the place sitting in total darkness. It was the only house on the block without power. She did not want to move.

She was fine sitting here holding her gun, soaked from head to toe, scared to death. She knew something had knocked the power out in the sheriff's house, and it wasn't the storm.

Her mind told her to sit and wait, but her body betrayed her. She was back up on her feet and heading around toward the backside of the house before she could stop herself.

She crept to the corner of the home, leaning back against the white-vinyl siding. She gripped her. pistol tightly with both hands, drew in a deep breath of the cool, moist air and steadied her nerves as she looked around the corner.

She smelled and felt the horrid breath of the monster; her mind barely had time to register the disgustingly warm aroma of death before she could react. The shock of its presence held her for the few seconds it took the beast to grab her by the back of the head, smash her face into the side of the house and hurl her backward through the air by her wet ponytail.

As she crashed to the ground, she registered the pain in her face. Her nose was definitely broken, and so was her left cheekbone. She had landed on something hard and couldn't catch her breath—she was guessing broken ribs. She was having trouble staying conscious, until she heard the growl.

*Grrrrrrr*

Her eyes fluttered open, fighting to remain that way, with the heavy raindrops landing on her face, making the simple task difficult. The beast rose before her, and she screamed.

Mel heard something that sounded like a woman's squeal come from outside, though it was hard to differentiate with the howling wind and pounding rain whipping against the house. Still, the shriek sounded more human than she wanted it to. Her eyes had adjusted to the darkness, and even though she couldn't see details of the objects around her, she could make out shapes to avoid as she headed toward the door in the back corner of the spacious kitchen.

She placed her nose to the glass, her hands wrapped around the sides of her eyes as she looked out. She didn't see anyone.

She could make out an old metal clothesline blowing in the wind. It was hitting up against a small wooden building that looked like a storage shed. She was surprised the old clothesline had lasted this long. It looked ready to bust apart and fly away. There was a knocking sound caused from one of its bending metal corners bouncing off the side of the shed, but nothing that looked like it would make a screech like the one she had heard.

*Of course not. That's because it came from a person. It was a scream, not a screech. Somebody's hurt out there.*

# BLOOD AND RAIN

She cursed her mind for being overactive, and then cursed herself for spending too many Friday nights watching horror movies. She moved down the hall off the kitchen, trying the light switch at its entrance, knowing it wouldn't work. The dark hallway led to a bathroom. She saw a window on the far wall and slowly made her way over to it. She wasn't sure why, but she felt like there was something waiting for her.

*Paranoia, Paranoia. Something's coming to get me.*

Fitting lyrics from some stupid song she couldn't remember the name of scrolled across her mind. She placed her back against the wall and peered out, being more cautious than she had reason to be. She could see the neighbor's fence and a light coming from a second-floor window.

The house next door had power. She looked diagonally across the street. Lights were on there too. The fear and panic that had been threatening her paranoid mind for the last twenty minutes took hold of her. She felt a cold chill scrape its icy fingers of dread deep into her spine. Her hands began to tremble as she slid her rump down the bathroom wall to the floor.

Something banged against the wall behind her.

She jumped. She began to crawl on her forearms, her belly touching the cool floor, away from the wall, scurrying close to the ground like a private on a boot-camp obstacle course. Her mind raced with terror. She crawled up next to the toilet, wrapping her arms around it, and stared wide-eyed over her shoulder toward the window across the room. She saw a flash of lightning cut through the blackened sky and waited for the thunder.

The deep rumble that followed was much too loud and much too close to be from the storm. She let go of the body of the toilet and sunk down behind it as far as she could get. There was no place else to hide, and her fear wouldn't allow her to stand up, lest she be seen by whatever manner of death stalked the dreadful night outside.

Dwayne Clarke sped up Hilton Street, followed closely behind by the sheriff and his Range Rover. They had both shut their sirens off as they closed in on the sheriff's street. Dwayne started to slow to a stop three houses down from the Fischers' when he caught sight of the darkened cruiser at the other end of the street. It was Shelly's.

He pulled up to the curb, Joe following behind him. Dwayne grabbed his radio.

"Shelly? Shelly, do you copy?"

"Dwayne? Is that you? Where's my dad?"

"Sonya? Where's Shelly?"

"I don't know. Where am I? Where's my dad?"

"He's right behind me, sweetheart. We're down at the other end of the street. Can you see us?"

"Yeah, yeah, I can see your car. Why am I way over here? Where's Shelly?"

"Sonya. Stay right there. I think Shelly's at your house. She thought she saw...something."

Joe came up to side of the car.

Dwayne rolled down the window. Rain whipped in with the wind. "Sonya's in Shelly's cruiser down at the end of the street. I told her to stay put. Shelly's not with her."

Joe looked down toward the car containing his daughter. "Let me see the radio."

"Dwayne? What's going–?"

"Hey, baby, it's Daddy."

"Daddy? What's going on? Where's Shelly? What the hell did she see?"

Joe had held back long enough. Besides, she'd already seen one of the monsters. She deserved the truth. "We're not sure, but we think there's another werewolf."

"What?"

"Shelly said she saw it go behind our house as she was pulling in, bringing you home. I want you to stay put, do you hear me?"

"Dad, what do you mean there's another one?"

"We don't have time, honey. We need to make sure Shelly's okay. I need you to wait right where you are. Shelly should have another gun in the glove box. Take it out and sit tight. Wait for us to come to you. Do you understand me? Wait for me or Dwayne."

"I just want this to all be over. I just want this to be a bad dream..."

He could hear her crying. His heart lurched. "I know you do, baby. Just stay right there. This will all be over soon." He gave the radio back to Deputy Clarke and disappeared back to his truck.

Dwayne placed the radio back on the receiver and stepped out into the wet and wild night.

"Dad? Daddy? Dwayne?"

Dwayne heard Sonya's sobbing as he closed the door. He felt bad for her, but there simply was no time to console the wounded girl. He needed to find Shelly.

Joe met him a few seconds later. He was carrying a large green military duffel bag.

"What do you have in there?"

Joe moved past him. "Let's hope you don't have to find out."

They made their way over to the freshly trimmed shrubs of Joe's neighbor Marv Thompson. Joe didn't despise many members of his community, but there were always the exceptional assholes. Marv Thompson was the biggest exception, and Joe had the great pleasure of living right next door to him. The man was an old army vet who thought his time served protecting his country entitled him to do whatever it was he wanted to do. Whether it was pruning his stupid shrubs at five fifteen in the morning with a gas-powered trimmer and waking up the whole neighborhood, or his penchant for throwing cans of Fresca at the misguided teens of Gilson Creek who often loaded his lawn with piles of dog shit. The man was the epitome of the term asshole.

Joe scanned Mr. Thompson's windows to make sure the crotchety old man wasn't peeking out at them. The only light in the house was coming from the kitchen. It was the light that he left on every night. He was most likely in bed for the evening. That was good.

Joe whispered to Dwayne, "Stay with me."

He led them down the length of the shrubs, right to where they ended next to Thompson's house. They stayed ducked down, glancing just over the top of the shrubbery. From here, they had a clear view of both Joe's front and backyards.

The rain persisted. The neighborhood seemed to be waiting for something to happen. His house sat before them in complete darkness, in sharp contrast to the surrounding houses that had lights in various windows.

That's when they heard the loud smash come from the other side of the house, and Mel's blood curdling scream.

"What the fuck?" Heath brought the Jetta to a complete stop. There was a cop car in the road and a second vehicle on the shoulder.

"No..." Kim recognized Alex's Camaro, beat to hell and off the side of the road. "Sonya!"

She burst out of the Jetta.

"Kim, Kim!" Heath tried to grab her. He followed her.

"Oh my God, Heath. That's Alex. That's Alex. He's, he's..."

There was a second body. Heath dropped down to his knees in front of Alex.

Kim had to find Sonya. She checked the second body. It wasn't her. It was Deputy Hines, and his arm was missing, among other things. She gave the cruiser a quick glance. There were no signs of the vehicle having been involved in any kind of collision.

She trotted to Alex's broken car. The Camaro was empty. The windshield was missing. There was blood inside on the front seat. The whole roof was caved in as if something huge had crashed down from out of the sky and landed upon it.

*What the fuck is going on here? And where the hell is Sonya?*

She made her way back over to Heath and placed her arms around him. "I'm sorry."

Heath shook his head as he rose to his feet. "Is Sonya in the car?"

"No. We need to get into town and find out what the fuck is going on. The sheriff should be out here by now."

She pulled her cell and tried the station. "I can't get a damn signal on this stupid road."

"Come on," Heath said. "We have to go find the sheriff."

"Can we please try Sonya's first?"

Heath put the car in gear and eased the vehicle around the scattered debris of the Camaro.

Kim looked at his moist eyes. She hoped somehow that Sonya had made it out of this mess okay. Maybe her dad had already been here and picked her up. But, then, why wasn't there anybody on the scene now?

·❦·

Melanie Murdock could do nothing but scream as the beast came smashing through the window. Shards of glass and wood rained down across the bathroom floor. The beast landed on all fours, locking eyes with her. Mel couldn't quite make out the face of the gigantic animal before her. She had never seen an animal of its size before, at least not outside of the York Zoo. It looked more like one of the monsters from her Friday-night movies.

It just sat there, facing her, staring at her. The soundtrack of the storm outside was the only audible noise registering outside of her head. Inside, her heartbeat was hammering within her chest like an incensed monkey in a cage.

The werewolf normally known as Stan Springs broke into another smile and let out a snort followed by a sound that resembled a laugh. It watched Mel Murdock's shocked reaction to its vocal giddiness. If it could talk in this form, it would. Instead, it derided her whining by making its own whiny, whimpering noises.

The large mass of fur and muscle crouched before her, and it had just laughed at her. It was mocking her. The beast began inching itself closer. Backed against the wall, she trembled from head to toe.

The cold nose at the end of its snout made contact with her forehead. She could smell its ghastly warm breath as the putrid scent buried itself in her nostrils. She fought the urge to throw up. The beast pulled back its dark lips, revealing an intimidating arsenal of teeth, opened its mouth, produced its pink, sandpaper tongue and lapped her face from chin to nose, leaving a trail of snot-textured saliva on her face. There was something strangely sexual in the way it performed the act, slow and drawn out, as though it was enjoying tasting her.

She couldn't hold back the vomit any longer—she spewed right into the mouth of the beast.

The werewolf grabbed her by the throat and flung her effortlessly across the open bathroom. The back of her head smashed into a mirror placed above the bathroom sink.

She came down hard, her tailbone connecting with the cold, white porcelain sink. A hot flash of pain shot up her spine as she fell forward off the sink's edge and landed face-first on the hard blue tile below.

*I'm going to die. Oh my God, I'm going to die. I don't want to die. God, please...*

The beast grabbed her by the ankles, its sharp claws digging into her flesh through her cotton socks. It pulled her body beneath its mass. Its breathing quickened as its primal urges took full control of its actions.

Mel craned her head back. Her threshold for pain and horror, which she figured was about maxed out, intensified as she registered the creature's intent. She kicked her legs, she clawed at the tile and she caught bits of shattered glass from the broken window beneath her fingernails. She screamed.

The werewolf easily overpowered her. She felt its heavy hand rake down across her back, its sharp nails slashing her open. It did this repeatedly, all the while making its crude attempts at laughter.

She screamed out against the whole maddening scene and at the world for harboring such a vile creature in its realm. The sudden panic that struck her accompanied a surge of adrenaline. She had to fight.

With every bit of her strength, she swung her arms wildly, she flailed her feet, she tried to buck beneath the weight of the monster, but to no avail. The beast was too large, too powerful. As a last-ditch effort, she reached for its leg. She caught hold of a fistful of fur and yanked as hard as she could.

The beast let out a howl of pain as her hand pulled free with a patch of black fur. Her small victory only enraged the creature. She clenched her eyes shut and prepared for its retaliation.

# CHAPTER FORTY-FOUR

**JOE AND DWAYNE** rushed around the back of the house, hearing the screams and thrashing coming from just ahead of them. As they rounded the corner of the home, they noticed two things—the body of Deputy Shelly Glescoe lying facedown in the puddle of mud next to the fence that divided the Fischers' property from the Nelsons' and the large hole in the side of Sheriff Fischer's home, from whence the screams came.

Joe spun around in time to see the werewolf slam its fist into the back of Melanie's skull. Her screams fell silent. Joe hesitated long enough for the monster to take notice of him and propel itself in his direction.

Dwayne could no longer hear or see anything around him. He saw nothing but Shelly lying facedown in the muck. He felt weak, he felt useless. He stepped toward her with his hand out; the rain began to fall harder, heavier. That's when he heard the gunshot just before something crashed into him, sending him sprawling to the fence and into the mud.

Joe's shot had missed. The werewolf was on top of him. His gun fell from his hand, disappearing into the mire. The beast clawed through his jacket. It slashed him across the

281

nose and then across the left side of his head, scraping half of his left ear off. Explosion upon explosion of searing pain burst to life in the wake of each strike. The creature was toying with him, like a cat with a moth. He was no match without his weapon, and it knew it.

The werewolf grabbed him by the shoulders of his jacket, lifted him into the air and stared into his face. Joe reached behind his back with his left hand, searching for his backup pistol. It was gone.

The monster held him there, his feet up off the ground by a good foot, and stared at him.

*What the hell is it waiting for?* Joe thought.

He watched the beast looking at him as the rain mixed with the blood from his facial wounds and flowed down his face. There was something about the thing that felt familiar. He was certain that this was the werewolf he had shot, burned and buried all those years ago. The thing he witnessed kill young Brett Curry. The monster responsible for the deaths of Michele Stahl and the rest of those poor kids. This beast killed Jack and Kelly McKinney. But there was something else—Joe could swear he recognized something else in its yellowy eyes. Something far more revealing than this beast being the beast from seven years ago. He couldn't quite grasp it.

Before he could ponder on the thought any longer, or try anything else to get free from its grip, he was sent backward, his body hurling through the air and through the red wooden fence that he himself had built. He tried to get to his feet before the beast could get to him, but it was too fast. As it slashed out at his chest again with its wicked claws, he grabbed a broken piece of the fence lying next to him, sat up and jammed it into the monster's side.

# BLOOD AND RAIN

Dwayne picked himself up out of the mud. His head was fuzzy. He had no idea what had hit him. He just remembered rounding the corner of the house, and the werewolf—then he saw Shelly lying in front of him. Tears filled his eyes as he crawled through the rain-drenched ground, over to her body. As he rolled her over and looked into her battered face, he heard the howl of the werewolf. It shook him back to the here and now. *Joe.*

Sonya's thoughts were all over the proverbial map. She thought of Alex. She thought of the creature that took his life, of its yellow eyes, of her father and of Deputies Clarke and Glescoe. What had her father said?

*Shelly had seen another werewolf?*

He had also told her to stay put, to stay here...alone. Her thoughts returned to Alex. She would never get to see him, kiss him, talk to him...Her chest started heaving again at the realization of the true loneliness that was now upon her.

A howl pierced the rage of the storm.

*Daddy.*

She opened the glove box, reached in and pulled out the gun. It was heavy in her hand.

If she got the chance, she wouldn't hesitate to fire. Not after witnessing the horror...She wiped the tear rolling down her cheek, pulled the hood of her light-blue sweatshirt up over her head, and stepped out into the once-again blustery wind and pouring rain. She ran, gun in hand, down the sidewalk and toward the sound of the beast. For the second time tonight, she was disobeying her father's wishes.

Joe felt the werewolf's howl of pain and violent anger hit him like a shock wave. He felt its energy reverberating down through its hind legs as it stood over him. He needed something else—his gun, his bag. He needed silver. He had none of those things. He scurried out from beneath the beast as he watched it pull the piece of fence from its side. He scrambled to his feet. The Nelsons' backyard was suddenly flooded with brightness.

The werewolf turned its attention to the source of the new light. Joe used the diversion to make his play. He ran, diving past the monster, back into his own yard. His green army duffel bag was on the ground before him.

As he reached down for the zipper, the beast crashed into him. They both slammed into the side of his house. Joe felt his right arm and shoulder shatter as they were pinned between his body and his home. The impact, knocking the air from his lungs, caused Joe to see black dots.

The werewolf grabbed him by the throat and lifted him up over its head. Joe couldn't breathe. He felt the crushing strength of the beast depleting him of his own.

"Hey!" Dwayne's voice broke through the nightmare.

The beast turned its head and felt the blast of two shots slam into its left leg. It spun around, flinging the sheriff at the deputy who had fired the shots.

Joe crashed into Dwayne, sending both men tumbling to the ground. Dwayne recovered almost instantly as the sheriff rolled off to the side.

Dwayne raised the revolver again, but the beast swiped at the weapon as soon as he did.

The gun, along with his trigger finger, went sailing into the night. The werewolf pulled its arms back, bent down inches from his face and let loose a ferocious roar.

Blood and spit sprayed Dwayne's face, temporarily replacing the cold rain. His life flashed before his eyes.

"Daddy!"

The beast spun at the sound of Sonya Fischer's cry for her father. It could already feel the poison from the wounds in its leg spreading and creeping up through its veins. The werewolf made its way down the fence toward the distraught girl, the two men on the ground behind it already forgotten.

Dwayne pulled his damaged hand to his chest and moved as quickly and quietly as he could over to Joe's green duffel bag. He struggled to unzip it with his left hand. He had to bring his damaged right hand down to the bag to get it open. Reaching in and fumbling around, he found what he was looking for—Joe's .44 Magnum.

He looked up as Sonya let out a scream, followed by number of gunshots. The monster continued, undaunted. Either she had missed hitting it completely or the bullets weren't silver. It was totally possible that Shelly hadn't thought to load it with tonight's ammo.

The beast was almost to her. Sonya was backing away.

"Run!" Dwayne strode forward, pointing Joe's massive gun at the beast.

"Daddy!"

Dwayne couldn't take the shot. The monster was almost upon Sonya, but he didn't feel confident pulling the trigger of the small cannon in his left hand. Not with Sonya so close. If he didn't do something now, Sonya would be next. He lowered the gun and ran at the beast.

The werewolf limped its way toward the sheriff's daughter. It relished the fear and pain in the girl's desperate and useless cries for her beaten father.

As it reached out for the broken angel standing before it, the beast heard the footfalls of the approaching deputy coming up from behind.

As the officer jumped through the air, the creature spun and backhanded him. The deputy's eyes rolled up in the back of his head—he was sent to the ground and knocked unconscious.

The werewolf focused its attention back on the screaming beauty.

Inside, the beast that had been Stan Springs thought of the ways he was going to devour this young one. He crept his way closer to his prey as she fell to her knees, drenched in rain and complete defeat. She was his.

"Holy shit, what the fuck is that?" Heath said.

Kim stared through the rain. Sonya was stumbling toward the road with a gun in her hand.

"Oh my God, Sonya!" Kim said. She felt the car begin to slow. "What are you doing?"

"That's, that's..." Heath stammered.

Kim stretched her foot over and pressed the accelerator. The Jetta shot straight for the beast.

This time the monster didn't have a chance to move. The black car seemed to have come from out of nowhere. As the werewolf broke its salacious gaze from the girl in the road, toward the speeding black vehicle darting in its direction, it looked ready to let out yet another enormous howl.

Kim held the wheel with one hand and braced herself with the other against the dash.

Neither she nor Heath was buckled in.

Sonya barely saw the car coming until it smashed into the beast. She flung herself backward. The gun slipped from her grip. She covered her head as the vehicle crunched into the creature and then spun out of control. She looked up as it smashed through the tall red fence that skirted her house.

The compact Volkswagen plowed through the fence to the Nelsons' driveway and came to a halt as it crashed into Mr. Nelson's Chevy Suburban.

Sonya lifted her head. Water dripped from her face. The beast temporarily forgotten, she stared through the shattered fence toward the driveway. There was a black Volkswagen Jetta—*just like Heath's.*

"No...no...no..."

She picked herself up off the waterlogged road, feeling all of whatever life energy she had left fleeing her as she baby-stepped her way over to the car's passenger side. She brought her hand to her mouth. Her knees weakened. She fell into the door and began to sob. Kim's lifeless eyes stared straight at the bloody and splintered windshield.

Over Kim's shoulder, Heath's bloody face lay slumped against the steering wheel. Sonya steadied herself enough to grab the door handle and open the door. She reached in and clutched her best friend's shoulder. Kim's head rolled toward her hand as her lifeless body shifted and slumped toward the door, Sonya dropped down on her knees and put her arms around Kim. The girl had been her closest confidante since her mother passed away, and knew all of her gravest fears, all of her aspirations, and was the only person who knew she had almost been raped in eighth grade by her sophomore boyfriend, Jake Collins. And now, she—along with Alex and her mom— was gone. She reached down, found Kim's cold hand, and held it tight. "Why, why, God?"

She was grabbed by the hair and yanked up and backward. Her feet left the ground as she was sent somersaulting through the air. She landed hard, coming down on her left knee.

Something in the joint popped.

Forced onto her back by the strong arms of the beast, she wanted to reach for the pain that was bursting to life in her back. As she looked away from the disgusting face of the creature, and gazed at Kim who was now spilled out onto the wet driveway. Sonya had no fight left in her. She just lay there as its saliva dripped down onto her cheek. She closed her eyes.

The werewolf reached down and grabbed the young girl's leg. It was getting weaker by the minute. The poison in its leg from the silver bullets was working on its internal functions. The sheriff's daughter cried. It lowered its mouth to within inches of her nose and lapped at her tears. Still, she did not fight, did not move.

The monster started to rise and then stumbled. Between the silver ravaging its inner workings, and the injured hip from the impact of the vehicle that had struck it, the beast knew it was in trouble.

*I can still rip this little bitch in two from the inside out.*

It raised its snout to the raging sky, letting out a howl.

The katana blade slammed into the side of the monster's neck and continued straight out the other side. Joe Fischer's momentum spun him around. He stumbled to his knees.

The beast's decapitated body fell and landed next to his little girl. He let the sword fall into the mud, shuffled forward on his knees, and placed his hand to his daughter's face.

Her eyes remained closed.

"Sonya? Baby girl, it's all right. Everything's going to be okay. Can you hear me?"

She opened her eyes, pursing her lips tightly together as the tears flowed from her eyes. She nodded.

Knowing his daughter was okay, Joe felt the last of his strength fade as he collapsed to the ground beside her. Growling at the pain in his ruined arm, he shut his eyes, clenching his teeth. When he opened them, he was staring into the dead face of the beast.

Despite all the pain racking his body, Joe found the strength to grin.

*Got you this time, you son of a bitch.*

# EPILOGUE

**THE MIDNIGHT HOUR** leaned heavily on the tired eyes of Sonya Fischer as she sat at the computer desk trying to finish an essay for her senior English class. It was titled "Christianity in Today's America: A Matter of Convenience".

Prior to the events of the past summer, she had never really given much thought to who, or what, she actually believed in. She'd occasionally gone to church with her dad, always making an appearance on the big holidays, mostly just Christmas, Easter and Thanksgiving. She even liked the way Pastor Lionel Peabody ran the whole holy shindig, but she never talked with him about her personal life or beliefs. She never really gave a thought to God, or Allah, or Yahweh, before the tragic deaths of the July Blood Moon.

She remembered praying to the higher power for help, for understanding, for intervention. In the course of that one dark and stormy night, she lost nearly everyone in her life that she cared about.

The official death toll at the hands of the "wild animal" (that's what the media outlets were told) tallied twelve. The deaths of Kim Donaldson and Heath Jorgensen were reported as accidents due to inclement weather.

There was also a fifteenth unofficial victim, Nick Bruce. The former *Crypto Insider* writer had disappeared from the town altogether. His body was never found. Officially, he was just a missing person. The select few who knew the real situation included him in the tally of victims of the unnatural force that tore through this small community.

Families and friends of both the official and unofficial victims mourned together in a candlelight vigil led by Pastor Peabody at Saving Grace Baptist two days after the tragedies.

Now, six months later, the city had returned to normal, but her father had resigned from his post as sheriff. Deputy Dwayne Clarke had since taken up the well-respected position. A new crop of deputies was transplanted from surrounding towns to replace the small force that had served Gilson Creek. Her father had used his savings to acquire Melanie Murdock's café, taking over as owner/co-manager, splitting managerial duties with Mel's top cook, Vinnie Castagno. She wasn't sure what kind of relationship her father had entered into with Mel before her death, but knew that it must have meant something tremendous to him. He even kept the name Mel's Café.

For the most part, life in Gilson Creek went on. It had no choice. They had no choice. Sonya decided that she wanted to join the force. She wanted to take up arms and defend her town, which surprised her as much as it did her classmates and her father alike. She had once aspired to be a singer, or a doctor, or a marine biologist, but those aspirations died with Kim and Alex.

Shortly after coming out of the five-month haze of depression that sat upon her heart and mind following that tragic night, she discovered an inner strength she never knew she possessed. It was inherited from her father, no doubt, and it—along with her equally surprising newfound relationship with God and the church—gave her the empowerment she so needed to lift her chin, raise her head and reopen her heart to the world.

# BLOOD AND RAIN

As Sonya was finishing her paper, there was a soft knock on her bedroom door.

"Mind if I come in?"

"Sure, Dad."

He stepped into her room.

She moved to the bed.

He walked over and sat down next to her. He gazed at her for a long time. He wore a smile upon his face comfortably, lifting his left hand up and tucking the loose strands of her long blonde hair behind her ear. "You're as beautiful as your mother was on the day I married her. You know that?"

"So you've told me." She returned his warm smile as her gaze drifted from his to the prosthetic arm he'd gained from his battle with the monster.

"C'mon now, we both know that we suck at lying to one another. What is it?"

"It's just that sometimes...when I notice your arm... it...it..."

"It all comes back?" he said.

"Yeah." A tear rolled down her cheek.

He wiped it away. "It's over, dear. You know that."

She managed a smile. "You made sure of that."

"Yeah, I sure as hell did."

She hugged him as they both allowed themselves to relax and laugh together.

When she let go of him, he stood up, kissed her on the forehead and went back to the door. "If you're done singing my praises as being some big monster hunter, I want you to hit the hay. I'll be doing the same myself in a little bit."

She smiled at his attempt at comforting humor. "I will. I finished my essay just before you came up. I've been ready to close my eyes for the last two hours."

"Well get some sleep then, kiddo. I'll see you in the morning. I love you."

"I love you too, Dad. Good night."

"Good night."

Joe pulled her door closed, and his smile immediately evaporated from his face. He'd never been very good at lying or keeping things from her. That was, until that awful night. Since then, he'd become quite adept at putting on the perfect smile and being the rock she needed to lean on whenever her rebuilt strength and confidence wavered.

He never said a word about leaving the body of the other werewolf in the woods off Old Gilson Creek Road that dreadful night, to come rescue her...and Mel. He never spoke of the fact that he had not driven the steel katana blade across the throat of the first beast they encountered that night. He kept it to himself. He'd even managed to tell Dwayne that he decapitated the monster before following him. He should know better by now. It was the only time he had ever lied—to himself, to the town or to the people who he cared for most in this world, and it always, always came back to haunt him.

Joe Fischer dreamt of blood-red moons, walking beasts and a slaughtered community. The recurring visions woke him up every morning at 3:00 a.m. Under the last full moon of February, rousing from the latest of his nightmares, he heard something that commanded every hair on his body to rise—a single howl rang out through the darkness.

Spring was coming—the time when all that was dead returned.

**GLENN ROLFE** is an author from the haunted woods of New England. He has studied Creative Writing at Southern New Hampshire University and continues his education in the world of horror by devouring the novels of Stephen King, Richard Laymon, Brian Keene, Jack Ketchum, and many others. He and his wife, Meghan, have three children, Ruby, Ramona, and Axl. He is grateful to be loved despite his weirdness.

He is a Splatterpunk Award nominee and the author of *The Window*, *Becoming*, *Blood and Rain*, *The Haunted Halls*, *Chasing Ghosts*, *Abram's Bridge*, *Things We Fear*, *Boom Town*, and the collections, *Slush* and *Land of Bones*.

Look for his next novel, *Until Summer Comes Around*, coming from Flame Tree Press in 2020.